PRAISE FOR *F*

In *Peyton's Promise*, Calumet Castle comes to life with visual detail, experience as Peyton Quinn makes her mark in the world by striving against the norms of society. I applauded Peyton's efforts and integrity and loved the way Mathis wove in mystery and romance. If you enjoy historical fiction as much as I do, get a copy and start reading.

~ **Marilyn Turk**
Award-winning author of *Abigail's Secret*

Mathis enchanted me with this tale set in New York's Thousand Islands. I'll revisit this story again with its lively description, realistic dialogue, and unable-to-put-the-book-down tension. I relished the cast of unique characters and loved her depiction of the Gilded Age. I cheered Peyyton on as she faced the twists and turns that complicated her life. If you appreciate inspirational historical romance, I highly recommend this travel back in time.

~**Anne Greene**
Author of *Trail of Tears*

Mathis weaves together fact and fiction in another richly detailed historical romance. As Peyton and Patrick become reacquainted, they face mutual foes, moments of joy, and weather tragedy. This tale of love, renewed faith, and forgiveness will hit the spot for fans of historical fiction.

~ **Kathleen Rouser**
Award-winning author of *Rumors and Promises*

Mathis discloses emotional complexity as Peyton deals with enlightenment and suffrage. She and childhood chum, Patrick, face testing by danger and illness, sabotage and vandalism, challenges to faith, and the hard road to forgiveness. In addition, the story has the right touch of historical detail as well as the charm of living on an island in a castle at the turn of the twentieth century.

~**Janet Chester Bly**
Best-selling author

Peyton's Promise is filled with suffragette sympathies and her struggle with faith. Mathis has penned a timely story for our day, although set at the beginning of the previous century. The setting is spectacular, the descriptions vivid, and the historical detail is accurate and interesting.

~Norma Gail
Author of *Within Golden Bands*

Peyton's Promise is a fast-paced tale from the days of ballrooms, gowns, and grandeur. Peyton's struggle for women's suffrage and the desire to chart her own path in a man's world makes her a champion. Readers will turn the pages with delight from Mathis's skillful prose.

~ Alice J. Wisler
Author of Christy Award finalist *Rain Song*

Author Susan G Mathis paints a beautifully written portrait of love between two people caught in issues that could tear them apart unless they are able to discover the special path God has prepared for them. Highly recommended.

~Nancy Mehl
Author of the Quantico Files

From the rich history and exquisite setting woven through the story, to the secrets both main characters hide from each other—you won't want to put this book down until you've consumed every word. Highly recommended.

~Donna Schlachter
Author of historical fiction

Peyton's Promise is delightful mix of fiction, history, and devotional food for thought. Peyton's plight causes one to consider that a woman's place in twenty-first century American culture had to be fought for.

~Judy Keeler
Coauthor of *Meandering Among the Thousand Islands*, second edition

Peyton's Promise

SUSAN G MATHIS

An Imprint of Iron Stream Media
Birmingham, Alabama

Peyton's Promise

Iron Stream Fiction
An imprint of Iron Stream Media
100 Missionary Ridge
Birmingham, AL 35242
IronStreamMedia.com

Library of Congress Control Number: 2022930760

Scripture quotations are from The Authorized (King James) Version. Rights in the Authorized Version in the United Kingdom are vested in the Crown. Reproduced by permission of the Crown's patentee, Cambridge University Press.

ISBN: 978-1-64526-344-9 (paperback)
ISBN: 978-1-64526-345-6 (ebook)

1 2 3 4 5—25 24 23 22
MANUFACTURED IN THE UNITED STATES OF AMERICA

To my real-life Peyton Pie, whose smile lights up the darkest day and whose sweet spirit inspires me to find joy and hope, no matter what.

To my precious daughter, Janelle, who never fails to amaze me. Thank you for blessing me with four beautiful granddaughters, including Peyton Quinn, who inspired my character of the same name.

And to my precious husband, Dale, who even from heaven encourages me to continue the great adventure of writing. I know you are up there cheering me on.

You are gifts from God.

ACKNOWLEDGMENTS

THIS HAS BEEN SUCH a fun story to write that when I finally wrote "The End," I felt a little sad. I hope you'll enjoy this third book in The Thousand Islands Gilded Age Series. Thanks to so many of you who participated in making this story special. I'm so grateful for your encouragement and support. I pray this story touches your heart.

Thanks to my readers who share my stories with their friends and family, especially the Thousand Islands River Rats and those who enjoy the tales of my Thousand Islands stomping ground. When I posted pictures on Facebook of Calumet Castle and the island and asked you for your input, I got such creative and interesting—and real—stories that I implemented many of your ideas into the novel. I'm thrilled you are a part of *Peyton's Promise,* and I'm grateful for you spreading the word through your reviews, social media comments, and personal recommendations.

Thanks again to Judy Keeler, my Thousand Islands historical editor and president of the Alexandria Township Historical Society. Your input on all of my books has been invaluable.

Thanks to Laurie Raker, Donna Schlachter, Barb Beyer, and Davalynn Spencer, who so willingly and lovingly pored over the manuscript, chapter by chapter, and gave me great suggestions and input to make the story even better. Thanks to Pastor Moreno who provided valuable spiritual insight. You are priceless.

Thanks to the stellar team at Iron Stream Media/Heritage Beacon, especially Denise Weimer, who is not only an incredible editor but has become a friend and helped make this book everything it can be. Without your faithful, hard work, this book wouldn't shine as brightly as it does.

Thanks to Mike Strauss for giving me a personal tour of the island.

There's nothing like experiencing the sights, sounds, and smells of the island and hearing its stories. My time there helped me create vivid descriptions and tell a better story.

And a special thanks to Mike Swisher for sharing your fireworks expertise to make those scenes historically accurate. So grateful for your help.

Thanks to my many writer friends who have helped me hone my craft, encouraged me to keep on writing, supported me through my writing journey, and prayed for me. There are too many to mention here, but you know who you are.

Thanks for the support of my fellow authors in the Christian Authors Network (CAN), the American Christian Fiction Writers Colorado Springs chapter (ACFW-CS), the Writers on the Rock group (WOTR), and, of course, my fellow authors at Lighthouse Publishing of the Carolinas.

And to God, from whom all good gifts come. Without You, there would never be a dream or the ability to fulfill that dream or even the opportunity to write *Peyton's Promise*—or any other book. Thank You!

CHAPTER 1

Summer 1902
Calumet Island
Thousand Islands, NY

"LA, LA, LA, LA ..." Peyton Quinn started to hum, balanced her basket on her hip, and gave a little twirl, entranced by the beauty of her surroundings. Would she really get to work in the largest and finest privately owned ballroom in all of New York State?

Goodness! Even Watertown's renowned Woodruff Hotel couldn't rival the paneled mahogany wainscoting and ceiling and rich green walls. The four huge, rounded alcoves with their massive windows. To her left, the enormous fireplace. The floor-to-ceiling gilded mirrors scattered around the room. How luxurious for an island summer home.

"As I live and breathe, could it be the fair young lassie who stole my heart while I was still in breeches? Where be your buttercream braids and toothless grin?"

Peyton almost dropped her heavy basket of treasured upholstery tools—the tailor's chalk, rubber mallet, scissors, stapler, and so much more she'd worked so hard to obtain. She spun around, searching for the owner of the familiar voice. High atop a ladder that had to be ten feet tall, a man chuckled, backlit by the morning sun shining through the window. She couldn't identify his face or make out his features, but she knew that voice, that endearing tease in his deep Irish lilt.

"Paddy? What in heaven's name are you doing here?" Setting the basket at her feet, she moved closer toward her long-lost chum.

She'd not seen him in nearly three years, ever since he'd taken a carpenter's apprenticeship in Ogdensburg, New York, fifty miles north. A year later, she'd traveled twenty miles south to Watertown for her upholstery apprenticeship with Mr. and Mrs. O'Cleary. She'd heard tales of Paddy's success as a finish carpenter, working for the famous architect, J.B. Reid. Yet she'd not been informed of his return nor that he'd be working on Calumet Island in the castle with her.

"What are *you* doing here, Miss Peyton Quinn?" Paddy descended the ladder and stood mere feet from her.

She wobbled back on her heels and gasped. He was much taller and handsomer than she remembered, and his shoulders had broadened. His short, well-trimmed beard appeared soft to the touch, not wiry like her father's. When did that scrappy lad become a man?

"Peyton Pie? Did you lose your tongue, my fair lass?"

He stepped closer and scooped her free hand into his, planting a kiss on it and holding it until she replied.

"I … I am bewildered at your presence, is all. No one told me you'd be here."

Peyton's heart raced, and she swallowed hard, blinking back her surprise—and her ire at the memory of their last curt words, words that cut to the very depth of her heart. She withdrew her hand.

"Are you vexed, oh dearest of my childhood friends? I hope not, for I believe we will be working toward the same goal of preparing this fine castle for the grand affair in just two months." He winked, sending her nerves soaring like he always did. "And it is Patrick Taylor, if you please. Paddy was a skinny, silly Irish lad who finally grew into this strapping man you now see."

When he thumped his chest, chin high and smile wide, she giggled in spite of her ire, relaxing under his easy way she so well remembered. "Patrick, it is. Or is it Mr. Taylor, since you're the Calumet Castle carpenter?"

"Patrick, please. We've too much history to plod through formalities." He shrugged, waving toward three empty chairs perched against the wall. "Shall we? Just for a moment?"

She peeked back toward the doorway through which she came. She'd been sent to the ballroom to await the mistress of the castle and to assess the work required on those very chairs. Sitting on them should be fine … for a moment.

Peyton sashayed toward them and took a seat on the faded, lime-green velvet padding. Against the elegant, forest-green walls, the color clashed hideously. No wonder the missus bid her come and reupholster them.

"I'm sorry for the loss of Aunt Bess, Peyton. Truly."

Patrick's deep, silvery eyes shone with sympathy. He'd always been a kind-hearted boy. Though more oft than not teasing, joking, and jesting, he'd never embarrassed or wounded her with his words. Until the day he left her in tears.

"Thank you. I returned home when Auntie passed on, to be with Papa and help manage the household. But then Mrs. Emery summoned me to recover these chairs for the grand ball, and Papa insisted he'd be fine."

He patted the seat, turning up his nose in a boyish scowl. "Good thing. Such a ghastly color these are."

"Indeed." Peyton gazed at her friend and then to the door again. Seeing no one, she continued. "Apparently, the missus is a very modern woman, wanting to reupholster many of the dated furnishings in the castle. Seems she's taken a fancy to the Art Nouveau style that's so popular in France and with aristocrats and the upper class around the globe. I have to agree, for the Art Nouveau patterns—the birds, the flowers, the bright and vibrant colors of nature—are quite appealing."

"Ah, she's found her tongue."

Patrick leaned in closer, but Peyton scooted onto the next chair. She had to create enough distance to catch her breath.

Just then, footsteps hurried through the doorway. She quickly stood and smoothed her skirt. Scurrying to retrieve her basket, she met the missus halfway. Peyton curtsied, lifted her basket to her hip, and dipped her chin.

"Welcome to Calumet Castle." Mrs. Emery's smile was kind, but then she wrinkled her nose and shook her head. Soft, feathered lines around her eyes revealed a much-lived life. "Mr. Emery may call it the 'Stone House,' but I cannot speak of it as such. It is a castle, don't you think?"

The woman, likely in her fifties, reminded her of a well-endowed snowman. Working for her promised to be amenable, as her gentle demeanor and cultured voice portended a friendly relationship.

"Absolutely, and a fine castle it is." Peyton surveyed the ballroom, and although she'd not yet seen the rest of the residence, she imagined the layout like the castles of old that one might view in the finest parts of Europe.

"This furniture simply must have a makeover before the Grand Ball. I haven't time to order new, but I did procure bolts of fabric with which to do your magic. I've been told you're quite accomplished and that you upholstered an extensive number of furnishings at the Woodruff. I see you've brought your tools of the trade."

Peyton's face warmed at Mrs. Emery's kind words. "Yes, missus. I am here to serve and will do my best."

"Good. Then let's get started." Mrs. Emery waved her arm toward the chairs she and Paddy—uh, Patrick—had just sat on. He tossed Peyton a wink and returned to his work.

"There are twenty-three of these that need recovering and more scattered around the castle that we'll use for the ball. Once you're done with the chairs, I have scads of other furnishings that need updating. You've been informed this is a summer-long position?"

"I have, and Mrs. Milton also said I'd be staying in the castle."

The missus waved a hand as if to dismiss such trivialities. "Yes, yes. She'll arrange all that. Now come with me, and I shall show you some of the other work you'll be tackling."

When Mrs. Emery turned back toward the entrance door, Peyton followed. Before crossing its threshold, she slowed her steps, motioning to her basket. "Excuse, please, missus. May I leave this here while you conduct your tour? This is ever so heavy."

Mrs. Emery consented. "Of course. And I'll have the staff bring down the sewing machine from upstairs and place it in one of the alcoves so you can do your work more efficiently here."

Peyton set the basket near the wall. "Thank you, missus."

After passing through a hallway, they entered an octagonal room. "We use this room for reading and quiet family evenings." Mrs. Emery's chin tweaked toward the shelves of books, then she surveyed the fireplace. "We have six fireplaces on this floor, including this one and the one in the ballroom. As I'm sure you know, it can get quite chilly on any given summer's eve here on the island."

"Yes, ma'am. I've lived in Clayton all my life." Should she be offering the missus such personal information? She bit her lip.

"I hear the winters are dreadful." Mrs. Emery tilted her head as if waiting for more. "Or was that mere gossip intended to scare me away?"

Peyton wet her lips with her tongue. "Up to ten feet of snow can fall each winter. But it's beautiful, nonetheless."

Mrs. Emery shivered. "I married Mr. Emery last winter in London, and it was very cold and snowy, but nothing like that."

"It's the Arctic winds that pick up the moisture from the lake and river and plop it down here. Several days each winter, we can't get out of our house."

What a chatterbox, and to the likes of the missus. What was wrong with her? Nerves. Her mouth always went to jabbering when she got nervous. She bit her tongue this time.

Mrs. Emery surveyed her for a moment. A twinkle in her eyes and a slight smile told Peyton that the missus wasn't vexed. "Yes, well. This settee needs refurbishing, as do several pieces in the great hall, the dining room, and the two other drawing rooms."

The missus led them into an enormous central hall. To her left, a wide staircase led to a landing where a balcony overlooked the great hall. Behind it, a large, pink-and-violet stained-glass window sent rays of sunshine dancing on the floor, walls, and furniture.

"Magnificent," Peyton whispered. Realizing she'd said it aloud, her cheeks warmed. "Sorry, missus."

"Exactly. And that's precisely why I want pinks and purples to grace this area. The fabric I've chosen will make this large room come alive." Mrs. Emery took a few more steps and pointed to the colossal fireplace. "The material has a cream background, just like the inside of this fireplace."

Across the high-ceilinged hallway, they came to the dining room. "The servant's wing is just beyond the butler's pantry. Mrs. Milton will show you around that area." She waved a hand toward the open pantry door before turning to the table. "Since these dining chairs weren't properly covered before closing up the castle last year, mice and other vermin have made a mess of them." She twitched her nose and put a finger to her chin. "Let's make these your first job and the ballroom chairs after."

Peyton counted eight around the dining table and four more encircling a round table in an alcove at the end of the room. "Of course, missus."

Mrs. Emery snapped her chin and quickly turned back from whence they came. Returning to the great hall, she stopped. "There are four more dining chairs here, and those two settees need recovering. I suppose they should all be done at the same time." She clicked her tongue and sighed. "Well, now, that should keep you quite busy." She pointed to two closed doors near the main entrance. "Once you've completed that, there are less urgent upholstering jobs I have in mind for the two drawing rooms."

Peyton curtsied. "Yes, missus. Thank you for putting your confidence in me. I shall do my best to make you proud."

Mrs. Emery turned to the butler standing by the front entrance. "Duvall, would you make Mrs. Milton aware that I'm finished with Miss Quinn?"

"Of course, missus." The large, balding, imposing man bowed, hurried toward the dining room, and vanished from sight.

Before ascending the stairs, Mrs. Emery addressed Peyton. "I shall turn you over to Mrs. Milton now. Wait in the ballroom. Good day, miss."

Peyton curtsied. "Thank you, missus."

Patrick chewed on the inside of his cheek as he concentrated on the intricate touchup work he'd accomplished so well before Peyton appeared like a ghost from his past. She'd haunted his dreams for nearly three years, and now she was here. Some of those dreams were sweet—of walking along the shore of the St. Lawrence arm in arm with the girl he'd loved ever since he was knee-high to a daddy longlegs.

As childhood best friends, they'd shared everything together. Their favorite fishing and swimming hole in a little cattail-sheltered inlet of French Bay just blocks from their homes. Studying in the same one-room schoolhouse, albeit he was a year ahead of her, and she was much smarter than he. Secrets and tears and laughs—oh, so many laughs. He'd quoted the Irish saying to her, *A best friend is like a four-leaf clover; hard to find and lucky to have,* time and again. Indeed, he was a lucky young lad.

He loved to make her laugh, to hear that captivating little snicker. Not quite a laugh. Not quite a giggle. A fanciful pixie sound he called a *liggle*. Oh, how he loved—and missed—that sound!

Really, he couldn't ever remember not loving her, not dreaming of growing old with the flaxen-haired lass with her haunting green eyes and soft, sweet lips. He'd kissed those lips once. His body quivered at the innocence of that childish moment.

While he fished on one hot summer's day, Peyton had fallen asleep in the sunshine, beads of moisture wetting her brow, yet her placid features didn't flinch in the heat. He'd probably been about eleven years old and just couldn't help himself. Studying her angelic face, he'd bent down and touched his lips to hers. Barely. She didn't even stir, but that stolen kiss became a golden badge of courage to him. He'd never told her—or anyone—about it. But it rarely left the recesses of his memories for long. And he'd never kissed anyone since.

But then, there were those troubling dreams. Dreams of what might have been. He'd been a selfish clod the day he'd left for his apprenticeship. A foolish schoolboy eejit who'd botched the special moment he'd meant to tell her how much he cared but instead blurted out some curt words. As he said goodbye, the vitriol in her retort had knocked the wind out of his bagpipes and had torn the song from his heart for nearly three years now.

Yet now, here she was—a chance at redemption. A jolly, grand opportunity to correct the wrong.

He could do it. He had to do it! But how?

Her eyes and the way she'd scooted a chair beyond when he'd leaned close to her told him she still stung. Why hadn't three long years healed those wounds?

Footsteps yanked him from his thoughts. "Peyton. Hello again. How'd it go with the missus? Isn't she crackin'?"

Peyton concurred, stopping to retrieve her upholstery basket. "Mrs. Emery is ever so nice, and it looks as though I have a shipload of work to do here."

When she scanned the room, he descended the ladder and headed her way. "Are you missing something? Can I help?"

Peyton shook her head. Her golden curls, puffed and waved into one of those fancy pompadours the maids prattled on about, tilted forward over her soft forehead. Somehow, it drew him to notice the

S-curve of her lovely silhouette. When his gaze swept back up to her eyes, those green gems had narrowed.

Peyton rolled her eyes and blew out a breath. "The missus said she'd have the sewing machine brought down and placed in one of the alcoves so I can work here."

He waved his arm toward the far-left alcove, then led her to it. "She must mean here. The two center alcoves have staircases and doorways—one up to the billiard and recreation room, one down to the terrace and out onto the balcony."

Peyton set her basket down. "With these huge windows, this is a perfect place to work. And how large it is!"

Patrick couldn't believe his luck. She'd be right here in the same room as he. "A full eighteen feet 'round, these towers are. This is truly a grand place."

"Yes, it is, but the missus has a full schedule set for me, and I mustn't be distracted. Do you understand?" Peyton's brow furrowed, and her eyes narrowed, just as they had when she'd scolded his childhood mischief. But he was no longer a child. He was a man.

"I, too, have much work to do, miss. Every nail hole must be hidden. Every mar or imperfection must be made flawless. This ballroom shall be immaculate for the guests. Yet we will have time to catch up, shan't we?"

Peyton took a deep breath. "I suppose we will. But for now, I need to know how to proceed."

"Shall I inquire for you?"

"No. The missus said Mrs. Milton would meet me here."

"There you are!" The housekeeper waddled through the doorway, dish towel thrown over her shoulder. She wiped her brow with the back of her sleeve, abruptly stopping in the middle of the ballroom. "Come here, girl, and stop fraternizing with the help."

CHAPTER 2

As PATRICK RETURNED TO the ladder, Peyton hurried to Mrs. Milton's side and curtsied.

"Yes, ma'am."

He'd observed the same body language when that terrible Mrs. Hostler was their school teacher. Stiffened shoulders. Straight back. Hands clenched at her sides.

"I don't know what kind of spell you've cast over Mrs. Emery, but I strongly disapprove of your unconventional ways. You should be reporting to me, not galivanting around the castle with her. You'd better watch yourself, missy, and not be thinkin' you're so high and mighty just because you've been working in the city. Here, you're nothing more than a servant."

Peyton curtsied low, dipping her head. Her shoulders sagged as she withstood Mrs. Milton's verbal lashing. "Yes, ma'am. I understand."

"Furthermore, you shall not be fraternizing with the carpenter, is that understood?"

The housekeeper pointed her fat finger toward Patrick. Ever since he'd been working at the castle, that woman had scolded each of her staff whether they needed it or not. Even those who weren't under her direction. Thank heaven, he reported to Duvall.

Peyton glanced his way and inclined her head. But, to his surprise, she wisely kept silent. Perhaps she'd learned a thing or two while in Watertown. She'd always been one to speak up for herself, even as a wee thing. That earned her several swats of the teacher's pointer.

Mrs. Milton let out a huff so strong it almost blew him from high atop his perch. "Well, then. I shall have your sewing machine and the fabric sent here. You'll work in that alcove to the left, as the missus commanded, but you'll not be a nuisance to anyone. You are an unexpected addition to the staff, and I shan't have time to be bothered with you. Don't even let me know you're here. Is that clear?"

Peyton acquiesced, her shoulders a bit straighter. She always was a quick learner. "Yes, Mrs. Milton."

"Furthermore, you shall take your meals with the staff and room with the housemaid, Rachel. She will fetch you for the noon meal and show you about. That's enough for now. Settle in and no shirking."

"Yes, ma'am."

Peyton curtsied in submission. Once the housekeeper made her way through the door and Patrick was sure she wasn't within earshot, he descended to the floor and let out a chuckle.

"That woman just berated me, accused me, and flogged me with her words—without cause—and you think it's funny?"

Peyton's perturbed expression brought him a measure of shame. He hurried to her side and took her hand. "Pardon, I was not mocking you. Just letting off a wee bit of steam. Remember that Irish proverb I oft quoted? 'Humor to a man is like a feather pillow. It is filled with what is easy to get but gives great comfort.'"

Peyton's shoulders relaxed and she smiled, just a little. "I remember." She wiggled her hand free and took a step back. Her gaze went to the floor, and a frown crossed her lips.

Patrick raked his hand through his hair. "I was about to forewarn you. Mrs. Milton scolds, berates, and reprimands every one of her staff, no matter how small the infraction or even when there is no error. She's a bitter woman who rules her kingdom with an iron spoon. Pay her no heed."

Peyton bit her lip, her eyes sad. "I must report to her, yet I cannot stop Mrs. Emery from talking to me."

"Aye, you cannot." Patrick grinned, his tone light and gentle. "But you can steer clear of the housekeeper as much as possible and play along when she does vent at you. You did a good job of that already."

"Thank you." Peyton ducked her head.

Patrick grinned. "To lighten the moment, I have a riddle."

"What's that?" She looked up, cautious but definitely intrigued.

"Why are Christmas trees so bad at sewing?"

Peyton huffed, looking to the mahogany-paneled ceiling for answers. "I cannot say."

Patrick shrugged. "Because they drop all their needles, silly."

Peyton's eyes danced, and she *liggled*. There it was, that sound he longed to hear.

"That's a good one—I'll give you that."

Peyton couldn't help laughing at Patrick's joke. He had always made her laugh, no matter how sad she was, how fearful or frustrated, how perplexed or perturbed. Even as a child, when she'd fretted, he'd tossed out a joke, challenged her with a riddle, or turned a phrase that made her cast her cares to the wind. She'd missed that.

But she checked herself and peered toward the doorway. Had that awful Mrs. Milton heard her laugh? "But hush."

"I love your *liggle*, Peyton Pie."

His sparkling silver eyes spoke volumes just then. Tomes she wasn't prepared to read. She dipped her chin.

The ensuing silence was deafening.

Footsteps patted down the hallway, so Peyton scurried farther away from Patrick.

Into the ballroom stepped a young woman the size of a child. "Good day, miss. I'm Rachel, your roommate and a housemaid here at the castle. Welcome to Calumet."

Rachel stood barely five feet tall and couldn't weigh but ninety pounds. But she was a pretty little thing with her gentle countenance and dark brown hair pulled back in a chignon.

"Thank you. I'm Peyton Quinn, and you may already know Mr. Taylor." Best not disclose their childhood friendship. At least, not yet.

Rachel bobbed a quick curtsy toward Patrick. "Yes. The missus sent for your sewing machine, and I am to show you upstairs and then bring you to the staff luncheon. Ready?"

"Thank you. Yes." Peyton followed the girl, but before she exited the ballroom, she tossed Patrick a quick wave and mouthed, "See you later."

They hurried through the library room and into the great hall, where the maid promptly stopped them. "Never use the main staircase unless the Emerys are not in residence. It isn't proper."

Peyton nodded. "Certainly. The hall is quite an imposing room, don't you think?"

Rachel canvassed the room as if she'd never seen it before. She mumbled, "It is."

Then she hurried through the butler's pantry and into the servants' wing. Only then did she puff out a breath, her shoulders relaxing.

They wound their way up two flights of servants' stairs that led to a long, narrow hallway. A dozen or more closed doors looked like soldiers at attention.

Rachel pointed. "Our room is down there. These are the female staff rooms. The men are in the servants' dormitory, a separate building at the far end of the island."

Peyton and Rachel walked past a crossing hallway with even more bedrooms. At the end of the main hall, a small balcony with glass doors let in the bright morning light.

Rachel pointed to the right and whispered. "That's Mrs. Milton's room."

Across from that, she turned the doorknob and stepped aside for Peyton to pass. "This is our room. There is a gigantic water tank on the other side of that wall, so it can get a little noisy. But we have this lovely dormer window that opens."

Peyton's carpetbag sat on the floor, welcoming her to her new summer residence. A cool breeze blew into the room, making the curtains dance and refreshing the third-floor room. "It's quite nice. Thank you."

Two small beds, a washbasin, and built-in cupboards made up the entire room. One of the beds was unmade, with sheets, a blanket, and a pillow folded neatly on the foot of the bed. She went over and sat on it. "Let me guess. This is my bed."

Sitting on the other bed mere inches away, Rachel giggled, then sobered, and she glanced at the door. "I think we'll get on just fine. But … may I warn you of something?"

Peyton raised a brow. "Mrs. Milton?"

Rachel's head bobbed vigorously, her mobcap dancing precariously atop her head. "She has ears everywhere and seems able to hear through the walls. Any infraction brings swift and sometimes harsh retribution. She may even swat you with her spoon or whatever she has in her hand."

"Goodness! I shall pay heed to your counsel." Peyton stood and set the bottom sheet in place. "But surely, Mrs. Emery doesn't approve of severe treatment of her staff. I should think a progressive woman such as she would not tolerate such activity."

Rachel shrugged. "Perhaps Mrs. Emery isn't aware of her methods since she only arrived in the States in April." She stood and helped Peyton by stuffing the pillow into its case. "Do you really know how to recover furniture? Isn't that a man's task?" Rachel drew back as if she'd said something improper. "Forgive me for prying."

"I do, and it was a man's occupation. My mentors, the O'Clearys, are a very modern couple who live without the male-domineering ways of the past. Mr. O'Cleary is a skilled tailor who taught his wife, and then she taught me. My papa said I can do anything I put my mind to do, and I agree with him. After all, this is the twentieth century.

Things are changing."

"Not here. Not now." Rachel bit her lip and plopped back down on her own bed. "I had to leave school in sixth grade when Papa died to take care of my brothers and the house. Now I'm here, but it's no easier than it was at home. I shall forever be a servant, doing the bidding of others."

The forlorn look in the girl's eyes hurt Peyton's heart, and she sat beside her. "Times are changing. I'm a modern woman and a—"

"Shh." Rachel grabbed her arm and squeezed. "Don't let Mrs. Milton hear that. She'll have you out on your ear. She hates anything modern. Won't even let us have a mixer in the kitchen."

Peyton took to whispering. "She can't hear us if we whisper. As I said, I learned to be a modern woman in Watertown. Mrs. O'Cleary is a secret suffragette and leads women into the new age set before us. She has secret meetings and everything. Though I don't consider myself a suffragette, I long for the vote, for women to be free of the social constraints we face. It can be done. It will be done."

Rachel's slate-gray eyes grew teary and her face as white as the sheet. "Not here it won't. And though I wish that for all of us, you must take care, miss, who you speak of this to. There are tattling toads among us."

As genuine as Rachel seemed, she was too fearful and timid. Peyton would have to help Rachel overcome such female weaknesses. "Well now. Let us move on, shall we? Tell me more about yourself."

Rachel stood. "Shall we walk while we talk? We mustn't be caught shirkin'."

Peyton agreed as she rose and followed the girl back through the hallway and down one flight of stairs.

Rachel pointed to a door. "That's the second floor. The Emerys' bedroom suite and four guest bedrooms are there. There are other guest bedrooms above the ballroom." She continued down the stairs, but instead of going into the servants' area, she exited to the outside. Rachel closed her eyes and took a deep breath. "A bit of fresh air before lunch?"

Peyton looked down the hill and to her right. "Where do those steps go?"

Rachel waved in that direction. "To the terrace that overlooks the lagoon. The ice house is also down there. Then, if you continue past the wooded area, you'll find a walkway that winds along the edge of the lagoon. We must ask permission before venturing too far in case Mr. and Mrs. Emery are out for a stroll. Or if they have guests here, we don't want to disturb them."

"Of course. When I came here, I saw other buildings on the island."

"Yes, but you'll need to see them another day, I'm afraid. We mustn't be late for luncheon." Rachel turned back toward the castle but led Peyton to the right and onto a terrace at the back of the residence. "You may enter the castle the way we came or through the servants' dining room here."

She opened the door to the sound of a dozen or more people chatting, dishes clanging, and Mrs. Milton scolding. "Hush ... all of you. You needn't make so much noise. Be seated and eat your meal quietly."

The entire room grew silent. Several staff members who were already seated scowled. Others served their plates gingerly and almost tiptoed to their places.

Rachel went to the stove, ladled some stew, and grabbed a hunk of still-warm bread. Peyton followed her lead and joined her at the last two seats near the end of the table. Several of the staff glanced at Peyton, some following her with lingering stares.

Mrs. Milton clanged her fork on her glass. "For goodness' sake, you are all so nosey." She huffed her irritation. "This is Miss Peyton Quinn, the staff seamstress. She's here for the summer, reupholstering some of the furnishings before the Grand Ball. She's rooming with Rachel and is working in the ballroom, so don't disturb her, or you'll have me to answer to. Now eat!"

A few nodded a welcome, and Peyton acknowledged them. But most kept their heads bowed and ate in silence. Was every meal to be this somber? She hoped not.

At home, mealtime conversations were lively and fun. Papa talked about his latest fireworks display plans, or Auntie Bess shared the gossip from her daily outing to town or the store. And they always talked about the Lord—about the Sunday sermon or what they'd read in their Bibles that day. Peyton prattled on about this or that happening at school or, if school was out, her adventures with Paddy—Patrick. How could she get used to such a formal name? He'd always been Paddy to her.

Even meals with the O'Clearys had been something to look forward to. The three of them had talked about the fabric shop, their customers, or the news out of the *Watertown Daily Times*. They'd dedicated evening mealtime to discussing the suffrage movement, the plight of women, the politics of the day. But to her regret, they never talked about spiritual things—ever.

Rachel elbowed her and shot a glance toward the sink. There Patrick stood, sipping his lemonade and staring at Peyton, a twinkle in his eye. He winked, a big grin passing his lemonade-moistened lips.

Her insides danced with emotions. Her face flamed, and some observant members of the staff smirked, but no one said a word. She picked up her glass, hiding behind it as the housekeeper's stern warning echoed through her mind.

No fraternizing!

CHAPTER 3

PEYTON DIDN'T MEAN TO slam the servants' hall screen door, but its spring snapped it shut hard. She jumped at the startling racket. She'd needed air—and freedom from the tense staff luncheon. The stuffy atmosphere. The staring and studying her. Patrick's flirting. And Mrs. Milton. Hopefully, the rest of the day would be far too busy for the housekeeper to bother with the likes of her.

Patrick slipped from behind the pillar with a quirked eyebrow and silly grin, making her gasp. "Are we vexed, my lovely lass?"

"Stop calling me terms of endearment! People might hear. And there is no *my.*" Peyton scanned her surroundings. Thankfully, no one could be seen nearby. She left him standing there as she hurried along the outside perimeter of the ballroom.

"Do I embarrass you?" Patrick followed her like a pet weasel, his words dripping with challenge. "Am I too lowly for you now that you're so accomplished?"

"No, but there's to be no fraternizing, remember? It's my first day here, and I need to make a good impression." Peyton gave him a warning glare as she scurried around the two towers to the entrance.

"You can go through the library, you know, as long as the Emerys aren't there. Or you could go upstairs and descend the circular staircase, if need be. Why take the long way 'round?"

"I enjoy the fresh air and sunshine—as I always have. *Remember?*" Her mocking tone surprised even her. "I'm sorry. I didn't mean to sound so ... so shrewish."

"Oh, I remember ... everything."

Patrick's tone was anything but mocking. It held a longing and cherishing that scared her. She shivered and rubbed her arms, even on this hot, sunny day. What was it about this man that confused her so? Oh, but he could be such a pest, just as he had when they were childhood chums.

Apparently, he wouldn't be dissuaded. "Just before lunch, they brought in your sewing machine and fabric. I made sure they set it up so you'll have the best light." His tone turned prideful. "I even found a table in storage for you to use to cut your fabric."

"Thank you." Peyton hurried even faster. She entered the ballroom, almost running to her sewing station. A Singer sewing machine and chair, a large table mounded with an immense pile of fabric, and her upholstery basket waited for her in the chosen alcove. A sheet of paper lay on the table too.

"A Singer model 127? I've always wanted to try one of these. The O'Clearys only had a 27."

Patrick's brow furrowed. "What's the difference, pray tell?"

Peyton clasped her hands to her chest and nearly giggled. "Scads! Though both are lockstitch machines, this one has a vibrating shuttle that drives the bobbin. It's supposed to be ever so much more efficient."

"Guess you've learned a thing or two at that fancy apprenticeship."

Because his teasing irked her, she challenged him with pursed lips. "More than you know. Isn't that what apprenticeships are for? Didn't you learn much?"

Patrick shrugged, his eyes sad. "I must return to my work."

When he shuffled back to the ladder with shoulders sagging, she pondered her words. Perhaps she was a little too harsh? But somehow, he stirred up all those feelings she'd worked so hard to bury. Confusion, anger, sadness. He also prompted warm memories of freedom and fun from their childhood romps and rambles. Oh, men could be so exasperating!

She examined the paper on the table and, recognizing Patrick's familiar script, slipped the unread note into her pocket. She wasn't ready to tackle its contents just then.

Patting her pocket, she surveyed the bolts. Sure enough, Art Nouveau fabrics littered the pile. Running her fingers over the heavy material, her excitement grew. She'd use many of them, some with modern geometric shapes of arcs, parabolas, and semicircles. There was lavender ribbon with pink roses, rosettes, and other flowers on a cream background for the great hall. And even bolder fabrics with peacock feathers and poppies.

Behind her, Patrick ascended the ladder, humming, "It is Well With my Soul," a song that had become her papa's favorite. Sad, melancholy, yet uplifting and reverent at the same time.

"Patrick, do you know the story behind that tune you're humming?" Papa had related it to her just last week. Perhaps sharing it now might soothe ruffled feathers.

Patrick paused, shaking his head as he stopped filling a nail hole. "Nae, I don't. Please tell."

Peyton drew closer, as the touching tale did not lend itself to shouting. "There was a man who lost his little boy in the Great Chicago fire of 1871, the fire that also hurt his business badly. Two years later, he sent his family to England, but the ship sank, and all four of his daughters died. Only his wife survived and told him of the tragedy in a telegram. When he went to meet her in England, his ship passed near where the girls died, and he wrote this song about it."

A woman's voice commented instead of Patrick's. "I didn't know that. How tragic!"

Peyton spun around to find Mrs. Emery with a man who she assumed to be her husband.

Caught shirkin', as Rachel had called it. Peyton's face heated, and she curtsied low. "Forgive me. He was humming my papa's favorite tune, and my tongue flew into the tale."

The missus laughed. "And an interesting story it was. No harm. This is Mr. Emery." She inclined her head toward her husband. "We've come to examine the fabric I've chosen."

Mr. Emery barely acknowledged Peyton as they crossed the ballroom to her workstation. He harrumphed. "I don't know why you sense the need for this, my dear."

The woman kissed her husband on the cheek. "The dining room chairs started it. But you know how I adore splashes of color and the current Art Nouveau style."

Mr. Emery shook his head. "In this Stone House, I can't see how these modern prints won't be distracting. But if it makes you happy, my dear, I'll forfeit my life savings."

The missus tittered. "Thank you, dear. I'm sure they will liven up this great castle and make it even more stunning than it already is."

"Carry on, then." Mr. Emery patted his wife's hand, turned, and exited the room without so much as a fleeting glimpse toward either Peyton or Patrick.

Mrs. Emery pulled the printed lavender ribbon out of the pile. "You've probably guessed this is for the great hall."

"Yes, and it's stunning. But what do I use on the dining room chairs? They are the first priority, correct?"

"Yes, yes. Let me contemplate this a moment." The missus tapped her forefinger on her chin, tilting her head and exploring the pile of fabric. "Let's do the purple and blue poppy and butterfly fabric. So lovely and chic. And the purple will accent the lavender when the extra chairs are scattered about the great hall."

Peyton sucked in a breath. "Splendid! And the darker blue background will hide any spills which might occur at the table."

Mrs. Emery laughed, patting Peyton's hand. "Exactly. I think you and I shall get along just fine, my dear. Well, toodles. I'll leave you to it."

"Thank you, missus. I shall begin at once." Peyton curtsied, then waited for Mrs. Emery to exit the room. She pulled out the intricate poppy-and-butterfly fabric. "Hmmm ... this shall be a challenge to match up."

"Did you say something?" Patrick. On the ladder. She'd forgotten he was there.

"No ... just assessing my work." She paused and took a step. "I need to gather chairs from the dining room. I could use your help."

"Aye, a fair maiden such as yourself shouldn't be hauling furniture through the castle." Patrick chuckled, bowing to her as soon as he stepped onto the floor. "Back shortly." He scurried out the door before she could thank him.

He'd always been so willing to assist with anything. Even as a boy, he'd helped her papa paint the porch, till the vegetable garden, and sow the seed. He'd weeded and even harvested the produce. Papa had once said that Patrick was the son he'd never had, to which Peyton asked if he wished he'd had a boy. The hurt in his eyes still stung, but he'd promptly kissed her and told her God had given him the greatest gift on this earth—her, his daughter. He vowed he'd not trade her for a hundred boys.

The memory warmed her heart as she laid out the poppy fabric and made her plan of attack. Hopefully, she wouldn't have to piece together any of it since she'd need only cover the seats.

Before long, Patrick had returned, carrying two chairs. He set them down and wiped his hands on his pants. "Those sure are solid chairs, unlike the rickety ones at home."

"Thank you, Patrick. I appreciate your help."

She must be careful with her praise else he would get the wrong idea. Surely, those few words wouldn't lead him astray.

Patrick chuckled, daring to touch her forearm and receiving a shock that skittered up his arm and straight to his heart. It warmed him to his toes and sent his senses reeling. "You're most welcome, and when you're done with those, I'll fetch you two more. Just consider me your long-lost go-fer."

Peyton, however, appeared as if she'd just been stung by a bee. She grimaced, withdrew her arm, and rubbed the spot he'd barely touched. She gave him a look as if to tell him to leave her alone.

He silently complied, nodding and returning to his work utterly confused.

What had happened to the carefree and happy-go-lucky lass he'd known? Life with her had been so easy, so comfortable. They'd played together, learned how to dance together, and laid in the summer darkness and counted the stars together, hoping to catch a glimpse of one falling from the sky so they could make a wish. And when he did, he wished for only one thing—her.

But now? A simple touch irritated her.

Did she have a beau, or had some cad broken her heart back in Watertown? If so, the man would have to answer to him. He'd have to explore those details with her when the time was right.

Heaven help him if he didn't win her heart afore the end of the summer!

Duvall, the butler, called from the doorway. "Patrick. A word, please."

"Aye, sir. Be right there." He scooted down the ladder and joined the formal yet kind older servant who waved him toward the butler's pantry.

"Shall we?"

Patrick followed Duvall and waited while he closed the door. Had he committed some infraction? Had Duvall caught him flirting or heard him speak to Peyton so intimately? Had someone overheard and told tales?

The butler cleared his throat quietly. "Besides your normal work, I'd like you to help our new hire, Miss Quinn. Seems Mrs. Emery has tasked her to work on much of the furniture, and Mrs. Milton can't be bothered. I won't have a dainty woman like her carting chairs and settees through the castle or imposing on the housekeeping staff to fetch what she needs. I'd like you to do that, and if you need a hand with the settees or whatnot, conscript another man to help."

Patrick let out a puff of relief. "Be glad to, sir. I already fetched two chairs from the breakfast room for her. I'd be happy to help in any way I can."

Duvall dipped his chin. "Good. I'd also like you to help familiarize her with the island. After dinner, please show her around Calumet— where to go and what to avoid. I doubt Mrs. Milton would give Rachel the time to do it."

"Be honored, sir." Patrick gave the butler a slight bow, a hand behind his back as if he wore a fine livery instead of paint-stained work pants.

Duvall waved him off. "Fine, then. Be about your work, and if the seamstress needs anything, please inform me."

Patrick almost danced a jig. "I will, sir."

Energized by the luck of the Irish, he hurried back to the ballroom. Surely, the good Lord had His hand in all this. Why, just a week ago, he'd wondered if he'd ever see his bonnie lass again. Now, here she was right under his feet. Under his tender, loving care.

He'd always liked Duvall. The man's receding hairline and clean-shaven, wrinkled face revealed his half-century or more of life. But his dark eyes shone with a gentle strength Patrick wanted to emulate. He looked up to the man, and now, he liked him even more.

So much more than his own father—the town drunk. The embarrassment of his existence. He hadn't seen the man for almost three years. Whenever he ran an errand into Clayton, he snuck around the back of the house like an alley cat just to say hello to his ma and avoid his father.

He looked up to Peyton's pa, too, trying not to be jealous of the close and warm relationship she had with her father—something he'd never have with his.

Peyton, now removing the chair bottom and the old material,

wiped her brow with a shirtsleeve, but the joy on her face revealed her pleasure in the work. She'd always embraced a challenge, loved learning something new, and bent toward the next thing, the newest gadget, the most modern fad.

He, on the other hand, wanted the comfortable, the predictable, the safe—the qualities lacking in his home. Fads and change be gone!

"Can you help, please?" Peyton yanked him from his musings as she pulled and pried on something. "Unless you're too busy."

"Be right there." Patrick didn't care if he ever finished hiding the nail holes. In a flash, he was by her side.

She blew an exasperated breath. "I can't get this to come loose." She indicated the bent head of a large tack that refused to release from the wood.

"You've got yourself a predicament, for sure. You know what the Irish say—'Many hands make light work,'—and I'm here to lend two hands." He took the tool and pried at the tack. "Actually, Duvall has tasked me to lend my hands to you on a regular basis. Apparently, Mrs. Milton suggested it, and I'm happy to help." The tack yanked free, and he laid it on the table.

"Thank you, Paddy."

He handed the tool back to her and gave her the kindest smile he could muster. "Welcome. Say, did you hear about the cat who swallowed a ball of yarn?"

Peyton rolled her eyes, shaking her head.

"She had mittens." He guffawed, and Peyton *liggled*, sending waves of joy down to his toes. He'd have to resurrect other old jokes and riddles and find some new ones just to hear more of her laughter.

"Well … thanks for your help … and to Mr. Duvall for his." Peyton pulled off the material. "I should have both of these done within the hour."

Patrick gently corrected her. "It's just Duvall. No *Mister.* And I'll be glad to return these when you're done and get you two more. Looks as though Mr. and Mrs. Emery will have new seats for breakfast. Well done, miss! And here I thought only a man could do well at this type of work."

Peyton's face reddened, her eyes narrowed, and her lips thinned. He'd seen that face and knew what was coming.

"Excuse me? I've studied and worked hard on my craft for three years. I recovered an entire dining room full of chairs at the Hotel Woodruff, if you must know! I'm quite accomplished, and I dare say, no man could do better."

She always could be so stubborn and self-assured. He stared at the chair. "Yet I needed to help you with that tack."

Her cheeks turned crimson, and he immediately regretted opening his big mouth. Again.

"How dare you! You know nothing about my life, my accomplishments, my dreams and desires of these past three years. You've been in your own world, and I've been in mine." She drew in a deep breath, swallowing hard. Her eyes filled. "I've faced ridicule, mockery, rebuke, and persecution trying to better myself, trying to prove myself, trying to succeed in this man's world, and I don't need you to pour any more of it on my head! This is exactly why I share the ideals of suffrage and fight to see women everywhere freed from the constraints of such a narrow, man-centered mindset."

Patrick's chest squeezed as he drew in a breath. How could the sweet girl he'd known have aligned herself with such a radical faction of society? "You've taken up with agitators? Honestly, I'm dumbfounded at such a revelation."

A tear tumbled down her cheek, her face paling. "Of all the people, Patrick. I'd expected more."

But his disappointment in her overpowered his pain at hurting her. Patrick shook his head and walked away.

CHAPTER 4

PEYTON'S HEART POUNDED IN her chest, but not from excitement. No, Patrick's gentle retort had cut her to the quick. He stomped out of the ballroom without a word of contrition or even an explanation. If he didn't believe in her, who would? Why did men dismiss women's goals with barely a turn of the hand—especially him?

She took a sip of her water, then finished her first chair, pleased at the outcome, and tackled the next with a vengeance. The tacks released easily. No need for help from a man, thank God.

Patrick had always been so supportive of her unorthodox ideas, even as a child. She'd never fit in with the girls in her school who only talked of marrying their Prince Charming and having babies. She'd always had dreams of more, so why the animus now?

Before she had the chance to explore those thoughts more deeply, he returned to the ballroom, red rings circling his silvery eyes. Had he been crying?

Patrick came closer, holding a bouquet of wildflowers. He thrust them toward her. "I know they're your favorites. Whenever I see wildflowers, I'm reminded of my chum who was one day a tomboy, the next day a Sunday school sweetheart, and every day, my best friend."

Peyton raised a brow. "Anyone ever tell you that you're a flirt?"

Patrick shrugged, a mischievous twinkle in his eye. "Ach. Never.

But many have told me I'm handsome, charming, and extremely talented."

That took her aback. But she was ready with a comeback. "So that's why you've been sent to this isolated island to work?" She took the flowers and buried her face in them, just for a moment. "Thanks for the flowers." She set them in the glass of water she'd been drinking and sneezed.

He cleared his throat. "Bless you. May we continue the prior conversation, please? I acted like a dunderhead when I walked out on you. Forgive me?"

She tipped her chin. "And I can be too hot-headed and impassioned regarding the topic. Forgive me?"

Patrick's brow quirked, and he bobbed his chin. "I have to ask—and please don't be angry with me." He paused and held her gaze, apparently making sure she wouldn't explode. "Where is your faith that God will change things in His own good time?" He swallowed, licking his lips and sucking in a deep breath as if to gain courage. "You cannot fight what society deems right, Peyton Pie. They will ridicule you. They'll whisper in the streets. You'll be ostracized from here to New York City."

Peyton waved a hand of dismissal. "Oh, I've already endured three years of that. I'm used to it. But men live such exciting, rewarding lives, free from social constraints, and women cannot. Men can talk about business and politics and enjoy every new-fangled invention of the day without a thought of ridicule. They can do anything without others whispering, accusing, condemning. Yet as women, we are relegated to the home and nothing more."

Patrick held her gaze. "I can see where that could be frustrating."

And that was all he had to say? She bit her lip. "Don't you see? It takes sacrifice to change things. We women have been ignored for too long. We are looking forward to a time when every little girl is equal to every little boy. We don't want to be lawbreakers—we want to be law*makers*. We just want to define our own destiny."

"Thank you. I may not completely understand, but I'll try." He took her hand, and his touch rattled her more than she'd expected. He was her childhood chum, for heaven's sake! Her heart jumped three beats as her blood rushed to her head, making her woozy. Her cheeks warmed as if she had a fever. What was the matter with her?

Peyton slipped her hand from his and stepped back. "I'm not a radical like Susan B. Anthony, but I do have an open mind to hope for a better tomorrow. And I cannot be the wimpy, whiny, submissive woman who hides in her home and tends babies. I shall likely continue to work and become an old maid like Aunt Bess. I must keep working, and if I marry, my husband must allow that as well as the freedom to learn, even though I shall be glad to nurture my family as well."

Patrick raked his hands through his hair. "I'll be jiggered. You've given me a lot to ponder, my lovely lass." He tossed her a wink as he returned to his work.

Thank goodness, her words appeared to make things right between them.

She also returned to her work, carefully cutting the material and tacking it to chair number two. For her first day of working here, she was making marvelous progress.

As always, Patrick brimmed with wit and charm, and this new manly version of her childhood friend held the perfect balance of masculinity and boyish mischief. But he was also gifted at sweeping his pain—or the pain and concerns of others—under the rug and dousing his world in sunshine and rainbows.

Patrick sanded a rough spot in the mahogany wood. He ran his hand over it. Such a warm, fine-grained hardwood from West Africa.

He found it so much easier to bury himself in his work than to face difficult concepts, confusing thoughts … or hurtful memories. If work wasn't at hand, he'd use whatever was necessary to cover the pain. A smile. A laugh. A clever riddle or joke or quip.

Peyton, too, had been a hiding place. His *favorite* hiding place. Thoughts of many hours with her by the river's edge warmed him. Fishing. Swimming. Just sitting and watching the sun melt into the St. Lawrence as they kissed the days goodbye.

But that was then, and this was now. Things had changed. *She* had changed. Her radical ideas pelted him with fear, worry, uncertainty. The question was … could he accept the profound changes in her?

He pondered it while he worked, then while he ate dinner with the men. As he enjoyed his dish of chicken and dumplings, he stole glimpses of Peyton with the women as she picked at her food. He needed to pry her from her work and show her around the island—as Duvall had requested.

Once dinner was done, the staff meandered out into the fresh air. Some who worked on the other side of the lagoon in the boathouse or the like headed that way. Others returned to various parts of the castle. Waiting for Peyton, he leaned against a tree and tried to appear as if he hadn't a care in the world while, inside, his mind and emotions swirled. Finally, she opened and gently closed the screen door.

He hurried to her side before she could embark to places unknown. "Good evening. Duvall has instructed me to give you a tour of the rest of the island. And you know what the Irish proverb commands, 'Never put off to tomorrow what you can do today.'" He grinned and waved his arm in the direction of the steps that led to the lagoon.

"But I was going to work on another chair until dark." Peyton snatched a look toward the ballroom. "I can't be shirkin'."

Patrick guffawed. "You've completed two already. That's a jolly good day's work, if you ask me."

"Well. All right, then. I'd like to experience it all as I saw only a bit of the island from afar as we entered the lagoon this morning."

"Perfect timing, then. The Emerys have gone to the mainland for the evening, so we have more freedom than usual to explore."

Instead of going to the lagoon, he led her around the outside of the castle to the front terrace. She started down the stairs facing their hometown of Clayton, but he gently stopped her, turning her toward the castle by her shoulders. At his presumption, her lips parted.

My, but she was altogether breathtaking.

"Before we go around to the lagoon and the far side of the island, I wanted to give you a bit of a lesson on the place you'll be living for the next few months. How does that sound?" Hopefully, she'd agree. He'd been trying to recall the details for most of the afternoon.

"You know how I love facts and such. Don't forget how I always beat you in the history bowls in school." Peyton's eyes glistened with mischief. "Carry on, then."

Patrick rolled his eyes. "Rub it in." He gestured toward the castle. "This three-story, thirty-room castle is made of Potsdam Sandstone. I saw the quarry during my apprenticeship in Ogdensburg, and it was dandy. The castle's Imperial Classicism style with its Dutch tile roof is not unlike grand European castles of old."

Peyton leaned her head back to look up. "You sound more like an architect than a carpenter, sir. But it's impressive, I'll give you that. I love how the veranda stretches across the front and runs all the way around the right side of it. How pleasant it must be to sit there at night and listen to the crickets chirp and gaze at the stars."

"I agree. Remember how we'd do that in our secret hideout?"

Peyton sucked in a breath, and her eyes narrowed at his confession. He'd made her uncomfortable—again. He had to rectify it and fast.

He snapped his fingers. "While I'm thinking about it, how about a fabric riddle? What's the opposite of irony?"

Peyton's face relaxed until she brightened. "You and your riddles. You always could stump me."

"My only way to beat you. The answer? Wrinkly. Get it?"

She *liggled*, her laughing giggle warm with amusement. "I always love your wit. It's quite … unique."

"Aye. Thank you, fair lass." He teasingly bowed and then inspected the castle to regain his focus—even though he'd rather focus on her. "Observe how the castle was built on the highest rise of the island facing Clayton. Mr. Emery wanted this to be the first castle ships saw as they returned to the sea from Lake Ontario. Let's meander over to the other side of the island before the sun sets."

He offered his elbow, but Peyton's pretty face scrunched up in dismay.

"Wouldn't it be fraternizing to take your arm?" Her eyes revealed clear concern.

He shook his head. "This is part of my job, remember? Duvall instructed me to show you around. I'm just being a gentleman." He gave her a wink, his way of putting her at ease.

"All right, then." Peyton slipped her hand into the crook of his arm, and he patted it.

He led her down the path to the boathouse.

"This is the path and pier that brought me here." Peyton pursed her lips, her eyes dancing.

"You just rhymed. Perhaps I'll make a leprechaun out of you yet."

He grinned before turning them to walk along the lagoon. "The lagoon has been dredged to allow even the largest yachts to dock safely in its harbor. Mr. Emery welcomes anyone to shelter here during a storm."

"How kind. I expect it could hold a dozen or more." She pointed to steps and a small building to their left, questioning him with her gaze.

"Yes, those are the steps that lead to the lower terrace and the servants' area. And that is the icehouse. To your right is the powerhouse, which holds the most modern machinery."

Peyton beamed. "I remember when all this was being built. There were newspaper articles and gossip galore. I'd just turned thirteen, so Papa had me read them. Said it was a special moment in our history. Remember how proud we were to have such a castle built right off our shore? I always wanted to explore it up close. I can't believe my luck. Eight years later, and I'm here for the entire summer!"

Patrick clicked his tongue. "I wonder if it's Irish luck or providence. Perhaps the good Lord has a bigger plan in mind for this summer, do you think?"

Peyton released her hold on his arm. "I don't know about that. I've come to believe that much of providence is simply circumstances of our own making. I subscribe to the enlightened view that man—or woman—can make his or her own way in life and not just depend upon a distant deity to do everything for them."

Her words stabbed him like a two-edged sword. With all his willpower, he swept her revelation away to ponder another time.

As the sun slipped low on the horizon, Patrick sped up his tour of the island past the tool house, laundry house, and launch house until they came to the newly erected water tower.

"Isn't she a beauty in all her seventy-five-foot glory?" He pointed to a long building to the left of the tower. "That's where I live. It's the men's dormitory." Then he motioned to a large, white house. "To the right here, where this lovely home for the island's caretaker now stands, is the spot where the first island structure was built."

Peyton swiped at the perspiration on her temple. "What first structure?"

"A small cottage, 'tis all. But it was the beginning of all you see here." He led her a short distance to a bench near the western shore of the island. "Let's sit and watch the sunset, shall we?"

"Please. It's ever so warm tonight, don't you think?"

"It is rather humid, and the air is still, a strange phenomenon for this time of year. Usually, there's a constant breeze to cool us coming off the river."

Just then, a huge cargo ship sailed along the main channel, dwarfing the island. Peyton sat up straight and pointed.

"Goodness! That ship is taller than the castle and longer than the island. They don't appear half as large when I'm on the mainland. It makes me feel so tiny, so insignificant in the scheme of things."

"The ships are often this huge. Yet, though we may be small, each one of us is a child of God, and thus, we are never insignificant." He touched her arm, but she withdrew.

As the sun painted the river pink, purple, and then orange, squirrels played tag in the tree above them, skittering and scattering along the tree branches, scolding one another and jumping from one limb to another, too close to Peyton's head. She jumped up, scaring them away.

Patrick grabbed her hand, shooting a bullet of heat up his arm. "They won't hurt you, love … lovely lass." Goodness, he'd better watch his words, or he might frighten her right back to the mainland. Then where would they be?

She sat, and for a long time, they silently watched the fireflies dance all around them. But the humidity thickened, weighing them down until it was hard to breathe.

Peyton stood, smoothing the front of her frock. "I think we should return to the castle. I'm exhausted, but I thank you for the fine tour. It's nice to have my bearings."

Blathers! Their time together, cut short by the weather. Still, he obliged her, walking her back to the servants' quarters and bidding her a good night.

Something crinkled as Peyton climbed the stairs to her room. In her pocket was the note she'd found earlier on her cutting table. The note from Patrick. She'd forgotten all about it.

She picked up her pace. The gap at the bottom of her door was dark. Was Rachel still working this late? How she hoped she'd be able to read the missive in private.

Gingerly, she opened the door to find her room dark and quiet. As her eyes adjusted to the dim light, she gave a sigh. Rachel lay sleeping.

Confound it! How could she read the letter in the dark? She slipped it from her pocket and laid it on the bed. As she changed into her nightgown, the moonshine grew stronger, popping out from behind a cloud.

Her heart raced as she quietly scooped the paper up and hurried to the window. She unfolded the letter and tilted it toward the moonlight, but the screen and window seemed to obscure the light. What to do?

The balcony. She tiptoed to the door, opened and closed it, and in just a few steps, she was at the balcony door. Peeking through the glass and finding no one about, she stepped out, shutting the door behind her. There, the moon fairly glowed like midday, and she read the letter.

Dearest Peyton Pie,

What an incredible joy to see your lovely face once again! Memories of our childhood adventures flood my thoughts and warm my blood. I hope that providence has planned this reunion and we may renew our friendship, for I have missed it sorely. Many a night, I've thought of you, prayed for you, longed for you, and here you are in the very last place I'd expect. But isn't that how the Lord works? I hope for many fine jaunts with you in between our work-a-day world.

Forever your faithful chum,

Patrick

He thought God had brought them together? She was here to work—not to fraternize!

Now what?

CHAPTER 5

After reading Patrick's note, Peyton entered her room to find the lantern lit and Rachel reclining in her bed, reading a book. "Good evening. Did I wake you earlier? Hope I didn't disturb you."

Rachel closed the book and sat up, swinging her legs around to plant her feet on the floor. "It's okay. I heard you come in but wondered where you went in your nightgown." Her eyes narrowed as she quirked her chin toward Peyton's work clothes lying on the bed. "How was your work today?"

Peyton plopped down. "I've never been so tired in my life, but I covered two chairs."

Rachel brushed a strand of hair from her face. "Did you always want to be a seamstress?"

Peyton bobbed her chin. "A seamstress, yes. An upholsterer, no. I dreamed of making fine garments ever since I was a little girl, sewing clothes for my doll. But I never envisioned working with textiles and learning a male-dominated trade like upholstering. Still, Papa never discouraged me from doing anything, even boy things, all my life."

Rachel's eyes grew wide. "Don't people talk?"

Peyton let down her hair and reached for her brush, running it through her blonde tresses. "Oh yes, but I try and pay them no mind. When my superiors object, I have to swallow it—and it doesn't taste good, I'll tell you. But when my peers prattle about me, I always let them know what I think. After all, it's my life, not theirs."

"But that doesn't make you many friends, does it?"

Rachel's frown revealed her disapproval. Peyton had received that expression far too often.

"No, but I've had one good friend all my life, and that's all that matters." Patrick's face ran through her mind, and she paused to braid her hair. "How was your day?"

Rachel began sharing about her dusting, cleaning, sweeping, and scrubbing. As she did, Peyton slipped into bed. What would she do about Patrick? Her face grew warm, and she snapped a peek at Rachel, who still recited her chores, not even realizing Peyton wasn't listening.

She swallowed her dismay over her own romantic conundrum. "That sounds like a lot of work."

"It's fine. It gives me a wage to send back to Mama and the boys."

Peyton punched her hard pillow, trying to find comfort in it. "How many brothers do you have? And your father?"

"Father died in a boating accident, and I have four younger brothers. Two of them help out on the docks now and then, but it's not enough to feed them all. So ... my wage is a mainstay." Rachel shrugged as if her mundane lot in life were as normal as breathing. "Nothing unusual about our family."

Unfortunately, the girl's situation was all too common for young women. "I'm sorry to hear that but glad you're my roommate. It's good to know you, Rachel." Peyton yawned. "I'm ready for sleep. You?"

When Rachel concurred, Peyton turned off the lantern, bid her new friend good night, and rolled toward the wall.

As tired as she was, she needed to think more.

Patrick spoke of providence. His faith hadn't changed through the years—of that, she was sure. His note and so many of the things he'd said told her so. Did she still believe in providence? The thought struck her like lightning. What had happened to her faith?

As children, she and Patrick went to Sunday school together and committed their lives to Christ within months of each other. He did first, but after she saw how God had changed her rambunctious, sometimes irritating, friend into a gentleman, she wanted to know Him too.

That was before her enlightenment. Before suffrage. Before she'd met the O'Clearys.

Under their tutelage, she'd discovered that her abilities could take her far. She had power in her own hands. Talents that made her popular with the patrons of the shop. New friends who embraced her rather than judged her. With it came a warm feeling that pulled her deep into a place she'd not known before.

She belonged.

After that, her Bible sat in the drawer, and she attended church only on Easter and Christmas. Yes, pangs of guilt and a twinge of regret niggled her, especially when Papa encouraged her to go more regularly. Her papa's strong, abiding faith pricked the secret places of her heart. What would he think of her lack of it? If he only knew…

If Patrick knew.

A shudder chilled her to her bones, even on this warm, summer evening. If he knew how she questioned her faith though he never had, would he stop being her friend?

Yet… he hadn't been enlightened as she had. He didn't understand modern ways. Maybe she could illuminate him.

Soon, her weary thoughts jumbled into a stream flowing slowly along tall grassy banks. Rocks jutted out, creating dangerous rapids. Troubling waters tossed her here and there all night long.

Rachel patted her shoulder. "Time to get up. Breakfast in ten minutes."

Peyton blinked the sandy sleep from her eyes. "Morning. Guess I was more tired than I realized."

She dragged herself out of bed and dressed as quickly as she could, pulling her hair into a loose, wavy bun at the crown of her head.

Rachel frowned at Peyton's personal ministrations. "Mrs. Milton prefers a tight chignon at the nape of the neck. She may object."

"Stuff and nonsense. I'm to work under Duvall, so she hasn't any say. Besides, this is a far more modern hairstyle." She gave her hair a little pat as she took one last glimpse in the small mirror on the wall. "Ready."

They hurried to the servants' dining room, where the staff waited for them. Mrs. Milton's scowl cast a dark shadow on the entire room. "You're late."

Rachel cowered as she slipped into her chair. Peyton squared her shoulders and took the remaining seat between a footman and a pretty maid. After Duvall murmured a quick prayer, she dipped her spoon into her steaming bowl of oatmeal.

Duvall cleared his throat. "We are expecting a storm this afternoon, so there may be several boaters seeking shelter in our harbor, as often happens. If that is the case, please have hot tea, refreshments, and extra towels at the ready."

The dark-haired girl to Peyton's right turned to her, a smile lighting her pretty face. "I love helping out with the boaters. Seems it's the only way to meet new people around here." She giggled. "I'm Edna, by the way."

"Pleased to meet you."

Mrs. Milton waved her spoon in their direction. "Stop the chatter and eat, or you'll go hungry, and it'll be no one's fault but your own." She glared at Peyton. "And quit distracting the staff."

Peyton gave a quick acknowledgement and returned to her bowl. Did every meal need to induce indigestion? Why couldn't they be a time to relax and chat freely as she was accustomed to? She assessed Patrick sitting at the far end of the table. She gave him a brief nod but returned to her oatmeal before he could respond.

When the meal was finished and her bowl and cup washed, Peyton stepped into the fresh air. Clouds gathered in the north—dark, foreboding ones promising rain. The wind pulled wisps of hair from her bun.

Mrs. Milton appeared in the doorway, eyes trained on her. "A word, miss."

Peyton gave a quick curtsy. "Yes, ma'am?"

"Fix your hair. A chignon. Here." She roughly tapped the nape of Peyton's neck. "Not this … this monstrosity." She spread her fingers wide as if to signal an explosion and scrunched her face into a frown. "It's unbecoming. Speaks poorly of your morals."

Without letting Peyton respond, the housekeeper turned on her heel. Several other staff shrugged, raised eyebrows, and gave glimpses of either disapproval or sympathy, but no one said anything. As usual. Best not cause a fuss over her hair. At least, not so early in her employ.

Peyton trudged back to her room to redo her hair, pulling it into a low chignon, albeit loosely and with a sweeping wave that gave it a softer feel. Just like while growing up, and now with Patrick, it appeared that nearly everyone had an opinion of everything she did. Most disapproved. Hadn't that been the way of it her entire life? Only her papa supported her unconventional ways.

And Patrick. He used to champion her. But now? How should she respond to him after their argument? After reading his note? Surely, she couldn't lead him on or make him think she had feelings for him. After all, he was like a brother to her.

Wasn't he?

Thoughts and feelings spun around her mind like a weaver's loom at full throttle. She had to slow them down and get to work. She had more than twenty chairs to upholster.

With a sigh, Peyton hurried for the ballroom to begin her day.

Patrick carefully spread a dab of stain on the recently sanded wood and chuckled at the memory of Peyton drawing herself up at Mrs. Milton's warning. So typical of her. So confident, even in the face of trouble. She'd often stood up to authority—just a bit—as gently and respectfully as she could. Though her strange ways often irritated or infuriated others, they amused him, making him respect her spunk and the unique way she looked at the world.

He loved her for them. Loved that she was her own unique woman. His face flamed as she entered the room and glanced at him as if she could read his thoughts.

Peyton hurried to her workstation. Something was different from moments ago. Her hair, perhaps?

"Top of the morning, sunshine. Here to brighten my day?"

Yes, she had a way of doing just that.

Peyton dipped her head, tossing him a tentative smile that didn't travel up to her eyes as it usually did.

"Did you sleep well?"

"Fine, thank you. You?"

She avoided his gaze and went straight to her workstation, a far distance from him. What was wrong?

"You know what the Irish say. 'A light heart lives long.' What troubles you, lass?"

He stepped toward her like a gentle shepherd, trying not to alarm her. When he got to her side, he touched her arm gently. "Don't let Mrs. Milton get your goat. She's all bluster and bluff."

Peyton took a tiny step away from him, disengaging his hand from her arm. She rubbed the spot. "I'm fine. Just have a lot of work to do today and don't want to be distracted."

"Oh. All right."

She always knew how to shut him down when frustrated or pained. With that tone. That blasted, empty, "I'm fine."

Patrick frowned and returned to his work. Why the change from her warmth the day before? If it wasn't Mrs. Milton, then what? Why, when he last saw her, all was well.

He scrubbed sandpaper over a rough patch of molding on the baseboard. Round and round he went, the rhythm soothing his soul. He loved the way he could smooth wood and make it beautiful. Just a touch of stain, and it would be nearly perfect. If only he could do the same with people.

They were so much more difficult.

Peyton's comments about providence and making it on your own returned to mind. Why, that had him up half the night. She was still his childhood friend, his Peyton.

But not.

Something had changed in the years they were apart, and he wasn't so sure he liked it. Maybe he'd write her ...

"Blathers!" He started at his own voice. The note! Perhaps that was what put her on tenterhooks.

"What did you say?" Peyton stared at him, seeking a reply with her raised eyebrows. "Were you talking to me?"

"Oh, nothing. I just realized an error I made." He set down his tools and strolled over to her. "Have I vexed you, miss? If I have, my most sincere apologies."

Peyton's face flushed a pretty pink, and she lowered her eyes. "No. I just ... we just ... can't fraternize, 'tis all. If others saw ..."

"How's it going today, miss?"

Duvall had entered the ballroom so quietly Patrick hadn't noticed. He stepped away, putting feet between himself and Peyton where, moments ago, there had been mere inches.

Peyton sucked in a breath and dropped her hammer, a loud thud reverberating off the walls. "I'm—I'm making fine progress, sir." She patted the chair, recovering her demeanor quick as a wink. She scooped up the hammer and laid it on the table. "I've nearly finished this chair."

Duvall crossed to her side, a smile lightening his otherwise stoic demeanor. "Well done. I saw the others you completed in the dining room. The missus is pleased. We didn't know you'd be so quick at your work. Carry on, then."

Peyton curtsied. "Thank you, sir."

"A word, Patrick." Duvall motioned for him to follow. When they reached the doorway, Duvall stopped. "The storm looks to be a doozy, so batten down the hatches in here. Doors closed. Windows tight. I know it might get stuffy, but we best not play with this one." He pointed to the nearest window and scowled. "Just look at those clouds."

"Yes, sir. I'll attend to it at once."

"And if we have visitors, I'd like you to lend a hand with serving them."

"Of course. It would be my pleasure."

Duvall nodded his approval and left, so Patrick returned to his sanding. He'd wait until the first raindrops fell before closing up the room. He snatched a glimpse of Peyton.

She tugged her heavy material into place over the seat, flipped it over, and carefully nailed a tack in place, her face scrunched up like that of the little girl he remembered. Her hair fell around her pretty face as she pounded the tacks in place, perspiration glistening on her temples. He'd observed that same determination many times.

Patrick grinned at her tenacity. "Need another chair, lass? Shall I fetch you a pair before the storm rises?"

Peyton wiped her brow with a piece of cloth and placed her hand on her hip. "Yes, please. And would you like some water? I'm thirsty, and you must be too."

"That would be crackin'. Thank you."

As if the heavens opened up, a quick thunderclap interrupted them, and suddenly, the deluge began. The wind blew in the open windows and doors with a fury, bringing rain in with it—onto the new floor, the walls, the fine wainscoting.

What a dunderhead! "Ach! I just promised Duvall I'd take care of this before the storm struck."

Patrick scrambled to shut the windows and doors as fast as he could. Peyton joined him in silent camaraderie, and before he knew it, they'd closed the room up tight. As he surveyed the scene, he gasped in dismay. Puddles on the floor. Wet spots on the beautifully painted walls.

"I'll fetch some towels."

Peyton scurried out the door and was back within minutes with a pile of towels. Together they worked in silence, mopping up the puddles, patting down the walls, and drying off the windows, the sills, and the doors.

Outside, thunder clapped loudly, and lightning struck in a steady rhythm. Rain beat against the building so hard they could hardly see anything out the window.

Peyton wiped her brow. "Are the storms often this fierce on the island? I don't remember them as bad in Clayton."

"I've just been here a month more than you, so I don't really know. But remember that storm when we hid under the boat at Mr. Preston's and fell asleep? Everyone thought we were dead. Scared the liver out of my ma and your pa, we did."

Peyton *liggled*. "You sure caught it on that one. Though I pleaded and pleaded for your pa to stop beatin' you, he wouldn't ..." Her voice caught in her throat, and her eyes brimmed with tears. "I'm sorry. I shouldn't bring up such things, especially on this stormy day."

He shrugged. She'd seen so much. "As long as no one else hears such tales."

She patted his arm. "I'd never, Patrick. It's our secret. Always has been. Always will be. I promise."

CHAPTER 6

PEYTON CHIDED HERSELF FOR bringing up Patrick's hurts of the past. Especially about his pa.

What a wicked man! She could never forgive Patrick's father for the way he treated his son. Indeed, he was part of the reason she'd embraced a more enlightened view of life. After all, if God allowed such a man to beat his wife and son like he did, a man who went to church and put on airs of being an upstanding Christian, well then, if that was Christianity, she wasn't too sure she wanted to join those ranks.

She gathered up the wet towels and pointed to a still-damp spot on the far wall. "Hopefully, that will dry soon, and it'll be all right. I'll fetch glasses of water. Back soon."

"And I'll get your chairs." Patrick raked his hair, blowing out a breath. "Thanks for your help with this kerfuffle."

She bobbed her head, hurrying out of the ballroom and peeking into the library to make sure the Emerys weren't about. After she'd slipped through the great hall and into the service wing undetected, she relaxed.

She deposited the towels in the laundry, poured two glasses of water, and returned to the ballroom to find the chairs but no Patrick. A glance out the window revealed that the rain still fell at a steady pace while several of the staff headed down the steps toward the lagoon.

Attending the harbored boaters, she supposed.

Under an umbrella, Patrick carried a tall pile of towels. But who held the umbrella for him, so very close they appeared intertwined?

Edna.

The pretty brunette turned her face toward the ballroom, mirth on her features. She looked back at Patrick, whose face reflected the same enjoyment. Were they a couple or just flirting with one another?

The prick of jealousy that blossomed in her heart startled her. She blinked, pulling herself from the scene to resume her labors. That's what really mattered. Accomplishing her work with excellence and receiving accolades for doing a fine job—the work of a man.

She returned to her upholstering with a vengeance, finishing the chair she'd almost completed before the rain started. Then she ripped the nasty, stained fabric from the other two dining chairs and tossed the material aside.

She enjoyed taking something ugly and making it beautiful. There was a sense of pride in completing the task, something rewarding.

Patrick seemed to view his work in the same way. She'd observed him lovingly run his hand along the part of wood he'd sanded, a joyful smile on his face. She knew that look well.

Still, he confused her. On the one hand, she enjoyed being near him, talking to him. But on the other, his very presence pricked her conscience, making her question the enlightened thinking she'd tried so hard to settle into.

And flirting with Edna? That certainly didn't square with the devoted friend she'd always depended upon.

Perhaps *he* had changed.

Footsteps clipped along the ballroom floor. Mrs. Milton waddled toward her. Peyton rose and hurried to meet her partway. She curtsied. "Ma'am?"

"I need you to come with me. One of the maids left the window open in the front drawing room, and the davenport is drenched. Drenched, I tell you. You may need to work on it now so mold doesn't set in. Come." Mrs. Milton fairly spat her disdain as Peyton followed her. "I don't know where I can find good help these days. Young people are all so giddy and distractible. Why, that maid will be chastised for leaving her duties unattended. Claims she is sick. There's no time to be sick in such a grand castle as this."

With a huff, the housekeeper swept the door open and pointed at a brown paisley davenport. "Just look at that!"

Sure enough, the rain had stained the heavy matching drapes and sofa. Peyton drew close and touched the damp material. "'Tis true. It is likely soaked through to the batting. I can fix it, and the curtains, too, if need be."

"That would be lovely, dear."

Peyton whipped around to discover Mrs. Emery standing in place of Mrs. Milton. Peyton curtsied. "I'd be happy to serve, missus."

"Splendid. I'd planned for you to recover this ugly thing, anyway. And thank you for fixing the chairs so quickly."

"Of course, missus. What material shall we use?"

Mrs. Emery scanned the room for several moments, tapping her chin as she pondered. "I believe I know just the thing. Let's peruse our pile of fabric."

Peyton followed the missus back to the ballroom. Once there, Mrs. Emery scanned the material and pulled out a bolt of embroidered fabric with flowers and birds on a black background. Pinks, maroons, and golds cast a most elegant design.

"This is perfect. I purchased it in Paris from the famous Scheurer Company, one of Europe's great textile manufacturers. Isn't it lovely? I think you'll have enough to make drapes too. Can you do that?"

Peyton examined the print before answering. "It appears the pattern isn't too difficult to match. I think so."

"Lovely. I'll have the settee brought here immediately." She inspected the completed chair and the two that Peyton had been working on. "Goodness! You're a quick worker. I daresay it would have taken a week for a man to do what you've done in just two days.

I'm impressed."

Peyton beamed. "Why, thank you. The settee will take some time, but I'll start on it immediately. The batting will need a day or two to dry out, so I'll finish these chairs in between."

Mrs. Emery nodded, clasping her hands together. "If you need more batting or whatnot, let Mrs. Milton know, and someone can fetch it. Carry on, then."

Peyton ran her hand over the material Mrs. Emery had chosen. Why, it must have cost a small fortune. She turned it over to survey the underside—tightly woven with impeccable precision. Heavy. Solid. Strong.

While she waited for the settee to be delivered, she worked on one of the two remaining chairs. The rain pattered to a halt, and sunshine soon beamed through the windows. The room had grown stuffy, so she opened the windows and doors to let a crosswind pass through, then she stepped onto the terrace nearest the back lawn for a breath of fresh air. Patrick and Edna returned to the kitchen, wet towels and laughter abundant.

With a huff of breath, Peyton slipped back into the ballroom. The nerve of him flirting with her. What about not fraternizing?

Two young men whom she'd seen at the staff meals entered carrying the damaged sofa. They stopped in the middle of the ballroom. "Where should we set this, miss?"

She motioned to the alcove. "Over here, if you please." She led them to her work area, where they set it down. Then she put out her hand. "I'm Peyton Quinn. And you are?"

"Charlie, and this is Sam. Pleased to meet ya."

She shook their hands as Patrick came into the room. He stopped, scowling.

Peyton ignored him, choosing to address the taller of the lads. "Would you be so kind as to return this finished chair to the breakfast nook in the dining room?"

Charlie complied, a kind smile crossing his lips. "Sure enough, milady." He scooped up the chair, and the two left the room, acknowledging Patrick as they passed him.

Patrick sauntered up to her. "What do we have here? A casualty of the summer storm?" He gawked at the newly arrived sofa. "Or merely another task from the missus?"

Peyton shrugged. "Seems a maid is in deep water over leaving a window open—which means my job has quickly shifted to repairing this."

"The sofa looks as though it took the brunt of the storm." Patrick ran his hand along the back, whistling low. "Exquisite, although the material is hideous."

"It is." Peyton admired the fine wood carving on the Victorian walnut settee. It boasted carved, gilt-wood flowers and intricate filigree. A most beautiful piece of furniture, to be sure. Peyton turned her gaze to Patrick's face. "And what have you been up to?" She held her breath. Would he confess his relationship with Edna?

"As Duvall mentioned at breakfast, I helped out at the lagoon. We had eight vessels seeking harbor—eighteen souls in all." Patrick paused, glancing out the door. "I suspect that by now, all are safely on their way back to where they came from."

"Who else helped the boaters?"

"Several of us. You've met Edna but not the others. One of the boats almost capsized, so it was quite a mess."

"Why Edna? What's her role?" Peyton surprised herself with the accusatory tone that came with her words.

Patrick's brows furrowed. "Why not her?"

Patrick shook his head. What was the meaning of Peyton's interrogation? What did she suspect him of? "Edna was tasked to help with the refreshments, 'tis all. Why?"

Peyton's face turned Christmas red, and she angled away from him without answering.

He took her arm and drew her back around. "Peyton Pie, what's the matter with you? You've been off-kilter all day."

"I'm sorry. You know how I can get a little topsy-turvy during storms."

Patrick chuckled. "Yes. I do remember how you'd fly under my wing when the thunder clapped or lightning flashed. You even cried on my shoulder a time or two." He stopped and tweaked her nose tenderly. "But that's our little secret. Besides, I think you got that fear from your Auntie Bess. She'd almost faint dead away when a storm came. Remember her ghostly face? Even when I was just a tyke, she'd hold onto me as if the world were ending that very moment."

Peyton's eyes twinkled, and she let a *liggle* pass her lips. "'Tis true. Auntie was afraid of a million things. Spiders. Snakes. Frogs."

Patrick gave her a safe, quick shoulder hug—like a big brother would. But it didn't feel like a brotherly hug. He bumped her playfully. "It's okay to be a wee bit sideways now and then, especially during thunderstorms."

Peyton blew out a breath.

What would she think of him if she knew what thoughts danced around inside his head? Would she run from him? He couldn't lose their friendship, even if it meant—

"Dear me. It's nearly dinnertime. Shall we? I shan't be late twice in one day. Mrs. Milton might stew me alive." She bit her bottom lip. "Not that I'm afraid of her. But, you know..."

"I missed seeing you chew on your bottom lip like that. You've done it since you were just a lass still in pigtails—especially when you were solving math problems." He smirked, hoping to ease her concerns. "Be careful, though. The boys won't want to kiss gnarled lips."

"Well, I miss seeing your cleft chin." Peyton tweaked his beard. "Hiding under all this."

"I thought you hated my cleft. You teased me mercilessly about it when we were schoolchildren." He touched his chin, rubbing his short beard in thought. "Maybe I'll shave it off. If you like."

Peyton just shrugged as they walked outside and down to the staff wing, dodging puddles and muddy spots in the grass and keeping a casual distance between them. She tilted her head to the sky and sucked in a lungful of the cool, humid air. "I may not like the summer storms, but I do love that it's so refreshing afterward."

"Aye, lass, I'll give you that."

After they fetched their plates in the dining room, which was unusually noisy and carefree after the storm, Peyton selected a seat across and down a few spots from Patrick. Why was she so concerned about being seen with him? Was she embarrassed by his small-town ways since she'd become a fancy city girl?

"That was quite a morning, eh, Patrick?" Edna sidled up to him and gave his shoulder an intimate rub. Then she took the chair next to him, scooting it a little closer than he appreciated. "I felt so much safer with you beside me."

Peyton's eyes narrowed and nostrils flared at Edna's actions. Was she jealous? Surely not. Still, he inched away from the forward maid.

"Safe from what, Edna?" Peyton jumped into the conversation with gusto, leaning forward as if she were a solicitor questioning a criminal. "Were you caught in the storm?"

Edna blinked before answering. "Yes. No. I mean ... Patrick and I helped with the stranded boaters. He bailed out a boat for nearly an hour, so the ship's mistress said he was her hero." She leaned toward him. "Mine too."

Just then, Duvall entered the room. Mrs. Milton was nowhere to be seen, so once Duvall gave the blessing, the staff enjoyed a lively conversation—or several conversations—free of the housekeeper's restrictions. What a difference her absence made!

Edna prattled on about the boats that sought harbor from the storm—some Canadian, some American. Most had been schooners, but there was also a yacht, a sailboat, and two small skiffs. His friend, Mitch, related how one young mother had tied her toddler to her with a rope for fear the child might fall overboard and drown.

Peyton's eyes widened. "Is the child all right?"

Mitch nodded. "The tyke is fine. Patrick gave him a peppermint stick to ease his tears." He paused and turned to Patrick. "Say, have another for me?"

Patrick shook his head. "Sorry, all out, mate."

Edna sniggered. "He gave me his last. I'm saving it for a sunset walk tonight." She peeked at Duvall, who was busy eating, then batted her eyelashes at Patrick. "With someone special."

Did she mean him? He certainly hadn't asked her.

Before Patrick could react, Edna turned her attention down the table. "Say, Peyton, how did you end up in such a strange occupation? I thought only middle-aged men with pot bellies and big cigars sticking out of their mouths were skilled at upholstering. Isn't it terribly complicated and boring?" Her condescending tone was unmistakable, a challenge that caused a dozen heads to pop up from their meals and stare at the two women.

Peyton's eyes flashed with anger, just like he'd seen them do when the lads and lasses picked on her in school and about town. "I apprenticed with two of the North Country's finest upholsterers and became quite accomplished, thank you very much. Yes, it is very complicated. And no, it's not boring at all."

Patrick coughed into his napkin. Blathers! If he came to her defense, she'd be vexed at him for fraternizing. If he didn't, what would the others think of her?

By the time the meal was over, Peyton's ire and Edna's flirting had given him a bellyache. Seemed he couldn't manage either lass very well. Perhaps if he walked Peyton back to the ballroom, he could soothe her battered ego.

Unfortunately, just as he took a step toward her, Mitch stopped to ask for help moving a piece of machinery from the dock to the powerhouse. Peyton left the dining room, no one saying a word to her but many—all too many—staring in judgment as she passed.

CHAPTER 7

"MISS QUINN, WHY DO you think that it's your place to disrupt peaceful meals time and again?" Mrs. Milton's red face accentuated her angry tone as she hovered over Peyton.

She'd barely taken her seat in the dining room when the matron bore down on her. She struggled to contain her surprise and dismay. *Now she's going to ruin dinner too?*

"Oh yes, I heard about the ruckus you caused at lunch. If you want to retain your position, you'd best mind your manners, young lady."

"But I—"

Mrs. Milton lifted her splayed hand high in the air. "Stop! Not a word. Excuses don't matter to me. Just be quiet or leave."

Peyton clamped her lips together. Tears burned her eyes, but she willed them away. She would not show her dismay to the likes of Mrs. Milton or Edna—who watched the scolding with a smirk—or any of the others who stared at her in judgment. At least only a handful of the staff was present to observe her latest tongue-lashing.

Sitting two places away and across from her, Patrick cleared his throat. "She didn't start the discussion, Mrs. Milton." Patrick's tone was respectful but determined. "She merely responded to an accusatory question from another staff member."

"That's none of my concern—or yours. The two of you have

positions outside my jurisdiction, but it doesn't mean you can run helter-skelter over my staff. The same warning goes for you, Patrick. Be silent or leave."

"Yes, ma'am." With a quick nod, he lowered his head.

As Mrs. Milton returned to the kitchen, Patrick caught Peyton's eye, tapping his hand to his chest, his middle and ring finger pressed to his palm.

She sucked in a breath. As a child, he'd taught her that sign—the sign for "I love you"—and used it whenever she found herself in a pickle. When she'd asked why, he'd said it was a sign of solidarity, of friendship.

Friendship … and only friendship.

Is that what it was now? If so, why did her heart speed up, her face flush, and a lump in her throat threaten to cut off her oxygen? She gave a nod of thanks and focused on her fish dinner.

Since arriving on the island, she'd sensed his feelings were different. But she couldn't figure out how. One moment, he disapproved of her. The next, he'd show his affection.

And her emotions? They staggered around like a drunken sailor.

Peyton ate a few bites despite her lack of appetite. One by one, the staff left the table. She nibbled at her bread. She'd wait until they were all gone so she didn't have to see their stares or listen to their opinions of her.

"Let's take a walk." Patrick stood behind her, ready to pull out her chair and escort her away from her humiliation.

She patted her lips, set her napkin on the table, and rose. "Thank you, sir."

In silence, they left the room and walked along the path and down the steps toward the lagoon. Keeping a circumspect distance, they waited until they were far from any staff member before speaking.

"Thank you, Patrick, for trying to defend me. That woman has it out for me, though I don't know why."

"You're different, and that threatens her control. She wants to be the general of her troops who all align with her rules, her dictates, and even her thinking. You're outside of that in every way, and it drives her to distraction."

Peyton giggled as she stopped to admire a huge freighter passing the island. The setting sun hovered low on the horizon as crickets took up their noisy good-night ritual.

"I thought Clayton was small and isolated, but this island is a tiny world all its own. There is beauty here, but I'm not sure I like the seclusion." She jerked her chin toward the passing ship as it gave three quick blows of its horn. "I wonder … what would it be like to sail the seven seas and explore this grand globe, not having to bow to the likes of a Mrs. Milton?"

Patrick chuckled. "Oh, I'm sure those sailors have Miltons in their lives. I'm told that many a captain has his sailors whipped when they don't comply with the rules, fair or not. Being a sailor would be like jumping from the frying pan into the fire."

"Perhaps I'm more of a city girl?" She wrung her hands. "Oh, I'm not sure where I belong anymore."

"Fear not. You'll find your place soon enough." Patrick touched her arm, bidding her to sit. "Come. Let's watch the sun set." He gazed up at the open sky. "And here, there are no squirrels overhead to disturb us."

She sat, and slowly her heart settled into its normal rhythm. Paddy always could put things into proper perspective when she was vexed.

After several moments of peaceful silence, Patrick cleared his throat, growing somber. "Peyton Pie, I have a question for you, and I hope you'll answer it honestly."

She shrugged, blinking in her confusion. "You always have questions for me, and I have never been untruthful with you, Patrick. You know that. Go ahead."

Patrick scooped up a nearby stone and tossed it into the water with a plop. "Why did you never return my letters? I wrote you every few weeks, but you never responded."

Peyton scowled. "What? I never received a single letter from you the entire time I was in Watertown. I even left you a letter every time I visited my papa. There must've been a half dozen in all. I gave you my address and begged you to respond, but you never did. I thought you didn't care."

"Care? Oh, Peyton, you know I care. You're my ... the best friend I've ever had." A catch in his words dripped with emotion. Emotion that frightened her.

Neither spoke for a long moment. If he'd written, where were the letters? And the ones she wrote him?

Peyton sighed. "I delivered each of my letters to your house. A few I even put directly into your father's hand. The rest I slipped under the door. None could be lost in the mail."

Patrick stiffened, his shoulders pushed back as he stood and paced. He worked his jaw, and his brows furrowed.

"Father never delivered them." He scowled at her, his eyes blazing. "That man is so dead set against his only son being happy that he probably burned them. Not only is he an embarrassment but also a detriment to my very existence. I hate him!"

"Don't say that. He's still your father."

Peyton stood and tried to slip her arm in his, but he shook it off.

"You don't understand what it's like. You have the perfect father who loves and supports you, while I ..."

Trying to divert Patrick's ire, she didn't respond but shifted the conversation. "I'm so sorry I didn't get your letters. Could the postal service be that negligent? Where could they be, I wonder?"

Patrick deflated like a balloon slowly losing its air. All those letters—gone. All the angst and wasted worry. And Father ...

He returned to the bench and plunked down, rubbing his face and raking his hair with both hands. He blew out a breath, trying to bring his anger under control.

It took a few minutes, but finally, he was able to speak. "It is quite a quandary. I must've written two dozen letters or more, and not one of them made their way to you? Nearly three long years? I assumed the city postal system would be extra efficient. Then, when I never heard from you, I figured that you had found someone else and couldn't be bothered with your small-town friend."

"How wrong you are, Patrick. I longed to hear from you." Peyton slipped her arm in the crook of his and laid her head on his shoulder. This time, he let her. Warmth emanated from her, healing warmth he needed just then. So ... she wasn't trying to rebuff him after all.

Peyton gave his arm a squeeze. "I also want to thank you again for supporting me at dinner and for our sign. I'd forgotten."

"You had?"

He took her right hand and bent her middle and ring finger toward her palm. Then he tapped it over her heart. She smiled the same way she had the first time he taught her. The memory softened him. Soothed him.

Since his grandfather had been deaf from childhood, he'd learned the signs from his grandmama. He couldn't have been more than six or seven, but when he shared the language with Peyton, and especially that sign, it became their special secret. Whenever she was scared or worried, he'd tap that sign on his chest to let her know he supported her, believed in her, loved her. And she did the same.

"Peyton, I still care. Always will."

Peyton pulled away, shifting to look him full in the face, her sparkling green eyes like priceless jewels. Tears rimmed the bottom of them, but not enough to overflow. For that, he was glad. He'd never been strong enough to handle her tears.

"I care, too, just you mind that. But we're on a tiny island with foes like Mrs. Milton—and Edna—waiting to catch us in an error." She almost spat out the two names before pausing—as if measuring her words. "We must be vigilant to avoid any appearance of impropriety. I want to leave this place with glowing recommendations, and you should too."

"For heaven's sake, woman. You've never feared what people thought until now. Where's your faith?"

Peyton's eyes flashed. "Faith in what? People who judge every breath I take? Superiors who pick at everything I do? Peers who mock, ridicule, and embarrass me? No! I guess I lack faith that this world will be fair to a working woman and give her the dignity and respect that's due her." Stiff, stilted, her voice quivered with dismay edged in irritation. "In the past few years, I've found that I can only have faith in myself, in my abilities and skills, and not much more."

Did he hear her right? What had happened to bring her to this point?

"Oh, dearest Peyton. Self-reliance can only get you so far. Sooner or later, you'll find that your beauty, talents, and abilities will fail you. And then what? Only faith in God will get you beyond your earthly limitations."

Mitch rounded the corner and joined them. "Good evening, friends. Is this not a beautiful evening?"

Peyton blew out a breath, giving Patrick an end-of-conversation glance. "The sunset is glorious." She scooted over, away from Patrick, patting the empty space between them. "How are you this evening? Join us?"

Mitch sat and tossed a lanky arm over the back of the bench toward her. "I've been wanting to get to know you. This scrappy lad here can't stop jabbering about you. Seems you've been connected at the hip since you were knee-high to a grasshopper. How'd you both end up on this tiny piece of nowhere?"

Peyton *liggled*. Could there be a prettier sound in all the world? "I wanted to be nearer to my papa, who lives in Clayton. I also thought this would be the perfect position for my career development."

Mitch chuckled, tilting his head, his dark eyes dancing in the evening light. "Career development? That's mighty modern thinking. I like an independent woman."

Patrick stiffened at the comment. Was the lad flirting with her?

Better not, or Mitch would have to reckon with him. He sucked in a steadying breath.

Peyton glowed, her eyes sparkling at the compliment. "Thank you. So ... what about you? From where do you hail?"

"Oh, I've been a vagabond of sorts. Signed on with a Chicago shipping company when I was but sixteen. Worked on a laker for near three years. But I tired of that when the captain's lash became a regular occurrence. That man was evil." He paused, shaking his floppy mop of black hair.

Peyton shook her head, her brow furrowing. "That's terrible. But why here?"

"Yes. Well, I'd traveled the main channel of the St. Lawrence River—back and forth and back and forth—and always wanted to explore these Thousand Islands. They've mesmerized me for years." He scanned the main channel as a ship passed. "Can you imagine being on one of those and looking down on these tiny islands with castles and mansions and fine summer homes? We all wondered—who lived there? What was it like to spend a summer there? I became obsessed with the idea until I quit the ship and found a job on Round Island at the Frontenac Hotel."

Peyton grinned. "I've always wanted to visit the Frontenac. Is it as wonderful as they say?"

"It is ... and more. I enjoyed four years there until some rich scoundrel accused me of stealing his watch. I was dismissed, but later, they caught the man red-handed, that very watch on his wrist. But it was too late for me. They invited me back, but being falsely accused soured my stomach for the place."

Patrick joined the conversation. "I hadn't heard that. Sorry, chap. Did they give you a good reference?"

Mitch brightened. "They did and even recommended me to the Emerys. I've been here ever since—two summers now."

Peyton's eyes twinkled. "Does the island not feel isolated after all the places you've been?"

She had always wanted to explore. She'd studied the world map on the schoolroom wall so many times that Teacher turned her desk away from it so she wouldn't be distracted. She even stayed in from recess to examine it—one more reason for the other students to ridicule her. They'd called her strange, odd, outlandish, and finally settled on a nickname—Peculiar Peyton Poo. She'd hated it, of course, and found herself in the corner more than once when she tried to make them stop.

Mitch lifted a shoulder in a half shrug. "I rather like the slower pace and quiet nature of the island. Besides, the Emerys are fair employers, and so is the wage. I may not be here forever, but for now, it's home." Mitch removed his arm from the bench and glanced Patrick's way. "Say, old chap, wanna play a game of horseshoes before the sun sets?" He smiled at Peyton. "You can be the referee if you'd like."

Before Patrick could decline, Peyton responded. "That'd be grand. I'd love to watch a lively game of horseshoes."

Foiled. Just when he'd hoped to dig a little deeper into Peyton's spiritual challenges. Now he'd have to wait until later.

The three stood, stretched, and headed for the horseshoe pit near the men's dormitory. Thankfully, no one was using it, so they began their game.

Halfway through, the sun dipping below the horizon lit Peyton's cheeks aflame. Patrick couldn't take his eyes off the beauty before him— not the sunset but the woman. She closed her eyes and embraced the warmth of the retreating orb just as she'd often done in their younger years. How he'd like to study that fair lass for the rest of his life.

"Wake up, old chap." Mitch tapped his toe, arms folded, a playful scowl on his face. "There's not much light left, and I intend to beat you."

"Sorry, lad. Shall we call it?" Patrick shrugged, glancing at Peyton, who'd come out of her trance. "I'd like to walk Peyton back to the castle before it's too dark."

"Fair enough. I win!" Mitch tossed back his head and guffawed.

"You've not beat me yet, old boy."

Patrick waved him off. "Good game, though I'll get the better of you next time. See you soon."

Mitch leaned in. "Hey, need a chaperone?" His smirk teased as it so often did. "Be glad to aid in your hour of need."

Peyton tucked an arm around both men's arms. "Yes."

"No need." Patrick shot Peyton a disapproving glare and rolled his eyes at Mitch. "I have a few things to say and don't need your big ears about."

Mitch tossed up his arms in surrender. "Whoa, boy. Just offering. See you in the room. Good night, Miss Peyton."

Peyton gave him a friendly wave. "And to you, sir. Nice to get to know you."

Mitch waved them off as Patrick bid Peyton take the lead back to the castle.

Peyton glanced in the direction of the path Mitch took. "I didn't know you are roommates. He seems nice enough."

"He's a fine chap, though a bit rough around the collar at times. Watch yourself around him. His charm can blind you to his faults."

"Forewarned is forearmed, right?" Peyton waved her arm. "Look. The fireflies are waking up. This is my favorite time of night."

"Mine too. How many lightning bugs did we catch as children? We must have murdered a thousand by imprisoning them in our jars for nightlights."

Peyton *liggled.*

Once they rounded the bend out of sight of Mitch, Patrick stopped and offered his arm, but Peyton shook her head.

"We shouldn't. Let's make a pact, shall we?"

"What kind of pact, Peyton Pie?" *Please, please don't say we can't talk to each other or be alone or be near one another. Please don't say we should be free or see other people.*

Peyton bit her index fingernail in thought. "First, we should never touch. Second, we must keep a safe distance proper to social etiquette.

Third, we must not let anyone think we're a couple in any way. We're friends. That's all."

"Friends? I thought you longed for my letters?" Patrick's heart began to beat hard in his chest, his stomach rolling. "Surely, that's more than friends."

"Whether it's more or not is immaterial. We are here to work, to earn a wage, to receive a fine recommendation. There mustn't be any question about a relationship, nothing to give pause to anyone. Ever."

Patrick stared at the face he loved and swallowed hard. She'd given him no choice.

Chapter 8

Peyton didn't mean to be so harsh, but Patrick needed some firm boundaries. She didn't have time to muddle her mind with notions of romance. She had a job to do. As she climbed the stairs, her heart quivered. Though deep down she had to admit his attentions flattered her, if she wasn't careful, they'd both get booted off the island.

Patrick had been a boundary pusher ever since he had four missing front teeth at the same time. How cute he'd looked as a seven-year-old trying to talk and whistle, failing terribly for several long months. When the other children teased him, Peyton got so mad that she pulled her desk mate's—Sally's—pigtail … hard. The teacher made Peyton stand in the corner for the rest of the school day.

After that, when Patrick set his mind to something, little could stop him. Determination had set deep into his bones. Now it seemed he'd set his mind on *her*, and for the time being, that was unacceptable. Perhaps she'd remain an old maid for the rest of her life, working on furniture and fighting for the rights of women everywhere.

Peyton opened the door to her room to find Rachel brushing her hair, a scowl on her face. "Good evening. And how was your day?"

Rachel's face relaxed. "I'm still shaking from my near disaster. I nearly spilled the inkpot on Mr. Emery's desk when I was dusting. Thankfully, I caught it just in time. Can you imagine?"

Peyton pulled back her grin into a compassionate smile. "Glad it turned out all right for you. Accidents happen, but it's always better if they happen to someone else, eh?"

Rachel giggled. "Surely, 'tis true. And I'm sorry for the mealtime drama you incurred today. That was quite the scene. Please forgive me for not saying anything. I can't afford to make enemies here and endanger my position."

Peyton let down her hair, recollecting that moment. "I understand, and I don't expect you to put your neck on the chopping block for me, though I was a little surprised that Patrick did."

Rachel set down her brush, her eyes growing wide. "Do you two know each other from the past? You appear rather chummy, as if you have secrets."

Peyton puffed out a breath. "Not secrets. Patrick was the brother I never had. He protected me, believed in me, scolded me, was there for me through thick and thin. He had a special way of making me feel I could do anything, even boy things, and never judged me when I failed. He has always been my best friend, ever since we were out of diapers, maybe before. All our lives, we did everything together, shared everything. Until the past few years when we were both away at our apprenticeships."

Rachel's brow furrowed so tight her brows merged into one. "That sounds like the makings of a wonderful marriage to me. After all, isn't that what couples do?"

Peyton shook her head. "He's not the little boy who once had a crush on me, and I'm not that girl. I didn't know he'd be here when I came to the island to work. And now he moons over me something awful. But we're different. We've changed."

"Isn't change what makes us grow and thrive? It sounds as though his love has grown from puppy love to mature, manly love. The question you have to answer is, has your love grown too?"

"Love? I don't know about that. What I do know is that he could spoil it all."

Rachel didn't speak for several minutes. They changed into their nightgowns in silence, but once they were both in bed, Rachel spoke into the darkness.

"What might he ruin?"

Peyton pressed her lips together. "Our chance at success. Our jobs might be jeopardized if he gets too close. He's always been a bit pushy, even during public school, so I must keep him at a safe distance."

Rachel giggled in the darkness, dispelling a bit of Peyton's tension. "He seems like a very nice young man. Always kind and considerate, and he has a wonderful sense of humor. Mind your p's and q's, but don't let him get away. He's a keeper in my book."

"Do you ... do you like him?" *Please say no.*

"Oh, not in that way. I just think you'd be a fool to dismiss his affections over a job of sticking fabric on chairs. No offense. I don't know how you feel about him, but by what I've observed and what you said just now, a relationship like that only comes once in a lifetime—if you're lucky."

Peyton sighed. "Thank you, Rachel. I'll ponder your words."

After wishing each other a good night, silence fell, but Peyton's mind whirled.

Do I love Patrick? Inconceivable. Impossible.

Maybe?

Her heart raced in his presence, her emotions danced when they talked, and her brain filled with thoughts of him. He made her go weak at the knees, and his attempts at flirting made her feel beautiful.

But no! She would not be shackled to a man, only keeping the house and raising babies for the rest of her life. She was a modern woman, for heaven's sake. A woman who wanted the right to vote, to have an equal say as a citizen, a person, a woman. She would not settle for the schemes of traditional life, even with Patrick.

Ever since she'd learned the importance of women taking their rightful place in society, that had become her goal in life—to prove to the male species that she was just as capable as they and deserved to be honored and compensated sufficiently.

Sure, it might be lonely, difficult even. But if she didn't fight for the cause, who would?

No. She had to keep her independence at all costs.

Once she finally fell asleep, the recurring dream haunted her yet again. Troubling waters swept her along the main channel of the great St. Lawrence River, past several of the Thousand Islands. People along the shore reached out, but they couldn't get to her. She stretched toward them to no avail. Twice, a large freighter almost ran her over. The second ship came right for her, so she swam away as fast as she could, but the current was too strong. It pulled her under—down, down, down into the darkest depth of the main shipping channel. She couldn't catch her breath or see where she was. Would she die there?

She awoke with a start, gulped in some air, and found she was safe in her bed in the middle of the night. Sweat poured off her, leaving her bedclothes damp.

She rose and went to the window, careful not to awaken her roommate. A gentle breeze caressed her, cooled her, calmed her. Why did she keep on having such dreams, and what did they mean?

Patrick worked his jaw as he shaved off his beard, nicking his right cheek in the process. He'd show her how much he cared for her. She missed his cleft? Well, there it was.

He tapped the small indentation at the base of his chin, groaning at his reflection. Now he'd have to shave daily. "Hope she's happy."

And what about the Peyton Pact? He'd been awake half the night brooding over her rules and regulations. What happened to the carefree lass who didn't give a whit about what other people thought? She'd always declared that whatever was in that person's mind was not her concern.

That girl, his best friend, hugged him with abandon when she was excited or appreciative. She'd plant her head on his shoulder and weep unabashedly. She'd even wrestled with him like he was her brother. But now she was constrained by society's expectations.

Ach. Women.

Patrick wiped his face with a towel and ran a comb through his wavy mop, flipping the front of it back in his signature style. With a force that surprised him, he blew out a breath, the air ricocheting off the mirror and mussing his hair. He added a dab of pomade and reworked the front flip. "Not that it matters what she thinks."

He hurried to the servants' hall. Were he late, Mrs. Milton's ire would be more than he could handle after a sleepless night.

Still, just the thought of seeing Peyton rewarded him with delicious goose pimples. And yet, her hoity-toity ways since she'd come back from the city often left him dumbstruck.

When he reached the dining room, Edna had her hand on the doorknob, but she let go when she saw him. An exaggerated grin lit her pretty face in the morning sunshine.

Blathers. She was the last person he wanted to interact with. He pasted on a half-hearted smile. "Good morning, Edna."

He opened the door for her, and she walked through it but abruptly stopped, causing him to bump into her.

She let out a loud giggle. "Oh, Patrick. Must you follow so close?"

Patrick's face flamed as several of the staff assessed them. Including Peyton. He gave Edna his most disapproving scowl and stepped away, hurrying to the opposite side of the table from where she was headed.

The only seat on that side was next to Peyton. He grabbed it and sat down with a huff.

"You shaved your beard." Peyton's emerald eyes twinkled. "You look—"

Duvall tapped his spoon on his glass. "Attention, please. Mrs. Milton is off the island for the day, so everyone will report to me. Housekeeping, you know your duties, but if you have questions, talk to Cook first. The rest of you, carry on with your work as usual."

The staff murmured their understanding, and breakfast began

after a prayer of blessing.

Patrick stole fleeting glimpses of Peyton several times, but with Mrs. Milton gone, she concentrated on chatting with the maid to her left.

When she finally ended the conversation and took a sip of her tea, he rubbed his chin. "So ... do you like it?"

"It's my old friend back from the dead." With a wink, Peyton leaned close and whispered. "But that old chum must remain a chum. Remember?"

To avoid responding, he shoveled an overly full spoon of oatmeal into his mouth. Everything in him wanted to slam the table with his fist and tell her to let it be. Stop throwing her blasted pact in his face. She could be so overbearing at times.

As he chewed, he perceived a pair of eyes on him, but they weren't Peyton's. He peeked up.

Leaning over her bowl, Edna batted her lashes at him. "I wanted to thank you, Patrick, for always being such a gentleman." She paused and turned narrowed eyes toward Sam, the lad who'd delivered the settee to Peyton. "Perhaps you could give lessons to some of the other young men on the island."

Instead of answering, he grabbed his tea and took a long, slow sip. If he kept eating and drinking to avoid conversations with these women, he'd get as big as a cow. He chuckled.

Edna's sudden scowl turned her face prudish. "Are you laughing at me?"

Patrick waved his hands. "That was nothing to do with you, I assure you, miss."

For the rest of the meal, he kept his head down and said not a word. After breakfast, Patrick fled to the ballroom. He hauled his ladder to the opposite end, near the fireplace—far from Peyton's workstation. There he could cool off. And maybe he could think.

Nail holes evident along the entire length of the baseboard caught his eye. He shook his head at the shoddy job of the previous carpenter.

As he climbed a few rungs and rubbed his hand on the mantel, Patrick clicked his tongue. "Even here, you can see them." By the look of it, he'd be puttying and staining a thousand holes or more.

A woman's voice nearly startled him off the ladder. "See what?"

Mrs. Emery?

He promptly descended the ladder and bowed. "Nail holes, missus. The carpenter who was let go did a terrible job of it." Small surprise that the man had been both fired and booted off the island in the dead of night. It was a wonder he hadn't broken the huge mirror when he'd hung it over the mantel.

"Yes, well ..." The missus scanned Peyton's empty workstation. "Do you know where the upholstery seamstress is?"

"Miss Quinn should be here presently. I saw her at breakfast."

"Here I am." Peyton bolted through the door and curtsied low. "Mrs. Emery, good morning. How may I help?"

The missus wrung her hands. "I'm in quite a quandary. We're having a dinner party tomorrow night, but the chairs are a disgrace. Mr. Emery forgot about the ... well ... I need you to finish eight more chairs before tomorrow night. Can you do that?"

Peyton's eyes grew wide, and her face paled. "I ... I can try."

Mrs. Emery assessed Patrick. "Can you help her, please? Our guests won't be entering the ballroom, so this isn't imperative." She waved at the fireplace. "She can show you how to assist her."

He consented. He was here to serve, but of all times, to work so closely with Peyton ...

The missus turned to Peyton and dipped her chin. "Can't you, dear."

It wasn't a question.

Peyton inclined her head and gave her a quick curtsy, her face filling with determination. "If I have to stay up all night, I will complete the task, missus."

Mrs. Emery wiped her palms together. "Very well. That's one less thing to worry about. If only he'd consulted me before inviting everyone on such short ..." Her gaze flitted toward them, her cheeks turning pink. "Never mind about that. I'm rather in a tizzy today."

Peyton spoke up. "Not to worry, missus. We'll take care of the chairs."

Mrs. Emery studied Patrick. He motioned that his lips were buttoned, and she tittered. "Thank you both. For your discretion and your hard work."

With that, she left the room, leaving behind a sweet scent of expensive perfume.

Peyton acknowledged him before hurrying to her station, but suddenly, she stopped short. "What? What happened here?"

From the other side of the ballroom, Patrick couldn't detect what she was talking about, so he returned to her side. "What happened, indeed?"

It was as if a tornado had touched down in the alcove where Peyton worked. Her tools had been scattered everywhere. Batting from the settee strewn about. The bolts of fabric unraveled on the floor. Upholstery tacks tossed all around.

Had animals gotten into the room during the night? But if that had been the case, they would have left droppings, and there was no evidence of that.

Patrick's blood raged through his veins, and he huffed. "This is sabotage. Someone is trying to thwart your success."

Peyton's eyes brimmed with tears. "But who? Who would do such a thing?"

CHAPTER 9

AFTER CLEANING AND REORGANIZING her workstation, Peyton decided how to efficiently complete Mrs. Emery's request in record time—with Patrick as her unskilled assistant. She'd employ the assembly-line idea.

But where was Patrick? He should've been back from the dining room with the chairs by now.

She scanned the now-tidy alcove. Who could have ransacked her workstation?

She let out a low groan. Why couldn't people leave her alone? Even in Watertown, shopkeepers had turned her away just because she worked for the *radical* O'Clearys. Such people didn't approve of the couple's viewpoints, so they took it out on Peyton. She'd endured enough persecution in that job and all the way back to her school days. She didn't need it here on this small island.

She'd wanted to be like the other girls—she really had. But having been raised without her mother and having a boy as her best friend—well, that didn't give her much feminine modeling. And despite her domestic skills, in both manner and appearance, Aunt Bess had been more of a drill sergeant than a lady.

"I'm back." Patrick's return dissolved her uncomfortable train of thought. He crossed the room carrying two chairs with ease. "Sorry it took so long. Duvall had me run an errand before I became your apprentice for the day."

"Thank you. I've got a plan that I think will work."

"You always did like making plans."

She shrugged. "The more efficient we are, the faster we can get it done."

Patrick gave her a sideways smirk and rubbed his chin. "Remember when you decided to show me how to dive but instead belly flopped into our swimming hole? That plan went awry. As I recall, you cried for almost half an hour."

Peyton rubbed her tummy. "It hurt."

"Your belly or your pride?"

"Both." She shivered. Many of her plans went awry. But at least she tried. "Enough of this chatter. To work."

Patrick clicked his heels together, saluting her. "Yes, captain. At your service, sir."

"At ease, mate ... ah, er ... Patrick." Mate? Where did that come from? Mr. O'Cleary would call it a Freudian slip. He'd devoured the new and controversial book from Dr. Freud that attributed many misspoken phrases to repressed desires.

"First, you have a pact, and now, you have a plan." His piercing, silver eyes threatened to make her forget what she had decided to do. "What's your plan, Miss Quinn?"

She gathered her wits, straightened her shoulders, and took control. "Let's form an assembly line. Whenever the O'Clearys and I had several bridesmaids' dresses to complete, we'd make them like the modern manufacturing systems. One of us did all the cutting, one the pinning, another the sewing."

Patrick rubbed his hands together. "Sounds good. Where do we begin?"

Peyton brightened, warmed by his amiable manner. "Let's get all the chairs lined up here. Since they're all the same, I can create a pattern and cut the cloth while you remove the seats and rip off the old fabric. As the Irish Proverb says, 'Many hands make light work.'" She tucked a strand of hair behind her ear. "Thanks for lending me your hands today, friend."

Patrick grinned wide, his eyes twinkling. He tossed her another salute and headed for the door. "Back with the chairs presently."

Before she could respond, he was gone. She'd forgotten how he beamed under any form of affirmation or the simplest adulation. Since he'd rarely received either at home, he must hunger for them. Well, if that's what it took to motivate him, she could do that.

Truth was, he was easy to affirm. A kind word went a long way. And, if she was honest, he had many positive traits to compliment. He was handsome, strong, smart, skilled, and full of faith.

"Got them all, Captain Quinn."

Patrick paraded in with Charlie and Sam following close behind. Each young man carried two chairs. She added one of the chairs he'd brought earlier to the line to make seven chairs, all standing in a row like soldiers.

After thanking the men and dismissing Charlie and Sam, Peyton surveyed the job.

"Yes. I think it will work. I've already removed one seat and will use the old material for a pattern." She pointed to the row of chairs. "If you'd be so kind as to remove all the seats and rip off the old fabric, we'll be on our way."

Patrick reached out to pat her arm but pulled his hand back. "Glad to assist, miss."

As they tugged and pulled, ripped and restored, Patrick kept a lively conversation going. He wanted to know her thoughts, her heart, for they seemed so different from what he previously knew.

"Did you read the speech President Roosevelt recently gave about Cuba gaining its independence? Quite smart, I'd say." He clicked his tongue. "I can't believe Teddy took the oath of office less than a year ago. It was a sad day when President McKinley was assassinated like that, aye?"

Peyton wiped her brow with a shirtsleeve. "It was. These are uncertain times, with the assassination, a new president, and the ongoing fight for women's rights." She stretched her back before returning to cutting. "Do you still enjoy reading the paper? I do. You might remember, Papa hooked me on keeping up with the news a decade ago."

He yanked at a stubborn tack. "I haven't always had access to a copy. But here, Mr. Emery gives one to Duvall, and when he's done with it, he saves it for me. It's a luxury, to be sure."

Peyton's green eyes danced with delight. "Really? May I have it when you're done? I read the *Watertown Daily Times* every day when I lived there, but Papa only gets the *On the St. Lawrence.* As you know, it's limited to a weekly during the summer and doesn't contain national or international news."

"I'd be delighted to pass it along, Peyton Pie." That would give them lots of safe topics of conversation. "Did you hear about the coal strike in Pennsylvania? My uncle was a part of it. Isn't that something?"

Peyton pulled on a stubborn nail. "It is. Could you help me with this?"

He hurried to assist, popping out the nail with ease while Peyton patted her glistening brow again. He handed her the offending piece of metal. "Shall we take a water break and get a whiff of the fresh river air?"

Peyton agreed, and the two poured glasses of water, taking them out onto the terrace. "There's something about the river breezes, don't you think? Somehow, they carry away the cares of the world. I'll never tire of seeing and smelling the St. Lawrence as long as I live."

Patrick studied her. "Didn't you enjoy the sights, sounds, and smells of the big city?"

"There were interesting people, events, and things to see and do in the city. But I missed Papa and the river and y—" She swallowed, scrunching up her nose. "I didn't appreciate the smell of burning coal or all the noises of the city."

Was she going to say she missed me? He'd observe her pact now if it killed him. Maybe that'd win her heart sooner rather than later.

Patrick downed the rest of his water. "There's no perfect place this side of heaven, I'm afraid. Here on the island, we have lots of beauty as well as Mrs. Milton and Edna. In Clayton, we have small minds and gossip, but we also enjoy community and small-town charm. Who knows what cities like New York might bring? No matter. As a clever young woman once said, we should appreciate the good things and bloom where we're planted, aye?"

Peyton *liggled*. "Tossing my words back in my face, are you?"

He shook his head. "No. Cherishing them. They've helped me through many difficult days. Your wisdom has been a blessing to me."

She blushed a pretty pink. "Thank you, kind sir. We should be getting back."

He agreed, and they returned to work. By lunch, all the seats had been removed.

Peyton placed her hands on her hips, tipping her head to one side. "We've accomplished a lot so far. Thanks, friend. I couldn't have done this without you."

Patrick waved off the compliment. "Glad to help. We'll finish the rest this afternoon and evening—no matter how long it takes."

Peyton echoed his words. "No matter how long."

After a refreshingly uneventful lunch—where neither Mrs. Milton nor Edna showed their faces—Patrick and Peyton returned to their work.

Peyton glanced his way, warming him to his toes. "I wonder who created the mess here this morning. I know of no one who would want to thwart efforts to make the Emerys' home more beautiful, do you?"

"Maybe someone who doesn't want you to succeed or is jealous of you? It wouldn't be your roommate, Rachel, would it?"

Peyton shook her head. "No, I'm sure she wouldn't. Though I don't know her too well, she seems like a girl of integrity and kindness. This sabotage, as you call it, would have to be from someone more sinister. Mrs. Milton, maybe?"

"Mrs. Milton isn't even on the island today. I know she doesn't appreciate you, but as the head housekeeper, she wouldn't compromise any work to beautify the castle." He evaluated Peyton. "Any men whose hearts you've broken?"

Peyton whipped around and gave him a narrow-eyed stare. Then she smirked. "Really, Patrick. Do you observe a string of beaus awaiting my hand? Of course not. What about you? A jealous woman in the shadows, perhaps? Have you been courting while I've been away? Perhaps it was Edna. She seems quite taken with you."

He blew out a breath. "Ridiculous. This line of questioning is going nowhere fast."

Peyton's tone edged with irritation. "Who, then? Why would anyone bother with me, a nobody in a corner alcove, cutting and sewing fabric?"

"We'll have to think on that one." Time to turn the conversation. "But for now, here's a question for you. How do knitters get into heaven?"

Peyton huffed a breath that melted into a soft *liggle.* "I cannot say."

"They go through the purly gates. Get it?"

Peyton slapped her thigh in an exaggerated fit of laughter. "Good one." She feigned exasperation, but he could tell she liked it. "Now get to work!"

An hour later, Patrick stood and twisted at the waist to release the tension of bending over for so long. "Ripping off the last of the seven."

Peyton stretched, arching her back. "I've finished cutting the fabric." She clapped her hands. "We may even have this done by dinner if we keep up this pace. Well done, my gallant knight in shining armor. I'd be working on this until the wee hours of the morn otherwise."

"We couldn't have that, now, could we? You need your beauty rest."

Upon realizing what he'd said, he bit his lip, praying she didn't take offense. Her eyebrows flew up. Somehow, she'd changed from his carefree playmate who took ribbing well to an enchanting and often exasperating woman who could misunderstood things all too quickly. "Just kidding. It's just a saying. You're the most bea—"

He stopped, the word sticking in his throat. He cleared it and turned back to his work. He'd not overstep her boundaries no matter how silly he thought them to be. "Did you know that last winter, the island's caretaker found a cache of hundreds of crates of fine, imported wine hidden in a solid rock cave behind a brick wall? Many of them were from France, but no one knows why they were bricked in."

Peyton quirked a brow. "Why would anyone do that? Did the Emerys know about it?"

He shook his head. "No. Mr. Emery and his first wife ordered the wine when the castle was first built, but the wall was a mystery."

The two fell silent as the mid-afternoon humidity sucked the air from the room. Sweat dripped from him, and perspiration beaded on Peyton's brow as they continued their work more closely now. Peyton placed the fabric on each seat, and together they turned it over and hammered the tacks in place. When that was complete, Patrick screwed the seat back onto the chair frame. They'd found an empowering rhythm to working together, and his mind turned to *what if.*

What if they were wed and worked together to build a home? Raise a family? Grow old together?

"Can you hold this fabric taut, please?" Peyton yanked him from his reverie and back into the ballroom. "If you're not too busy daydreaming."

"Most certainly, my captain." He chuckled, hoping she wouldn't ask what he was thinking. "Your wish is my command."

Minutes before dinner, Peyton laid her last piece of fabric on the seventh chair. Patrick grinned as he pounded in the tacks with the exact beat of Peyton's hammering. Yes, they'd make quite a pair—in work and in wedded bliss. But how to make her understand that?

Mrs. Emery entered the ballroom just as they finished the last chair. Peyton kicked the scraps of fabric into a pile, clearing the area, then she smoothed her skirts. By the time the missus got to the alcove, they stood ready.

"Goodness. It's a miracle—or, at least, a feat of extreme professional excellence. Well done, you two!" The missus inspected each chair and folded her hands gracefully. "And by a woman. Even better." She snapped wide eyes toward Patrick. "Not to disparage your assistance, sir."

Patrick waved his hands. "Just helped here and there."

Peyton shook her head. "Mrs. Emery, I could not have accomplished this so swiftly without Patrick's help. He was invaluable to the success of this project."

Patrick basked in Peyton's affirmation, hungry and happy to hear her words.

Mrs. Emery appraised him and then Peyton. "Well then, the two of you may have the entire day off tomorrow. I'll inform Duvall of my decision. Enjoy your Sunday respite, and thank you for achieving this job. Mr. Emery will be quite pleased, I assure you."

With that, she turned and left the room. He and Peyton cleaned up just in time for dinner. They walked in separately, ate at opposite ends of the table, and left at different times. But he waited for her outside the dining hall. "Shall we walk along the shoreline and make plans for tomorrow?"

Peyton beamed. "I'll meet you by the bench." Then she gave him a fleeting warning look, which he interpreted as *remember the pact.*

When she appeared, she shifted her weight from foot to foot, almost dancing. "Let's go to Clayton and visit Papa. Shall we?"

"That's a crackin' good idea." He skipped a rock on the water. An entire day in Peyton's company? He'd be the last to argue.

"I can't believe we get the whole day off." Peyton tittered, fairly skipping as she searched the shore. She picked up a flat, smooth stone and rubbed it as if she were enticing a genie out of it. "Especially since I've only been working at Calumet Castle under two weeks."

"It will be great to catch up with your father, thanks to your masterfully efficient plan today." He winked at her.

"Glad it was successful." Peyton tossed her stone into the river. Raising her chin to a teasing angle, she slapped a hand on her shapely hip and faced him with mischief dancing in her eyes. "Tell me this—who is the fastest, most fastidious, and fascinating fabric worker you know?"

"Tell me this first—who is the funniest, wittiest, most handsome assistant upholsterer you know?" As Peyton crossed her arms and tapped her toe, Patrick stooped down, grabbed a rock, and skittered it three times over the tranquil water. "And ... the best rock-skipper?"

With a laugh and a shake of her head, Peyton dropped her arms to her side. "In all seriousness, it really was nice working with you today."

Something tightened in Patrick's chest. "And in all seriousness, I'm so proud of you, Peyton Pie. Clearly, there's an art and skill to being a master upholsterer."

Her smile gave evidence that his praise took root. Had he finally found the way to her heart?

CHAPTER 10

AS PATRICK ROWED ACROSS the channel the next day, Peyton couldn't help but admire his strong muscles working hard and the contented smile on his face. But then he squinted over his shoulder at his destination, and his face grew somber. His jaw tightened and his rowing slowed.

She knew his angst—his father.

"Shall we surprise Papa and meet him at church?"

Patrick nodded, resuming his pace at the oars.

Clayton presented her with mixed feelings as well, thanks to the local gossips. She loved her hometown, but she'd embraced the big city of Watertown with its noisy streets bustling with buggies and shoppers and lovers walking around the square—though its center greenspace was actually oval. She'd enjoyed window shopping at the Paddock Arcade, the country's oldest covered shopping mall. Built before the Civil War, it boasted a large, pointed, arched window in its Gothic Revival interior. And oh, what delightful picnics they'd had at Watertown's City Park, built by one of the most famous park creators, Frederick Olmsted.

Though the novelty of her big-city experiences gave her a thrill she had never experienced in Clayton, her hometown hamlet offered its own charms. As they neared the docks, she anticipated the faces of her father and friends who would warm her heart and the familiarity of Main Street running along the shore. Both made her feel at home, like a cozy blanket in the dead of winter.

As Patrick tied the boat at the dock, a train announced its arrival with squealing brakes and three short whistles. But by the time they neared the station before turning onto John Street on their way to the church, the conductor's "all aboard" carried on the river breeze. In the distance, passengers milling about suddenly scurried like ants toward a jam sandwich.

Patrick jerked his chin toward the train depot. "It's been almost thirty years since they built the turntable and depot. Father worked on it as a young man." His face grew taut as it always did when he spoke of his father, but he continued. "What would this village be like without the New York City folk traveling here each summer on their luxurious Pullman Sleeper cars?"

"Papa said the train station has made it a very different town, especially in the summer. New Yorkers seem to overtake our tiny village."

"Many of the New Yorkers belong to a Yacht Club that has a special club car. It leaves Grand Central Station at three on Friday afternoons. After the passengers enjoy a leisurely dinner along the Hudson, they go to sleep and arrive at the dock in Clayton on Saturday morning. What might it be like to travel so freely? So easily?"

"And in such luxury." Patrick sighed. "As a lad, I often came down here on Saturday mornings to view all the yachts and steamers picking up such fine folk to take them to their summer homes on the river. On Sunday afternoons, the men return to the city for their workweek, leaving their families behind only to return the following weekend. Can you imagine?"

She shrugged. "I can't. From what I experienced in Watertown, even though it was a small city, the rich and famous carry their own troubles. Besides, here we can enjoy the river's beauty every day, not just on summer weekends."

Patrick gifted her with a gentle grin. "You're right, of course."

They turned onto John Street and, in a few blocks, came to Christ Church. Peyton surveyed her home church, and butterflies danced in her belly. Was her father already here?

With an open belfry and mission-style front, the brick church brought back many memories—and a little guilt. Why had she neglected her faith these past few years?

Patrick pointed at the roof. "The fish-scale slates, an early symbol of Christianity, are my favorite part of this building. What about you?"

She skirted two children tussling with each other as she joined the dozen or so worshippers heading toward the church.

"Seeing Papa." Without commenting further, Peyton climbed the steps and entered the familiar sanctuary. Several dozen people sat in the black walnut pews. A few whispered quietly in the corners.

The bell in the belfry rang, causing Peyton to startle.

Patrick chuckled. "A little jumpy this morning?"

She tossed him a warning glare. *Careful, my friend. I'm in no mood for teasing.*

As always, Papa sat in the third row, head bowed. She hurried up the aisle and tapped him on the shoulder. "Papa!"

As several parishioners cast her a disapproving glare, Peyton's cheeks warmed. She ignored them. She was here for Papa, not them.

Her father blinked and his brows furrowed. "What? How..." He patted the pew and grinned. "Lord be praised."

She whispered hello and kissed him on the cheek, sitting down beside him. Patrick slipped into the pew and nodded his greeting.

"Welcome, son." Papa reached over and patted Patrick's knee. "Glad you're here."

As the service began, Peyton relaxed. Sitting between her papa and Patrick, life felt right and at peace. The good-humored minister sported a wide grin, his dark eyes exuding welcome. Pastor Moreno had served here as long as she could remember.

Today he spoke on 1 Corinthians 1:26-31—how God chose the foolish and weak people to astonish the wise. Peyton had worked so hard to be self-reliant, strong, and rational that the very idea shook her. But he didn't stop there. He went on to say God uses our weaknesses so that we can't take the credit for our accomplishments—the very opposite of what the O'Clearys had taught her. They admonished her to use her own talents and skills and to rely on no one. To push through and make her own way. To never depend upon an undependable God.

As she pondered this dichotomy, she had to admit that, though the modern way felt better, God's way held more value. So where was she to go from here?

The choir sang the closing song, Pastor gave the benediction, and the service was over. She turned to her papa but caught Patrick ready to explode—his face red, jaw tight, and eyes narrowed into slits. She followed his gaze to Patrick's father standing in the back.

Peyton slipped her hand in the crook of his arm. He blinked and looked at her. "Do you want to see him?"

Patrick shook his head. "Let's get out of here." He checked the side door and begged with such a pained expression that she turned to her papa. "We'll wait for you outside. It's dreadfully hot in here."

Papa conceded but quickly excused himself from a conversation and followed them out the door. "What a treat to have you here. Both of you. So happens I caught several largemouth bass last night and am ready to feast. You?"

Peyton licked her lips. "No one fries them better. It's so good to see you. We have the entire day off."

Patrick scanned the crowd. Finally, he turned to Peyton and Papa and cleared his throat. "Your fried fish sounds perfect, Mr. Quinn."

They walked the few blocks to the Quinn home and found Lucy, their black-and-white collie, waiting at the front door, pressing on the screen as Peyton opened it. She bent down to hug her dear friend.

"Lucy Lu. How I've missed you." She snuggled into her fur and allowed her dog to lick her hand. "How's my girl?"

"She's a comfort and a joy, daughter." Papa's tender words touched

Peyton. She rose and embraced her father.

"And you are a comfort to me, Papa." Smells of home engulfed her senses. "You've been baking? Let me guess. Gooseberry pie?"

Papa chuckled. "A nose like Lucy. I have baked potatoes and fresh green beans from the garden ready to cook. Hungry?"

Patrick rubbed his stomach. "Starving for a home-cooked meal. The castle staff feeds us pretty well, but there's nothing like home."

Peyton wondered at his words. This tiny house had been Patrick's second home since they were small. His family house was just across the street and four doors down, so he'd come here often—especially when his father was on the warpath.

"I hope you'll always feel this is your home, Patrick." Papa winked at him and then at her. He chuckled as if he were up to something.

She needed to turn the chatter to a safer topic. "Have you taught Lucy any new tricks lately?"

"Taught her the two-step. Watch this." Papa grabbed a piece of raw fish. "Lucy, two-step." He gave a low whistle and held the fish over her head while the dog stood on her hind legs and stepped back and forth.

Peyton giggled, and Patrick laughed, dispelling the gloom that hovered around him. "That's crackin', sir. How's work?"

"Quite good this summer. I have five fireworks shows to do." Papa grinned as he cleared the table of an open newspaper. He shook it before laying it on the counter. "Did you hear that the U.S. just bought the Panama Canal from the French? Gonna finish that monstrosity to save the shipping industry time and money. It cost the American people a mere forty million. I wonder how much more it'll take to complete the job—and how many lives will be lost in the process."

Patrick answered as he helped her set the table. "I heard that. What else is new?"

The men chatted about local gossip and national interests while Papa fried the fish and Peyton finished the rest of the meal preparation, grateful for the cool cross breeze that blew from the front door to the back. Soon dinner was ready, and the three of them sat down to enjoy a fine Sunday dinner.

Patrick's emotions rose and fell with thoughts of family. Here, with Peyton and her papa, he belonged. This was family. And then he remembered seeing his father at church. Their eyes met only for a moment, so he couldn't decipher what mood the man was in or what he thought.

But then, Patrick never could. Father was erratic, sometimes irrational. Often downright mean.

"Did you know your father seems to have a new lease on life, Patrick? It's astounding. Off the drink. Back in church. Engaged in the community." Mr. Quinn took a bite of his fish. "Darn good, if you ask me."

Patrick refrained from a cynical sneer. *Another one of his attempts to deceive the good people of Clayton. Disgusting.* His father's 'new leases' never lasted. But Patrick held his tongue and took a bite of the fish. "This is delicious, sir."

"Don't believe me? It's true, son." Mr. Quinn set down his fork. "Patrick, I know you've been through a lot, and most of it has been terrible. I'm sorry about that. But your father has changed, and you need to change with him. Forgive him, son, and let the past go."

Just like that? Impossible. "I appreciate your concern, sir, but it's more complicated than that. The man should rot in a prison of his own making."

"But don't you understand? You're in a prison of your own by not forgiving him. That hurts you and those you love. You can't change him, but you can change your heart."

"Right." He couldn't breathe. "Excuse me. I need to visit the privy." He didn't wait for permission but stormed out the kitchen door, onto the back porch, and heaved a deep breath. His heart raced, his blood surging faster than a locomotive.

Forgive? How could he forgive?

He stepped down the porch steps and paced the Quinns' small backyard, glancing at the vegetable garden that took up half the yard. Life. Abundant life growing and thriving in the dirt.

He, too, was growing in lots of ways. Still, his father's dirt seemed to cling to his very soul. He scrubbed his face with his hand, trying to ward off the dark mood he found himself in. *Shake it off, lad. You've done it so many times before.*

After visiting the privy, he stepped out to find Peyton sitting on the back porch steps. "Can I help, Patrick? Please." She stood and held out her arms to him.

Patrick stepped close, tentative. "What about the pact?"

Peyton sighed. "That's for the island. Here, we're the friends we've always been."

He slipped into her arms, returning a much-needed hug. "It's too much to believe he's changed. I ... I can't forgive him."

"I know. I struggle with forgiving him too. But Papa says ..."

He gently pushed her away. "Let's drop the subject. And I hope your papa will too."

Peyton pulled him toward the kitchen door. "Let's finish our dinner and relax on our one day off, shall we?"

He agreed and followed her back into the kitchen. For the rest of the meal, none of them spoke of his father. Instead, Peyton told her papa about the castle, her work, the Emerys. He joined in the conversation now and then, but his stomach turned every time he thought of his father.

When dinner was done, Peyton insisted on cleaning up, and Mr. Quinn agreed. "Well, it is time for my Sunday afternoon nap. Do you mind? It'll just be for a little while."

Peyton kissed him on the cheek. "You go lie down. Patrick and I will clean up. Then we can all enjoy a quiet afternoon together. How's that sound?"

Mr. Quinn enfolded her in his big arms. "Perfect." He turned to

Patrick. "Thanks, son, for bringing my girl and helping out here." He glanced around the kitchen. "Sorry I made such a mess. Never been a tidy cook." He rumbled a chuckle and headed toward the stairs. "Be back soon."

Toenails tapping, Lucy followed close on his heels. Mr. Quinn turned partway up and waved at the dog. "Go play with Peyton. You don't need a nap, girl."

Patrick gave a whistle that brought Lucy quickly to his side. "Good girl, Lucy. Spend some time with us."

The dog plopped on his boots, paws under her head.

"I can't work with you on my feet." Patrick chuckled and slipped his toes out from underneath Lucy as he pumped the water into the pot to rinse the dishes.

Already clearing the table, Peyton smiled. "Lucy's always loved you, Patrick." Her emerald eyes turned soft, inviting. "She knows a good man when she sees one."

With that one compliment, the anger and angst swirling around him dissipated in an instant. "Thank you for that."

Bringing the last of the dishes to the counter, Peyton slipped her hands into the soapy water and began washing their plates.

He grabbed a towel and dried each one she rinsed. A comfortable silence reminded him of working on the chairs together. "This is nice," he said, more to himself than to her.

"I agree. So was working with you on the chairs." She paused, tilting her head as if to think. "Forgive me if I was harsh about the pact. I didn't mean to be. I just think we need to be extra careful on the island so we don't endanger our jobs or our reputations."

"You're right. But here, it feels so different, so free." Patrick set the plate on the shelf and reached for another.

"Free with us, but not with your father." Peyton's eyes flashed with … was it fear? "Papa's right, you know. Whether he's changed or not, I cannot say. But unforgiveness has you in chains, and I fear it will poison you if you let it."

Patrick didn't feel the usual anger. Instead, he felt … safe. "I know. I just don't know how to let it go."

"I'm not sure I do either. It's not as if I've been on speaking terms with the Almighty lately." Peyton's admission caught in her throat as she handed him a glass. "This life is a journey, Patrick, and its twists and turns can be scary, confusing, and sometimes misleading. But I do know that God is with us through it all, even in the deepest, darkest questions of our lives."

Patrick had so many questions about her journey in the past few years, but how to ask her without threatening her? "Your journey of late has had lots of twists and turns, aye?"

"It has, and it's given me more questions than answers. I thought I had to do it all on my own, but do I? Do you? I haven't the answers but would love to explore and maybe find them together?" Her eyes brimmed with tears. "You're my best friend, Patrick. I always want us to be friends."

"Peyton Pie, I l—" He swallowed the words he longed to say. "I want that, too, no matter how long it takes. And I understand your pact. I even agree."

An understanding smile swept the heartache away, and they turned the conversation to simpler things. Mr. Bryer's soft snoring during the sermon. The funny hat Mrs. McTavish wore. The Edwards' twin boys fighting during the benediction.

Mr. Quinn swept into the room as they finished their work. "That church service is a microcosm of life here in Clayton, aye?"

Peyton's brow furrowed. "Did you sleep in such a short time?"

He shook his head. "Couldn't waste time sleeping when you two are here. Let's sit on the porch and visit."

For the rest of the afternoon, they enjoyed lemonade and casual chatter, but all too soon, it was time to leave. Peyton hugged her papa. "Thank you for a lovely day, Papa. You're the best."

Patrick shook his hand. "I agree. Thank you."

As they walked back to the boat, Patrick kept his hands in his pockets and Peyton at a distance. But something had changed. The push and pull he'd felt on the island weren't there. Would it be the same when they returned to Calumet?

They passed a childhood friend's home, and Patrick chuckled. "I remember when Tommy used to beg me to go to Calumet with him so he could rescue the princess he was sure was held captive in the tower. He even claimed there was a dragon keeping her there. He was so insistent that I had dreams of her for years."

Peyton shook her head. "I hadn't heard that. Boys can be so funny."

He squinted her way. "So can girls."

Patrick returned to the island with a mustard seed of hope that he might win her hand yet.

CHAPTER 11

THE NEXT DAY, AFTER a delicious lunch of chicken salad, Peyton dabbed her lips and set her napkin down. She took a final sip of iced tea.

Across the table, Duvall addressed her. His white eyebrows twitched against creases that told the tale of time. "A word, Miss Quinn?"

Peyton stood and pushed in her chair. Then she curtsied and joined him at the far end of the room. "Sir?"

"Cook has an errand for you to run. Please report to her in the kitchen."

The butler's kind demeanor was quite the dichotomy to Mrs. Milton's. Was Cook like the housekeeper? Though she'd barely talked to Cook, she'd heard the woman was stern and opinionated.

Peyton entered the kitchen and curtsied when she reached the portly, wrinkled woman. "You needed something, ma'am?"

Cook acknowledged her, wiping her hands on her apron. "We have a worker from the mainland who's come to fix some gadget or another in the powerhouse. For heaven's sake—if they'd keep it simple around here and stop complicating things with new-fangled machines, the contraptions wouldn't break down, and we wouldn't have another mouth to feed." The woman huffed, her jowls and ample neck wiggling like jelly. "Regardless, the man needs to eat. Would you take him this tray? My staff are busy getting ready for a dinner party."

Peyton curtsied, then picked up the tray with enough food to generously feed her papa and her. "I'd be happy to help, Cook."

Who was this man to require such a feast?

She welcomed the opportunity to be out in the fresh air for a few minutes. The ballroom stayed fairly cool when the windows and doors let in the river's cross breeze, but the alcove grew rather stuffy and sticky in the heat of the day. She balanced the tray as she walked down the steps to the powerhouse, taking care not to spill the iced tea.

Once she got there, she found the door held wide open with a large rock. She peered inside. "Hello. Is someone here?"

A deep voice responded from the far end of a hallway. "Down here."

It took a moment for her eyes to adjust to the dim interior. Peyton followed the sound of the voice until the corridor opened into a wide space full of noisy machinery. The room was steamy and dank, smelling of oil and coal. A dark-haired man sat on the floor with his back to her, twisting something with a large wrench.

The tray wobbled just a tad, and she steadied it. "I ... I have some lunch for you, sir."

The man's head bobbed up suddenly, and he spun around on his backside. "I thought I recognized that voice. If it isn't the fair damsel of Clayton."

Henry Applebee? His tone teased, or was he mocking her?

The man's hawkish nose did nothing to help his looks. Dirt-brown eyes slanted a bit down, but somehow, his roguish smirk diminished his facial flaws. He hadn't shaved in days, and his black, curly hair reminded her of her dog Lucy's fluffy mop.

"Hello." Her voice sounded taut to her ears, and she gripped the tray tighter.

Henry's square jaw moved back and forth as he sized her up, his dark eyes narrow and scheming. When he stood, his lanky frame towered over her, sending a chill down her spine. The mask of his conceited sideways sneer, yellowed teeth displayed and gaze intensifying, made her heart begin to pound.

He reached for the tray and caressed her fingers, holding them there longer than was proper. She pulled away. "Let me help you with this."

She'd observed that smirk before. Peyton had thwarted his advances more than once when they crossed paths in Clayton.

"What's an innocent little lamb like you doing here?" As he spoke, his Adam's apple moved up and down, reminding her of the time when she'd seen a snake swallow a mouse whole. She'd lost her lunch back then, and she experienced a similar feeling now.

He set down the tray on a nearby barrel and faced her. "Come now. You're afraid of me? Am I not a fellow river rat?"

Peyton panicked and took a step away from him, but a coil of wire tripped her. She landed on the floor, her hands slamming against the hard stone. "Ouch!"

The man reached out, grabbed her arm, and yanked her to standing. Then he stepped forward until they were inches apart.

He didn't let go of her.

Her cheeks warmed, her breath coming in quick stops and starts. She sidestepped and tugged her hand away, running it along her skirt to both wipe away the feel of him and avert attention from her now-flaming cheeks.

He touched her cheek, anyway. "Aren't you pretty, with them rosy cheeks? When I'm done here, before I leave the island, I'd like to take a walk with you."

"No." She mustn't anger him. "Thank you, but I must return to the castle. I have things to attend to."

What was this reprobate up to?

Before she realized what was coming, Henry stepped closer and slipped his arm around her waist, pulling her to him. He pressed his lips to hers before she could object. Somehow, she slid her hands up to his shoulders and pushed, forcing him to disengage. Once she was free, she slapped his face as hard as she could. The sound reverberated in the enclosed room. His lowered brow and crinkled mouth gave her a measure of power—and satisfaction.

She turned and fled. But before she slammed the door, she stopped and yelled, "You repulsive blackguard! Mrs. Emery shall hear of this."

Peyton took off running as fast as she could but stopped as she neared the castle. Patrick. If he knew what that rogue had done, he'd likely kill the man in a fit of rage. She couldn't tell him. Couldn't endanger his work here. And what about her reputation? Women got the blame more often than not for this kind of thing, even when they were the innocent party.

Instead of returning to the ballroom, Peyton circled the castle and climbed the stairs to her room. She needed time to recover and freshen up, though she'd be late in returning to her post.

Relieved that Rachel wasn't in the room, Peyton plunked down on her bed. Tears fell. Out of fear or anger, she wasn't sure. How could that scoundrel behave that way? She had simply—and kindly—brought him lunch. How dare he?

Her concerns turned again to Patrick and her threat to report the event to Mrs. Emery. Anger tickled her throat, and the start of a headache banged against her temples. She stretched her neck and rolled her shoulders as she moved to the mirror.

What a mess.

During her mad dash back to the house, her hair had pulled out of its chignon in various places, and spots on her neck blazed red as they always did when she was in a tizzy. She rubbed them, hoping they would disappear so that Patrick wouldn't notice them and question her.

What would she tell him about being gone so long? Surely, he would ask.

She splashed water on her face, smoothing the red rims of her eyes. Then she refashioned her hair. And because her head pounded even harder, she took a dose of headache powders. Ah ... that's what she could tell him.

After one last glance into the small mirror, she pasted on a smile that didn't rise to her eyes. "That'll have to do."

As she entered the ballroom, Patrick turned from his work on the mantel, a look of concern on his face. "Are you all right? Where have you been? I was about to send a posse for you."

His sheepish grin dispelled a bit of her gloom.

She waved off his question. "Oh, I had the start of a little headache, so I went to my room for my powders. Guess I rested longer than I planned."

Patrick left his work to join her in the alcove. "I'm sorry, Peyton Pie. Do you need the afternoon off? I'm sure Duvall wouldn't mind."

She couldn't let him detect her distress. "It's all right. I'll be fine."

He came close but didn't touch her. His gaze slipped to her skirt, and he stepped around her to inspect the back of it. "What's on your skirt?"

Alarmed, she pulled her skirts around to view a large grease stain. Her heart pumped harder. What could she say?

Then his gaze caught a glimpse of her heart and laid it bare. "It's more than a headache. What's really wrong?"

Patrick shivered at the fear in her eyes. She looked as if she'd seen a ghost. And where had that grease mark come from? He knew of nowhere on the island where she could sit in a puddle of oil. He continued to scrutinize her dumbfounded expression.

She had no answer? Surely, as fastidious as she was with her clothing, she would have noticed acquiring the stain. Her frantic rubbing of the stain with a scrap of cloth—to no avail—only magnified the issue. She bit her bottom lip, the telltale sign she was near tears.

He mustered as tender a tone as he could. "What happened, Peyton Pie?"

"I have no idea where this came from, but I simply must change before the missus notices. Don't tell her anything. Please?"

Her voice cracked with a desperation he hadn't heard in a long while. Her eyes flashed with fear he hadn't detected since she almost fell off the cliff on the river's edge where they'd swum years ago.

Without waiting for his response, Peyton fled the room, leaving him alone with his thoughts and concerns. Something was amiss, but she obviously didn't want to reveal it to him.

Had she been reprimanded for something?

That wouldn't explain the stain.

As he returned to his work on the mantel, he lifted a prayer for her. Just yesterday, she'd been so carefree and warm. Even this morning, though professional, they'd shared a few laughs and memories. Now the panic in her eyes scared him.

Duvall stepped into the room, clearing his throat to draw Patrick's attention. "Where is Miss Quinn? Surely, she finished Cook's errand by now. I have a message for her from Mrs. Emery."

Patrick bobbed his head. "She was just here but soiled her skirt and went to change. She should be back soon. May I give her a message, sir?"

Duvall dipped his chin. "The missus would like her to finish the settee and curtains. Then, if there's enough fabric left over, she may use the same material for the chair and piano bench in that room."

"I'll tell her, sir. Thank you."

Duvall paused, and his gaze went to Peyton's empty workstation. "I hope the girl isn't neglecting her duties."

He shook his head. "She's not. She's a hard worker, sir. And very talented."

Duvall's brow furrowed. "I'll take your word for it, but I'll check back later. Be about your work, lad."

Patrick returned to puttying nail holes—thousands of nail holes. He loved his occupation, but redoing the shoddy work of another irritated him. Nevertheless, as he pressed the putty into the holes, he promised the Lord—and himself—he'd always do his best at any assignment.

Almost half an hour later, Peyton appeared, wearing a pale blue skirt and a crisp white blouse. He'd seen her in it before, but as she walked up to him, the light hit her face and set her eyes glistening a beautiful shade of green. Yet he also detected she'd been crying.

Carefully, he stepped closer. "Tell me. You've always felt better once you got a secret off your chest. I'm here to listen and help, if need be."

Peyton's tender eyes turned hard. "Stop it. Just stop trying to be my savior. I'm in no mood for you to brood over me like I'm a helpless child. I haven't needed your rescuing for several years now, and I certainly don't need it now."

After giving him a leave-me-alone glare, she stomped to her station, hands fisted. She kept her back to him and worked on the settee.

In the quiet of the ballroom, he resumed his labors to the cadence of Peyton's—tapping in tacks, grunting as she pulled the fabric taut. Patrick ached for an explanation, but he had to accept that none would be forthcoming now. Hadn't it taken nearly two weeks before she admitted her friend, Karen, had stolen her lunch that time?

Ah, well.

Suddenly, Peyton spoke behind him, causing him to jump. "I'm … I'm sorry, Patrick."

He slapped his chest. "You scared me out of my wits, woman."

A smile faltered over her face. "Sorry. I shouldn't have snapped at you like that. It's just been a topsy-turvy day. I'll be all right after a good night's sleep."

He acknowledged her with a wink. "Whatever's got you in knots, I'll not push you to explain. I'm always here to talk—or simply listen."

"There you are, miss." Duvall came through the door. "Did Patrick relay the missus' request?"

Patrick grimaced, giving her an apologetic shrug. "I didn't, sir. Forgive me?"

Duvall's brows furrowed, and he pursed his lips for a moment. "No urgency." He repeated the message about the chair and piano bench.

Peyton curtsied. "I think there will be enough material. I'm almost done with the settee."

Duvall snapped an appraising stare at Patrick and then back to Peyton as if to scrutinize their close proximity. And their relationship? "The mantel is looking splendid. Carry on, then."

"Thank you, sir." Once Duvall left, Patrick blew out a breath. "Sorry. In the commotion about your skirt, I forgot to relay his message."

Peyton gifted him with a genuine smile, the first he'd seen since lunch. "Seems it wasn't a problem. Duvall is a merciful and kind man, is he not?" Her eyes drifted to the door where the butler had exited. "I wonder if he ever married."

He shook his head. "Not likely. Most butlers dedicate their lives to their employers and loyally follow them wherever they go. I've been told that Duvall has served the Emerys for decades at their New York City residence, here, and abroad. Mr. Emery takes Duvall with him wherever he goes."

Peyton peered at the ceiling. "I can't imagine being in service all my life." She returned her determined gaze to him. "I'd like to enjoy a measure of freedom at some point."

"Freedom is a frame of mind. An Irish proverb says that a dog owns nothing but is seldom dissatisfied. We humans put far too much value in our things and our independence. Aren't love, joy, and peace better goals?"

Peyton shook her head as if she were a teacher scolding her pupil for giving the wrong answer. "I don't know about that. Virtues and freedom should both be attained. At present, women and servants lack many of the opportunities that men take for granted. 'Tis a shame that we all cannot be treated as equals."

"Equality isn't all it's cracked up to be, Peyton. Duvall isn't a slave. He isn't forced to be a butler. He could leave tomorrow and likely find gainful employment elsewhere, if he wanted." He paused, trying to calm his racing heart and tone down his passion. "Or he could retire.

Another saying goes like this—'Life is like a cup of tea. It's all in how you make it.' Apparently, Duvall has made a fine cup of tea and enjoys it, else he wouldn't be as content as he is."

Peyton cast him a dismissive glare and shrugged. "You're not a woman. You can't understand. I need to get back to my post."

With that, she returned to her work, not letting Patrick respond.

Whenever he said anything about her modern thinking, he was dismissed as if he were a wayward child. He huffed out a breath and sanded the dried putty with a vengeance. If only he could erase some of the influences of the past few years from the woman he loved.

CHAPTER 12

PEYTON SLIPPED OUT OF her petticoat and dress, let down her hair, and donned her nightclothes as she expressed her frustrations to Rachel that evening. "God gave all mankind equality when He created us. Equality isn't based on gender, religion, status, or race. Men can't understand how a woman feels. Even if we finally do get the right to vote, men won't assess us any differently than they do now. But at least society at large will be forced to take notice."

Rachel cast her a scowl. "I suppose. But I don't understand why having the right to vote for politicians will make us any better. Besides, only men can take those positions."

"But they won't always. One day, women will step up and be politicians too. We women just want to help make our country greater than it already is. Men think we can't help and we can't make wise decisions, but we make them every day."

"That may be true, but I doubt we'll experience such radical changes in our lifetimes." Rachel's reply dripped with skepticism.

Peyton shook her head. "Maybe not, but I, for one, want to try to make things better for our children and grandchildren. Change is rarely comfortable or fun, so most people settle for life as it is. But good enough is not fine with me."

Her gaze fell on her oil-stained skirt, lying on the bed. She picked it up and assessed it. "It's ruined." She let out a disgusted huff.

"What is ruined?" Rachel joined her and looked at the stain. "What happened to your skirt?"

Drat! I hadn't wanted her involved in this.

What to say? "I'm not sure what I sat on or where, but this skirt is ready for the rag bag." She threw it in the corner and changed the subject. "It sounds like rain. I love a gentle rainfall at night, don't you?"

Rachel concurred as she slipped under the covers and settled. "It lulls me to sleep, and I love the smell of it too."

Peyton, too, climbed into bed and lowered her lamp. A few minutes later, Rachel spoke. "I've never met anyone like you, Peyton. Your way of thinking is so ... grand. It makes me want to think about grand things too. Thank you."

Peyton scooted up on an elbow and looked at her roommate. "I think God gave women just as much ability to think deeply as men, but we've not had the chance to exercise our brains like they have. Cooking, caring for the house, and raising children are worthy skills, but they don't challenge our thinking as much as politics, science, and mathematics."

"True enough." Rachel yawned and turned off the lantern. "But right now, I need to let my brain rest. Good night, friend."

Peyton bid her a good sleep and snuggled under the covers.

A summer rain started as a ballet, raindrops pitter-pattering a dance on the roof. But then the wind picked up and howled like a violent, turbulent storm fighting against the house. What had been calming turned tempestuous.

Peyton's thoughts did as well. What about that cad, Henry, and her promise to inform Mrs. Emery? If she were to talk to the missus, surely, the staff and, by extension, Patrick, would find out about the scoundrel's actions. And perhaps the rumor mill would extend to Clayton, and Papa might hear. The very thought made her queasy. She couldn't endanger her already questionable reputation.

No. She'd swallow the bitter pill of the contemptible behavior of another to keep her good name safe.

Peyton thanked Sam and Charlie for moving the completed settee back into the drawing room. Then she supervised them as they hung the drapes. Once they left, carrying the piano bench to the ballroom, she admired her handiwork, a satisfied smile crossing her lips. The settee and the drapes brightened and modernized the room, and she even had enough leftover fabric for the chair and piano bench. Once completed, the space would look splendid.

She had rarely seen the outcome of her work in Watertown. One or both of the O'Clearys went to the fine homes that held their finished products. And even when they were contracted to do seamstress work such as wedding attire, she almost never attended the final fittings. As an apprentice, she'd been relegated to the back room and the mundane jobs.

But now, here she was, in a castle, working for a famous industrialist and hotelman and his new bride. No longer an apprentice. And the opportunity to enhance such a setting with her skillful upholstery work warmed her heart.

She slid her hand over the Victorian chair she was to recover, then patted the seat, which smelled musty when she pressed on it. It must be priceless, and even though it had soft, pliable stuffing and was covered by elegant, embroidered fabric, it was outdated.

Queen Victoria had died last year. The woman influenced so much of the world and continued to, even from her grave. Peyton wanted to be influential too. Not to the extent of a queen, but at least to make a difference in her world, much as her employers did.

Portraits of Mr. and Mrs. Emery with several younger couples, whom Peyton assumed were their children, graced a bookcase full of gilded volumes, trinkets, and treasures. She'd been informed that while Mr. Emery and his first wife had five children, their boy, Charles, died at age three, and Gertrude died as an infant, leaving Frank, Mabel, and

Francena. After his wife died, he married his current wife, who had two children from a previous marriage.

Peyton adjusted a large frame featuring a multitude of people. That must be them. Would she ever meet the rest of the family? If she wanted to, she'd best get busy.

She hurried back to her post, passing Sam and Charlie on the way. She nodded but didn't stop to talk.

Patrick had finished the mantel and was on the floor attending to the baseboards. He playfully peeped under his arm and grinned. "I wondered if the fairies stole you. Or maybe some handsome rogue swept you away on his sailing yacht to places unknown."

Peyton giggled. "I've only been gone an hour."

The affection in Patrick's eye was unmistakable. "But it felt like an eternity to me."

He was attempting to make amends for his challenging words of the day before. That was his way, and she admired him for it. Always trying to find peace. She'd experienced that sweetness many times before.

By the time they were fifteen or so, she'd become aware of his puppy love for her. He'd tried to woo her with his winsome ways, yet she always managed to turn it around and focus only on their friendship.

Until now.

Things had changed. She could detect it in his eyes. Hear it on his lips. She'd never guessed their friendship would turn into the pensive adult love before her.

She'd never encouraged romance. Or so she thought.

Before she could set him straight, Sam and Charlie brought in the chair. After they set it in the alcove, Sam took off his cap and wiped his brow. "Until next time."

She thanked them as they retreated, and Patrick joined her. "This is quite the piece. Just look at that intricate carving and the ebonized wood."

"What's *ebonized?*"

"It's when you stain or finish the wood in black to resemble ebony. It was quite the fad with the queen in her day. Does this gentlemen's armchair have a mate?"

"You mean an armless lady's chair? It wasn't in the parlor." She ran a hand over the floral tapestry upholstery and scrunched up her nose. "Pretty, but it smells of mold, cigars, and sweat. And it's terribly outdated. The missus is wise to recover it."

Patrick shrugged. "I rather like it myself. It has character. The fabric you will use on it will take away from the timeless beauty of traditional furnishings."

Peyton tapped her finger against her lips. "You may be right, but the missus has made her choice." She gave Patrick a sweet smile. She'd no desire to pick another argument today.

Patrick stifled a frown when Sam returned, handing Peyton a pillow of the same material as the chair. Sam barely said a word, but the young man's intensity revealed pleasure in serving Peyton. He'd best keep an eye on that lad.

He folded his arms over his chest, contemplating their interchange. Maybe she wasn't the radical he'd suspected her of being. After all, she did like the traditional chair. Didn't she?

Tossing a wave in Patrick's direction, Sam departed. Peyton hovered over the bench for several minutes before gathering her measuring tape and slipping it around her neck. How charming she looked, hard at work. She measured. Wrote down what he assumed were numbers and did it again.

Measure twice. Cut once. Same as a carpenter.

They weren't so different. They'd both honed a rather artistic skill. They both enjoyed their work. They both wanted to live and die in Clayton.

Didn't they?

Patrick loved Clayton, but his father's presence there gave him a bellyache. His jaw muscles tensed. Maybe he didn't want to make his home there, after all.

And Peyton? She wanted more. What that really meant was quite the mystery. How had this modern thinking planted itself so deep into her life in just a few years?

Patrick hiked his pant legs up before kneeling to work on a new section of the seemingly endless baseboards. Hopefully, he'd have it all completed before the Grand Ball in August. Just a month away? Blathers! He'd have to pick up his pace.

As he sanded and then puttied five- to six-foot sections, he continued to ponder his similarities to Peyton—and their differences. He much preferred focusing on how they could navigate life together, but he also needed to be realistic. If their differences were too many, could they make a happy home together?

His parents certainly couldn't. Their differences drove his sister away. His father's abusive ways had scarred him. His mousy mother had never stuck up for him. Never protected him. Of course, he couldn't protect his mother or his sister, either, so he had no room to judge.

But his folks' differences were far more diverse than being abusive or mousy. Father put on a pretense of being perfect. Mother hid from the public eye and almost became a recluse. Father would show up at church or other social functions bigger than life, while she slipped into the sanctuary only at Christmas and Easter and said nary a word to anyone. Indeed, his mother seemed invisible. No one ever spoke of her, asked about her, or worried about her welfare. And that hurt.

"Patrick. It's time for lunch." Peyton waved a hand, bidding him join her on the way to the servants' dining room.

They met at the door.

"I should be able to finish the bench this afternoon. It's a simple task." Peyton's smile made her green eyes dance. "The chair will be another matter." The tiniest frown crossed her brow.

"I wish my task yielded such joy and accomplishment. I fear I may not have the work done before the ball."

Peyton touched his forearm before a blink of shock preceded its quick removal. She'd almost crossed her own line. Broken her pact. "But you've come so far. You finished the upper level already, and the fireplace is glorious. You've hidden that wretched carpenter's mistakes impeccably."

"Thank you for that." He scratched his head. "I need to remember to count my blessings, eh?"

Peyton agreed. "You always needed to be reminded of all the things you do so well. And that Irish proverb, 'praise the young and they will flourish,' isn't just for children, you know. It goes for men and women, too, I think."

Patrick chuckled. "Then I shall praise you often, Peyton Pie, for I want you to flourish in everything you do."

Joining several others entering the dining room, Peyton responded to his comment with little more than a tender dip of her chin. Dare he sit next to her? Across from her? Oh, how he wanted to!

Thinking better of it, he took a seat far from Peyton where she settled next to Rachel.

Halfway through the meal, angry brouhaha from the end of the table drifted to his ears.

Mrs. Milton slammed her flat hand on the table. "You ain't right in the head, Miss Quinn. Women will discredit politics because they aren't ready to take on that responsibility."

"What wicked thoughts are you putting in this poor girl's head?" Mr. Brown, the older footman, pointed to Rachel, who cringed under his harsh tone. "You want the vote. What's next? My brother's business?" He shook his head, glaring at Peyton. "Why on earth would you want such a burden, anyway?"

Patrick gasped as Peyton stood and pushed in her chair, a little too hard. She pursed her lips tightly together, her fists clenched. The rage in her voice scared him. "I want the same freedoms you men have, that's why."

Duvall burst into the room. "What's the meaning of this disturbance? I could hear you all the way up in the butler's pantry. For shame. All of you. Quiet!"

The lot of them became silent at the gentle man's rare scolding.

He frowned at the housekeeper. "Mrs. Milton, what's going on?"

The housekeeper pointed her fat finger at Peyton. "She's a radical. I told you she might be trouble. Heard tales about her from my cousin in Watertown. Those people she worked for are rabid."

Duvall raised both palms to her. "Enough." Then he looked into the faces of each staff member before turning back to Mrs. Milton and then addressing the entire room. "I'll get to the bottom of this altercation, but for now, I want no gossip. Do you understand?"

Everyone murmured their agreement and stared at their plates.

"Very well, then." Duvall sat in his usual seat at the head of the table. "Finish your meal, and then you are dismissed." He paused, took a sip of his water, and cleared his throat. "And remember—no chatter."

Peyton slipped back into her seat and glowered. Her eyes glistened, her pretty mouth drawn into a sorrowful frown.

Poor lass. What could she have said to evoke such vehemence?

Patrick hurried to finish his meal, keeping an eye on Peyton. As he took his last bite of chicken, Peyton rose. He guzzled the rest of his iced tea and almost ran to join her.

Peyton's shoulders sagged. Her head hung, allowing her to avoid the gazes of other staffers. Though they complied with not spreading gossip for the moment, their stares and turned-up noses told everyone just what they thought.

"What happened back there?" Patrick kept his distance but would not be cast off, even if she shooed him away. "Tell me, please. Let's walk the shore, away from the elephant ears."

Surprisingly, Peyton complied. When they were a fair distance away, she exploded. "Rachel mentioned our conversation about the vote, and Mrs. Milton blew her stack. Nearly scared my roommate to death. Then the footman sided with Mrs. Milton and got everyone in a tizzy. I don't care a whit what they think. We've all got to slide into the twentieth century sooner or later."

Patrick sighed, low and long. "Mrs. Emery can afford to live with her modern ideas and ways. You cannot. Not here on this island or in Clayton." He paused to consider his next words. "Whether it's the vote or purporting your modern notions, you cannot force change on others, Peyton. Being a wife and homemaker is not an unworthy goal. Not here. Not now."

Peyton's eyes filled with tears, her words pouring out like a mournful waterfall. "You view me as a possession, a homemaker, and a mother only? I'm capable of so much more and have the right to use my talents and abilities. I won't be subjugated to male-dominated restrictions. I cannot."

No anger. No feistiness. Only melancholy that made the whole thing even worse.

But she wasn't finished. "I wish you weren't stuck in the 1800s, Patrick. It makes me sad to realize you think so little of me that I can be no more than a puppet on a string or a decoration on your arm."

"That's not true." Patrick's voice squeaked an octave higher than normal. He ran his finger through his hair and reached for a beard that was no longer there. Because of her. "Your ambition and desire to create a better world make me respect you, Peyton. So does your talent and your keen intelligence." He swallowed hard, praying the right words would find his tongue. "But you must take care to reveal your heart and your thoughts only to a trusted few. You cannot presume people will understand, for they often don't. Remember the proverb, 'who keeps his tongue, keeps friends'? Better heed it, friend."

She held up a hand to silence him. "Friend? Well, you certainly are not one of them right now." When he took a step toward her, Peyton shook her head. "Don't. Just don't."

Fine. He wouldn't.

CHAPTER 13

PEYTON HUFFED HER EXASPERATION as Patrick stomped away. Why did he feel he had the right to correct her—to scold her as if she were a silly schoolgirl? She was a woman. An intelligent, self-sufficient woman who wanted to make a difference in the world. Why couldn't he understand that?

As she stood on the riverbank's main channel, she contemplated the white-capped waves slapping the shore. Pretty, but with an edge. Was she like that?

At the moment, the St. Lawrence was a gorgeous deep violet speckled with white. Though its colors changed regularly, whether the day was cloudy or sunny, stormy or calm, the hues and shades were always stunning. She looked to the sky, where billowy clouds formed tall towers, their bottoms turning a dark gray, warning of a coming storm.

Peyton sat on a nearby rock, mesmerized. Like a mighty warrior, the river demanded respect. Its many moods fascinated her. It might be romantically serene one day and dreadfully frightening the next. One could embrace the emerald wonder one moment, then need to flee from an explosive fit of rage.

Just like with people.

She swiped at a few wisps of hair the burgeoning breeze pulled from her chignon. Thankful to be alone at the water's edge and have a few extra minutes before returning to her post, she pondered the lunchtime altercation—and Patrick. Perhaps he was right? But how could the suffrage movement—or any important change—happen if everyone kept silent? She couldn't reckon it.

As she stood, a gust of wind twisted her skirts about her ankles, temporarily trapping her in place. Even the elements of nature seemed against her.

Mitch sauntered up to her from behind. He whiffed the wind like a dog, making her shiver. "Windy day. Don't you love the smell of the river? So fresh and clean."

Peyton adjusted her skirts. "Yes, but the wind also twists a woman's skirts about her something fierce, though you wouldn't know the irritating nature of that."

"Agreed." Mitch chuckled. "It must be most difficult to navigate such attire day in and day out. The layers and complexities of being a woman seem much too daunting for one such as I." Once she settled her skirts, he gave her an inquisitive stare. "Say, where's our friend, Patrick? I have a message for him."

She shook her head and shrugged. "Haven't a clue, nor, at the moment, do I care."

Mitch gazed at her from under thick eyebrows. He folded his arms over his chest and chortled. "Having a lover's spat, are we?"

Peyton's face burned, and so did the blood in her veins. "We, sir, are not lovers. How dare you accuse me of such impropriety? We have only ever been—and only ever will be—friends."

Mitch's hands shot up in surrender. "I meant no ill, miss. I was only trying to find my roommate as Duvall requested."

As if popping a balloon, Peyton deflated. "Sorry. I seem to be out of sorts just now."

Mitch swallowed. He tentatively touched her forearm. "It's all right. We all have our moments. Sometimes Patrick can make my blood boil faster than a ship's captain, but he's a good man. The best,

I expect, in these islands. And his utter devotion to you is amazing. Don't give up on him too quickly."

He tossed her a wink and gently squeezed her arm. "I must be on my way." He pointed at the clouds. "Best get under cover before that storm reaches us."

She apologized again, thanked him, and followed his suggestion. Peyton hurried toward the castle, arriving just as several fat raindrops splashed on and around her. Ducking into the ballroom, she brushed droplets from her skirt and hair. But she didn't close the door. Instead, she stood in the opening and breathed in the fragrance of the rain, a freshness that soothed her soul.

Pulling herself from the reverie, she closed the door and the two windows that were letting in the wind and rain. She left the others ajar since the stuffiness became overwhelming when the ballroom was closed up. She'd keep a close watch on them in case the wind changed direction. How would they ever entertain two hundred warm bodies in here during the Grand Ball?

"Ah, well. I'll not be present."

Startled she'd spoken aloud, she scanned the room. Empty, save herself. Reassured, she let out a breath.

Patrick. Where was he, and what had he said to Mitch? The man obviously knew more than she about Patrick's feelings for her. Or did he?

Truth be told, she knew. Knew he cared for her beyond friendship. But what was she to do with that?

Get to work, that's what.

She had already finished the bench and had it returned to its place in front of the piano. That was a cinch, but this spoon-back chair would be more difficult. She sighed contentedly.

She did love a challenge.

Thunder rumbled in the distance, accentuating her determination. Rain pattered outside, but the storm didn't appear to be growing, at least on the island. Lightning pulsed intermittently as a gentle rain fell.

She assessed the piece of furniture like the O'Clearys had taught her. Mid-Victorian. Probably 1850s. Solid mahogany with intricate carvings. She ran her fingers along the upholstered arms that featured scroll ends and touched the stunning serpentine-shaped front rail frame. She bent down to observe that the cabriole legs had little toes, then noticed that the rear legs splayed like pigeon toes. It was a sturdy piece that would hold up under even the heaviest guest. She stood and pressed on the seat, delighted to find it had springs and, she guessed, horsehair stuffing. The problems of worn fabric and a few stains would become irrelevant as soon as she recovered it.

Yes, her mentors had taught her well.

She felt the deeply buttoned and braided chair back. These would take significant time to do properly. And she mustn't damage the immaculate wood while repairing the upholstery.

Peyton picked up her upholstery tools and went to work on the gentleman's chair, removing the charcoal linen fabric from the seat and pulling out the old horsehair stuffing. She'd work on the back and arms later. She sneezed as dust took to the air.

Mrs. Emery appeared as if out of nowhere, a soft chuckle in her voice. "Good afternoon, miss."

Peyton's cheeks grew warm as she imagined what a mess she must look. A thin cloud of dust still hung in the air, and her skin surely bore a layer too. Sweat trickled down the back of her neck and temples, and she sneezed again.

The missus took out a pink embroidered handkerchief and covered her amusement. "Gesundheit."

Peyton rose and curtsied, wiping her brow with a shirtsleeve as discreetly as she could. "Excuse me, missus. Dust always makes me sneeze."

"Me too. I'd like to speak to you a moment, please." Mrs. Emery waved toward a group of three chairs Peyton had not yet recovered. The missus stepped toward them, ran a hand over one, and sat. "You can do these next. The poppy-and-butterfly cotton should be lovely on all the ballroom chairs, don't you think?"

Peyton sucked in a breath. The missus wanted her opinion? "Oh yes. The purples, violets, and blues trimmed with gold will make the most elegant seating in this room and complement the walls perfectly." She bit her bottom lip. Had she said too much?

Mrs. Emery's smile ran to the creases in her forehead. "I agree. And now, to another matter."

As if on cue, a thunderclap pealed as rain came down in sheets. Peyton excused herself to close the other window and door, blocking out much of the summer storm's volume.

When she returned, Mrs. Emery's face was taut, concerned. "Mrs. Milton informed me there was a problem in the staff luncheon today."

Peyton's stomach flipped. Then flopped. She thought she might lose her lunch right then, but she swallowed back her dismay. What had Mrs. Milton said that the mistress of the castle would come to reprimand her personally? Surely, her roommate sharing a simple conversation wasn't reason enough to sack her. Or was it?

"I ... I only shared some thoughts with my roommate—about women getting the right to vote."

The missus put up a hand to stop her, so Peyton clamped her lips tightly shut. For a moment, she shut her eyes too.

"I haven't come to scold you for such opinions, for I, too, share them. We are shaped by our thoughts and beliefs, and they may eventually bring a mustard seed of change." Her tone sounded matronly rather than angry. "It is God who gives us the strength and ability to change. Sooner or later, women will have a say in our country's affairs. But it may take some time."

Peyton conceded with a single nod and picked imaginary lint from her skirt.

"But we must take care to whom we speak such radical thoughts. Men, especially, are fearful, suspicious even, of the thought of losing control of their wives and daughters." The missus' amused tone now turned to mockery. "Powerful men cannot envision a world where they are not the gods of their own empires." Her eyes grew wide, and she covered her mouth with a hand. "You see, I speak amiss even now. I came to warn you to be careful to whom you speak, and I spoke out of turn."

Peyton curtsied, her head bowed. "Your secret is safe with me, missus."

Mrs. Emery threw back her head and laughed with abandon. "I understand. It appears we are kindred spirits."

Patrick entered the ballroom to witness Mrs. Emery and Peyton laughing like schoolmates. But how could that be? He slipped into his place quietly, trying not to disturb the strange sight. The gaiety between mistress and servant puzzled him.

As did Peyton.

In a perfect world, there wouldn't be all these power struggles. Women would vote and share their wisdom and make the world a better place. Masters would pay servants their rightful due and grant them respect. But this wasn't a perfect world. So why rock the boat? Why threaten scandal and ridicule and worse?

Rain pounded persistently on the windows, beating a drum not too different from the feel of his heart when he thought of Peyton.

Just last night, he had admitted his affection for her to Mitch. No, more like poured out his love-struck guts and fairly whined his way through the revelation. Good thing Mitch vowed silence and didn't tease him, or the fellow might have a mighty big shiner to deal with. But Mitch was a good listener and spoke wisdom, suggesting Patrick give Peyton space to find her way instead of barking at her and pushing into things headlong like a puppy who'd not yet found his feet.

Patrick opened the can of stain and dipped his fine brush into it. Like an artist, he carefully swept the bristles back and forth, covering the baseboard areas he'd previously sanded. His meticulous work had paid off, for he couldn't detect a single brushstroke. Perhaps he should take a similar stance with Peyton and share his true feelings with her?

When the women's laughing and talking stopped, he glanced at the alcove. Peyton bent over her task, and the missus headed his way. He set down his brush and stood. "Good afternoon, Mrs. Emery."

The missus nodded. "And to you. A word, please."

He bobbed his head. "Certainly. How can I be of assistance, missus?"

Mrs. Emery cleared her throat. "I'm sure you're aware of the situation at today's staff lunch. It appears you have a cordial relationship with my upholsterer, so I'd like you to watch out for her. I fear retribution because of the ideas she's spoken about. I'm quite aware that some staff think little of her modern ways."

The rain settled to a gentleness that reminded him of the missus standing before him. How kind of her to care for one such as Peyton.

"I will, missus." Patrick clicked his heels together to punctuate his promise. "You can count on it."

"And if Mrs. Milton, or anyone, causes her grief, please let me know so I can deal with it properly."

"Yes, Mrs. Emery. And thank you for caring for your staff."

The missus turned but paused. "We are all God's lovely creation, are we not?" Without waiting for him to agree, she left the room.

The rain had stopped.

The silence was deafening.

Peyton had watched the interchange. Patrick waved and dipped his chin before returning to staining. But then she came his way. Perhaps they could put away their spat and move forward?

Peyton crossed her arms over her chest, her lips pursed, her green eyes narrowed. "What did the missus want from you?"

"Nothing to worry your pretty little head about. She just wanted me to assist her with something."

"Keeping secrets now, are we? I thought we were friends." A faint sheen of perspiration glistened on her upper lip, and eyes that had lost their luster revealed distress. "Or perhaps I thought wrong."

He had to address that statement. "In our last conversation, I distinctly recall you said I wasn't your friend. Which is it? You can't toss me back and forth like a ship on an angry sea."

Peyton's shoulders slumped. "I'm sorry, Patrick. You were right about being careful with whom I speak. I just wasn't ready to hear it."

"Forgiven and forgotten. Friends?"

He stuck out his hand, and although she shook it as though embarrassed to touch him, she rewarded him with a delightful *liggle*.

A bolt of lightning lit up the room, but not from the receding storm. From her touch. With increasing intensity, closeness to her meant his feelings grew deeper and stronger. How would he endure?

His collar constricted his breathing, and the closed-up room had grown balmy, the air thick with humidity. He waved toward the terrace door. "Let's take a water break outside, shall we? Give me just a quick minute ..."

Without waiting for her answer, he scurried about the room, opening all the windows and doors. Then he poured two glasses of water and bid her join him. But she stood where they had conversed as if stuck in cement. "Are you coming, Peyton Pie?"

Coming out of her trance, she hightailed it toward him at the door. "Coming." When she got to him, he took the glass and sipped from it. "Thanks. It's suffocating in there."

"Always is, especially when it's closed up. I thought you had turned into a pillar of salt back there."

"No. I was just ... thinking." She set her glass on a nearby table. "I need to tell you something, but you must promise not to retaliate."

What could require retaliation? His heart raced, and his beard stubble stood at attention as he firmed his jaw. "Retaliate? That sounds serious. Did someone harm you? Are you all right? I can't promise not to hurt someone who hurts you."

Peyton patted his arm. "Calm down. I'm fine. But you won't like the tale, so you must promise."

"I promise not to kill anyone."

She glanced at the view from the terrace. Tiny droplets of rain sparkled on the trees and grass as the sun popped from behind the clouds. Several moments of silence passed before Peyton was ready to speak. When she did, she told him of Cook's errand, the menacing mechanic, and the forced kiss. And she surmised that the oil stain came from falling on the mechanical room floor.

He pasted on a sympathetic smile. "I'm glad you're all right, Peyton Pie. With my very life, I want to always keep you safe from harm. Is the scoundrel still here? Who is he?"

Peyton shook her head. "He is not, so there's no need to worry."

He'd promised not to kill the man. But pummel, pulverize, persecute? Possibly.

CHAPTER 14

PEYTON HEAVED A GRATEFUL sigh as she pulled at the horsehair remaining between the springs. She'd smoothed things over with Patrick, and somehow, she hadn't divulged the cad's name. Yet this was a small island, and Patrick could find out if he tried. Hopefully, he'd drop the subject altogether.

Peyton turned to the new cotton batting for use in the chair. How luxurious that must be. She squeezed the softness and relished its pliability. She would carefully build it up, layer by layer, evenly and densely, without impeding the coil springs. A tedious job, to be sure. But she'd successfully completed several such projects while apprenticing, and she'd do it again.

As she worked, she reflected on her life with the O'Clearys. Had they been a help or a detriment to her? They'd taught her well the crafts and skills of upholstering and sewing. But did they serve her well in building her character? She hated to admit, even to herself, that she'd become hard, dogmatic, and opinionated. Traits that disconcerted her greatly.

And her spiritual life? She'd set that aside like an old, worn schoolbook. Guilt pricked her heart as she shoved the batting around the coils. In a quest to become successful, especially as a woman, she'd ignored that part of her life for the past three years, and it needed to change. But how?

She couldn't admit such folly to Papa or Patrick. They might cast her aside like a heathen from deepest, darkest Africa. Who could she talk to? Her few friends in Clayton were busy with babies and homemaking. The O'Clearys would dismiss her concerns. And Rachel? She hadn't conversed with her about faith, but perhaps she might have some ideas.

No, better not. Rachel divulged their private conversation about suffrage in public. How could she trust her?

When Patrick appeared almost at her feet, she pricked her finger on the end of a sharp coil. "Ouch!"

She'd been so caught up in her work and thoughts that she hadn't even noticed him approach.

Patrick's brows furrowed. "Are you okay? It's almost time for dinner."

He held out a hand to help her stand, and she took it, the coolness of his skin refreshing her. "You may want to freshen up before dinner. You've a fine layer of horsehair and dust hiding the beautiful woman you are."

Peyton looked at her hands and skirt. Sure enough. If anyone saw her in public like this—she stuck her finger in the air. "And a pricked finger. I'd better skedaddle, or Mrs. Milton will have my head on a platter if I'm late."

He shook his head. "Don't worry. I thought you might need a little time to primp, so I alerted you early. You'll be fine. Now off with you."

Peyton smiled. "That was thoughtful. Thank you, Patrick."

She hurried to her room to find Rachel changing for dinner as well. A whoosh of anger passed through Peyton's veins as she thought of her roommate's misstep.

Rachel turned, her face crimson. A deep frown and quivering voice begged her forgiveness. "Oh, Peyton. I am so very sorry for opening my big mouth and getting us both into hot water. I had no right. But I also had no idea the topic was taboo."

Peyton blew out a breath as she splashed cool water on her face and hands. "I'm sure you meant no harm. I just wish it hadn't happened."

Rachel whimpered. "Me too. I would never betray your confidence. Edna made a comment about her cousin being in the suffrage movement, and I got pulled into it. Knowing her, I suspect she'd planned to trap me."

As Peyton slipped out of her dusty dress and donned a fresh one, her frustration turned from Rachel to Edna. "I hadn't heard that part of the conversation, but I'm not surprised. She's a scheming one. We'd better watch our backs around her."

Rachel yielded. "True. Please know that I'll be on the alert and never speak of our discussions again outside of this room, okay?"

"Thank you for that. The same goes for me. From now on, what's said here stays here."

Rachel ran over and gave her a hug. "You're a good friend, Peyton. Thank you. I've fretted over this all day."

Peyton returned her hug. "So have I. But it's in the past now. Shall we enjoy a nice dinner, hopefully free from any drama?"

"Let's." Rachel laughed, fastening the last of her buttons and pinching color into her cheeks. "How's your work going?"

"Moving along nicely. Finished the piano bench this morning and working on the gentleman's chair. Can you believe I'm using cotton batting instead of horsehair for stuffing?"

"Gracious." Rachel gawked at Peyton as they descended the servants' stairs on their way to the dining room. "Such luxury. I've only had straw ticks for my bedding. It must feel like a cloud."

"It does."

They entered the dining room just in time and sat next to each other.

Unfortunately, Edna sat across from them, tossing them both an expression of sniveling triumph. "How are the radicals? What mischief do you have planned for tonight?"

Duvall interrupted her taunt with a blessing over the food and a few staff instructions. Peyton ignored Edna's comment. Small talk about the afternoon thunderstorm and a leaky roof ensued, and she was grateful to have dodged that bullet.

Peyton turned to Rachel. "So how was your day?"

"I spent hours in the root cellar dusting jars and fending off a slew of spiders and one little garter snake." She turned up her nose. "I think I killed a thousand spiders and good riddance."

Peyton shuddered. "I hate creepy-crawlers. Always have. Always will. When I was about eight, I was swimming, and a huge northern water snake joined me. It was longer than I was. I almost drowned trying to get away from it. Pat, my best friend, saved me, and I've been afraid of them ever since." She snatched a glimpse at Patrick, glad she hadn't said his name.

Edna snickered. "That species of snake isn't venomous. Why all the fuss?" She rolled her eyes and promptly turned to the maid next to her to join an animated conversation about the Fourth of July.

Peyton shifted in her seat, tossing Rachel an eye roll and exaggerated smirk. "Do you know my papa puts on fireworks? That's his job, and he loves it. He'll be putting on the Clayton fireworks this Fourth of July, just as he's done for as long as I can remember, and we'll surely have front row seats here on the island. Hundreds of boats from all over the islands come to enjoy the spectacle."

That drew a surprised glare from Edna, which Peyton ignored by turning a shoulder.

"Really? Have you ever helped him? I think I'd faint dead away to be near such dangerous incendiaries." Rachel's hand fluttered to her chest.

Peyton beamed. "Yes. I've always been his 'wee assistant,' as he calls me. Since I moved to apprenticing almost three years ago, I haven't had the privilege of helping, but I'd love to do it again sometime. I love the precision, the art, the thrill. If I were a man, I'd be delighted to take over his business one day."

Rachel swallowed her bite of food, her eyes wide. "But isn't it scary? The fire? The noise? The danger?"

Peyton sipped her lemonade before answering. "Not usually. We take every precaution to stay safe and avoid accidents. Papa has never had a problem, though I've heard things can go awry all too quickly."

Rachel touched the top of Peyton's hand. "Well, I'll pray for him this holiday. You can count on it."

Peyton smiled before taking a bite of cooked carrots. She hadn't prayed for her papa's safety in several years. Before Watertown, she'd never failed to ask God for protection. Where did that go?

Edna interrupted her musings. "Say, I bet my radical cousin in Rochester would like to meet you two. Betsy has gone and joined the likes of Susan B. Anthony and the National Woman Suffrage Association. That Anthony woman even made it possible for Betsy to go to the University of Rochester. Can you imagine? Well, the entire family has disowned her, and I'm glad. Such a disgrace." She then canvassed the table to make sure she had an audience. "Women deserving the same rights as men? Poppycock! As soon as the right man comes along, I'll be happy to focus my life on home and family. And you two will probably be in jail."

Chuckles and glares joined the conversation. Mrs. Milton watched the proceedings with arms folded over her ample chest, chewing on something like a cow chews her cud. She smirked at Edna and scowled at Peyton.

Peyton gave the housekeeper nothing more than pursed lips before casting a narrow-eyed glare at Edna. She refused to be pulled into either woman's web.

Patrick groaned as pork loin churned in his stomach. Talk of suffrage again? Why couldn't that woman let it go? He held his breath, praying Peyton wouldn't take the bait and say anything. To his surprise and gratitude, she kept quiet. But the room grew tense, and dinner was no longer a pleasant affair.

How could he make Peyton understand that this battle should not be fought in tiny hometowns or places like this small island?

Better to leave the skirmishes to big cities and groups of women who didn't know their neighbors or care what they thought. Here, in the Thousand Islands, life was simpler. For good or for bad, everyone knew everyone's business.

What if word got out that Peyton espoused such unconventional thinking? It was bad enough that she'd apprenticed for radicals and learned a trade usually occupied by men. Folks cackled about that already. If they learned of her involvement with such inflammatory issues as the vote for women, they'd squawk even louder.

Mrs. Milton interrupted his musings by addressing the group. "You're dismissed. And stay away from the veranda tonight. The Emerys are entertaining."

One by one, the staff members stood and left the dining room, but Patrick took his time. Perhaps he could walk with Peyton before sunset.

Peyton set her napkin on the table and rose, gathering her empty plate, glass, and utensils.

Mrs. Milton motioned for Peyton to resume her seat. "Stay behind. You, too, Rachel."

Patrick pretended to eat, though he couldn't imagine swallowing a thing. What ill intent festered in the woman's bosom? He peered at the two remaining men who shoveled food into their mouths like it was their final meal.

"Bringing dissension to the staff is grounds for dismissal. Do you know that? There will be no more talk of radical ideas such as suffrage or anything else of that nature. Is that understood?" After pointing her knife at Peyton and Rachel, she let it clatter to her plate.

Peyton bowed her head. "Yes, ma'am." Rachel merely nodded as she sniffled.

Mrs. Milton wiped her hands together. "I've seen enough of you two for today. Be off with you, and keep your mouths shut, or you'll leave this island."

Patrick's heart constricted when he beheld Peyton's downcast face.

As soon as Rachel reached the door, the tearful girl ran into the rain helter-skelter. He wanted to comfort both of them, but Peyton was his priority.

When Peyton got to the door, Patrick stopped her. "Shall we talk? The ballroom is private enough, I think."

She shook her head. "I should see to Rachel. False accusations and fear of losing her position must overwhelm the poor girl."

He touched her arm. "Please. A few moments won't matter. You'll have the whole evening with your roommate."

Peyton shrugged. "Oh, all right. But only for a few minutes. I should tend to her promptly."

As they walked to the ballroom, Peyton huffed. She groaned. But she said nothing. Patrick's hair prickled as if lightning were nearby. It was. The lightning was inside his precious Peyton.

She was ready to explode. He'd observed that same demeanor many times before. She wouldn't stand being falsely accused. Ever.

When they got to the ballroom, the lightning bolt cracked the atmosphere.

"I can't believe the nerve of that scheming, wicked woman. Threatening me. Taunting me. Teasing me. Well, I don't give a whit what she says. She has no right to question my beliefs, nor does she have the mental aptitude of a salamander. I doubt she's ever considered the viability or the necessity of women taking their rightful place in society. All she wants to do is wield her haughtiness over others and cause trouble."

Footsteps announced they were not alone, and Peyton pinched her lips together, her eyes growing wide as she turned. Her gaze drifted past Patrick to the entrance, and she flinched. He followed her stare.

Duvall. The butler's probing assessment incited fear. He'd heard it all.

As if in slow motion, Duvall stepped toward them, his footsteps like a gong ringing her conviction.

Peyton chewed her quivering bottom lip, her eyes brimming with tears. Yet she stayed silent, waiting for the butler's judgment. What could she say to dissuade his condemnation?

Duvall cleared his throat and shook his head slowly. "I am disappointed in you, Miss Quinn. I came to encourage you, but your words have nullified the faith I put in you being a woman of integrity and honor. I am distressed that you care so little for your position here that you would risk losing it this way. Mrs. Milton's warning may have disgruntled you. You may even disagree with her assessment of you and your ideas. But you may never speak about your superiors as you just did."

A tiny vein throbbed along the side of Patrick's right eye, pulsing to the tune of this scathing lecture. Peyton wasn't speaking about the housekeeper. Nae. Surely, she was addressing Edna's character.

Peyton's face turned ghostly white. Two large tears spilled over her cheeks. "But sir, I—"

Duvall held up his hand. "No excuses. I'll not hear of it. But know this—I expect you to tame your tongue and be respectful of Mrs. Milton. If I detect an eyelash of disrespect, I'll sack you myself. Is that understood?"

Peyton curtsied low, nearly kneeling in humility. "Yes, sir."

Duvall waited for her to straighten before responding. He studied Patrick. "And you, sir, as her friend and colleague, should do all you can to dissuade her from such folly."

"Yes, sir."

The butler clasped his hands behind his back and dipped his chin. "Very well, then. We'll leave it at that. Good evening."

Patrick stood next to Peyton as Duvall left the ballroom. Several moments of silence filled the room except for an occasional sniffle. What could he say to help her?

"Unbelievable. People and their judgments." Peyton stomped to her workstation, hands fisted.

Was her moment of humility an act?

He joined her, a calming hand extended, but she'd have none of it.

Shrugging away from him, Peyton stomped her foot. "He condemned me before he even knew who I was talking about. I was describing Edna, not Mrs. Milton, for heaven's sake. But he didn't give me a chance to explain. And Mrs. Milton threatened Rachel and me when it was only Edna who spoke up today. I'm so tired of being judged and accused and condemned. Women have a right to be equal to men and have their opinions heard and have the right to vote, and I'll go to my grave believing it."

Patrick heaved a deep breath. He had to lower the temperature of her near-boil. "Most men think women are too emotional, irrational, and unprepared to vote or do much else outside the home. Unfortunately, your behavior doesn't convince them otherwise. You're going to have to find a different way to make change than ranting from the rooftops, Peyton. And until then, your role in society entails marrying, having children, and allowing your husband to make decisions for the family."

That didn't come out the way he'd planned.

Peyton's eyes flashed with simmering anger so palpable that Patrick stepped back to avoid retribution. "I'll never conform to that role."

Patrick sighed. "But don't you see? Wisdom is learning how to work within the constraints we each may face, though they be different. And if you can't do that, the catty ladies will likely run you out of town on a rail. Then what will you do? Where will you work?"

The intensity of her tearful gaze made him shiver. "I don't care what they think. Nor you." She cast one last saber-toothed scowl at him before fleeing from his presence.

In the past, Patrick had always smoothed things over with her and helped her understand reason. For as long as he remembered, he'd listened to her thoughts and opinions and responded openly and honestly. He'd fumbled and bumbled his words now and then. But she'd respected what he had to say and most often took his suggestions to heart.

Until now.

CHAPTER 15

THE NEXT MORNING, PEYTON waited in the gentle shadows of the island's lagoon for her ride to Clayton. Dawn crept in on mouse feet. She loved the sunrise on the river, and her eagerness to visit Papa had awakened her far earlier than expected. Today was a new day, far from the concerns of Mrs. Milton, Edna—and Patrick.

She needed to resupply her quickly dwindling sewing notions, so she had gathered her courage to ask Duvall if she could visit her papa while in Clayton.

The kind butler nodded. "Please be back after lunch, and don't dally."

If she played it right, she could hand Mr. Burlingame her list and head straight to Papa, spend the entire morning with him, then return to the shop to fetch her wares in the allotted time.

Twenty minutes later, she sat in the skiff as her hometown grew closer and closer. A tiny smile played about her lips. How much nicer it was to work so near her papa. While living in Watertown, she'd only seen him once a month—or even less.

Peyton reviewed her list of necessities for accuracy. Hopefully, the store would have everything on hand, and she'd not have to order it and wait, which might impede her work schedule.

When the boatman pulled up to the dock and let her out, she

thanked him.

He tipped his cap. "I'll pick you up at one sharp, miss. Don't be tardy."

She waved, already in motion toward town. "Thank you, Mr. Beaman. I won't."

Peyton hurried to the Burlingame's General Store. As she passed the café, two women from her church sat at a table near the window. Peyton waved, but instead of waving back, the two turned up their noses and shook their heads.

What was their problem? She'd done nothing to either of them to warrant such treatment.

She willed the snub to roll off her like water off a duck, then entered the store.

Mr. Burlingame, a jovial chap with gray hair, a wide girth, and an even wider smile, greeted her. "Miss Quinn. It's been ages. I heard you were back in the village and working at the castle. How are you faring?"

She acknowledged his warm welcome with a nod. "Wonderfully, thank you. Calumet is a magical place, to be sure."

The man nodded, picked up a cloth, and wiped the counter aimlessly. "So I've been told, though I haven't had the pleasure of visiting it. I'd become acquainted with Mr. Emery and his previous wife—may God rest her soul—but I haven't met his new bride. How is the new Mrs. Emery?"

"The missus is a lovely person. She's been very encouraging and is making the castle into a spectacular summer retreat. The ballroom rivals the Woodruff Hotel's."

"Good, good. Are you here on business or pleasure?"

Peyton handed him her list. "I'm doing an extensive amount of reupholstery work on Calumet to get it ready for the Grand Ball."

Mr. Burlingame leaned on the glass counter. He held the list but didn't look at it. The man always enjoyed a chat with his customers. "I've heard about the ball, and the Emerys have an account with us.

Several of the servants have been here gathering supplies, ordering items, and preparing for the affair. I hear your papa will be putting on a lavish fireworks display to culminate the party."

Peyton blinked. "He is? I hadn't heard."

The man acceded, then perused her paper. "You're in luck. I think I have everything on this list. Do you want to wait while I gather it?"

Peyton glanced toward the door. "No. I've been given the morning to visit Papa, so I'll pick it up around twelve-thirty, if that's okay. And please charge it to the Emerys' account."

Mr. Burlingame chuckled, his belly jiggling like jelly. "Yes, miss. Say hello to your father."

Peyton thanked him and headed for the exit. But as she was leaving, the two women from the café entered. Peyton stepped aside and greeted them, but both women huffed, their narrowed eyes and frowns signaling disapproval.

Mrs. Chapman leaned closer to her friend and mumbled, "That one's been trouble from the start. A radical in our village. Wish she'd stayed in Watertown."

Mrs. Black scowled. "Yes. Girls raised without their mothers can be a nuisance. They belong in the city, not here."

Peyton pretended not to hear and hurried toward her home, but their comments hurt. Like always.

She picked up her pace, anxious to receive the love and approval Papa always bestowed upon her. A radical? She was no radical. Yes, she longed to see change, but she'd never harm anyone or do anything unlawful to get it. That's what radicals did.

She climbed the steps to her childhood home and opened the screen door. Before alerting Papa of her arrival, she breathed in the familiar fragrances. The smell of sweet Williams dancing on the breeze from the bushes outside. Papa said they were her mother's favorite, so he took great care to keep them trimmed and healthy. Bacon and eggs. Her papa's favorite—and almost daily—breakfast. And Lucy's scent too. Her heart warmed.

"Papa? I'm home."

Lucy came running and jumped up to meet her, licking her hand and wagging her tail viciously. "Hello, my sweet Lucy Lu."

She gave her dog a loving hug and scratched behind her ears as a chair scraped the wooden kitchen floor. Papa had probably been reading the paper and sipping tea. She met him at the threshold.

"Peyton? What are you doing here, my darling daughter? Merciful heavens. Just last night, I longed to see you, so I prayed you'd visit soon. I never expected my prayers would be answered this very morning."

Papa kissed her cheek, gathering her into a warm embrace. He heaved a contented sigh as he held her close for a long, long while. When he finally let go, Peyton studied his face. Tears glistened in his eyes.

Worry laced her happiness. "Are you all right, Papa?"

Stepping toward the stove, Papa shrugged. "I'm fine. Today is your mama's birthday—God rest her soul. I always get a little melancholy on this day."

Peyton sucked in a breath. She'd forgotten. Recovering quickly, she offered a faltering smile. "I remember, and I miss her, too, though I never knew her."

He touched her cheek tenderly, glancing into her eyes as if to study her soul. "You remind me so much of her. Always wanting to make the world a better place. Her big heart drove her like a ship's rudder. She'd be fighting for the vote, too, if she were here."

Papa continued to gaze into her eyes with such deep affection that it almost made her cry. He knew? Were rumors going around town about her? If so, that'd explain the church ladies' disapproval. But how? Who spread the gossip?

Peyton sucked in a deep breath to calm her growing angst. "Are people telling tales about me again, Papa?"

He motioned to the kitchen table. "Have a seat, darling. Breakfast?"

Peyton agreed, and he fried an egg while she poured some tea for both of them. When she sat, a troubled moan escaped her lips. "What are they saying, Papa?"

Papa flipped the egg and slid it onto a plate, adding two pieces of bacon before handing it to her. "Pay them no heed. Prattling prunes, they are. They have nothing better to do than gossip."

She nibbled her bacon. "I mean no harm. Truly. I just want to see that women are treated fairly." She patted her lips with a napkin, waving the bacon above her plate. "Crispy. Just the way I like it. Thanks, Papa."

He shrugged. "Your mama worked for the vote. Did you know that? She was discreet in her canvassing and rarely ruffled feathers. Instead, she quietly educated and informed women, encouraging them to believe that things would eventually change. She was a little ahead of her time, and I think you are, too, but it's a worthy cause."

Peyton hopped up from her chair and hugged him from behind. "You do understand. I was so afraid to tell you. Afraid you'd disapprove."

He gently took her arm and motioned for her to sit again. "I'd like to see everyone fairly treated. But discretion is the key to success here, daughter. You can rail all you want, and teems of women can rally. But change like this must be a grassroots effort. As your mama always said, 'you win 'em one by one.'"

Peyton sat up straight as that sank in. "Then I'm proud to be like her. And maybe I can apply some of her wise ways in the days ahead."

"That would be good." Taking a seat across from her, Papa rubbed the back of his neck. "Truth is, I'm worried about you, Peyton Pie, even as I tell you not to take notice of the town gossips. They're wagging their tongues something fierce. I just don't want you hurt, 'tis all."

Peyton waved a hand. "Oh, they're always babbling about something. When I was young, it was my friendship with Patrick and unladylike behavior. When I apprenticed, I was a thief for stealing a man's job. Now, it's this. Bah-humbug on them all, I say!"

Papa laughed. "Agreed. Enough of that subject. Tell me something about Calumet that I don't know."

Peyton pondered that a moment. "Did you know the island has cement sidewalks and gas lamps?"

"Huh. I didn't. Clayton doesn't even have those modern conveniences. Guess I'll have to speak to the town board about our town coming up to snuff."

She giggled. "You do, and they'll pronounce you a radical. Say, I hear you'll be putting on a fireworks show for the Emerys' Grand Ball next month."

Papa grinned. "Yes. And they are spending more on that event than the town of Clayton does for the Fourth of July fireworks— which, of course, I'll be doing in just over a week. I've chosen a few new items for both events. The crates of incendiaries were delivered yesterday by train."

"Wish I could be your 'wee apprentice' again. I miss working with you."

"I miss you, too, dear one." He leaned forward, his face twisting as he drew a breath. "Peyton, I have something to tell you."

The eggs and bacon soured in her stomach. "What is it, Papa?"

"I saw Dr. Whitmarsh the other day."

He reached his hand toward her, and to her horror, it trembled. The longer he held it there, the faster it wobbled until it shook violently.

She reached for his hand and kissed it. "What is it? Can he fix it?"

Papa shook his head. "It's the shaking palsy, I'm afraid. The Emery's Grand Ball fireworks and the Fourth of July will be my last jobs. I must retire. Alas, Quinn Fireworks will be no more. I'm sorry."

She hopped out of her chair and hurried around to hug him. Papa shifted to receive her embrace. For a long while, she held her papa as if he were a fragile child who'd tumbled down a hill. How could she help him? This precious man who had given her everything?

Her answers were few.

She could pray. Inside, she reached heavenward to a familiar place of peace. She prayed for her papa, for his work, for herself. She simply breathed a prayer, but it was genuine, and it felt so good. Papa softened under her hug, and she relaxed too. Could God come to their aid? Surely, He was still on the throne even if she'd wandered from Him.

Finally, she pushed back and looked Papa in the eye. "What will you do? How will you live?"

"Trust God. I always have. Always will. When your mother died, I wondered how I would manage raising this helpless little baby alone. God provided then. He'll provide for us now."

"But Auntie Bess isn't here."

"I've saved a fair bit, and the house is paid for. I'll manage—you just mind that."

When Papa let go of her, he pasted on a smile and patted her hand. "Enough talk of bad stuff. I want to show you the new rockets and how they work."

Patrick tossed a stone onto the placid river, skipping it not four but five times. He threw in another. Then another. Better to throw a stone than a person. His jaw muscles ached from grinding his teeth.

Why hadn't Peyton told him that the cad who accosted her in the powerhouse was none other than that rogue from Depauville, Henry Applebee? It wasn't hard to find out. Patrick simply asked which mechanic worked that day.

But why did she cover for him? Was there more to the relationship than she had divulged? Surely not.

Patrick cringed and threw another half-dozen stones into the river to dispel his frustration.

Applebee was well-known around the islands for bringing trouble wherever he went. Though a skilled mechanic, he partook of the drink far too often and engaged in barroom brawls on a regular basis. Indeed, many of the summer residents refused his services because of his reputation. Apparently, the Emerys hadn't heard.

But Patrick hadn't known he was also a womanizer.

He shot up a prayer for Peyton, for himself, for their future. Why was love so complicated? And how could he bring peace to the whole sordid mess?

Overhead, a large gander honked orders for the twenty or so Canadian geese to get in line and form a perfect *V*. The large gaggle complied, each jockeying for position. Why couldn't Peyton get in line with social mores and be content to glide on the current of others who fought for change? She'd have so much more energy for the journey of life—and not get into hot water as often. He gazed at the birds' beautiful formation as the lead gander slipped to the back and another took its place. Could he and Peyton perform such a skillful dance together one day?

Mitch strolled up and slapped him on the shoulder. "Hey, mate. Are you skipping lunch? I stopped by the ballroom and found it empty. Thought I'd find you here at your favorite thinking spot. What's up? Where's Peyton?"

Patrick smiled at his roommate's concern. The lad might be a bit rough around the edges, but he had a good heart. "In town for the morning. And yes, I'm here pondering some hard questions of life."

"Lovesick?"

Patrick nodded. "And more." He'd tell Mitch about Henry and Peyton's situation, but she'd be horrified if others knew what had happened. He swallowed the temptation, his jaw tight. "Life can get so complicated, aye?"

Mitch laughed, picking up a stone and tossing it into the water. "Where women are present, always. Is she vexed with you?"

"Aye." Patrick frowned, a deep sigh punctuating his admission. "Seems I continually say the wrong thing. It never used to be that way. I just don't want to see her get hurt."

Mitch stepped close to Patrick and bumped shoulders. "You're a good man. Be patient. You knew her as a girl, but now she's a woman who has grown a solid backbone. She'll be all right. But we won't if we're late for lunch."

Crickets chirped the end of the day, and long shadows signaled twilight drew near. Patrick intercepted Peyton as she exited the staff dining room. "Fancy an evening stroll with me?" She'd returned to the island with a cloud of sadness hovering over her, and he needed to know why.

He motioned toward the steps leading to the lagoon. Peyton walked beside him in silence but kept an appropriate distance. When they reached the bottom of the steps, they turned right and ventured past the boathouse until they came to the eastern lawn, where a tall flagpole now stood empty. Someone had already taken down the enormous flag that flew every day from dawn to dusk.

Lightning bugs slowly woke, and several dragonflies hovered over the river, searching for their dinner. A large ship broke the dead calm while smaller boats ran along the channel as if to race the steel monster. But other than that, a hush penetrated the evening.

Lacking even a whisper of wind it unusually and uncomfortably quiet. So did Peyton's pensive mood. Patrick broke the silence. "Sorry that I've been preoccupied. How was your day, and how's your papa?"

With eyes that had lost their luster, Peyton stiffened, and her face grew tight as she told him about her father's failing health and impending retirement. Her voice cracked several times. "What if I lose him? He's the only family I have."

He leaned forward, touching her cheek. "I'm so sorry, Peyton Pie."

She shivered under his gentle touch, a trace of fright in her anguished eyes. "But that's not all. Vicious rumors are spreading like wildfire in the village. Scandal that I've acted inappropriately and traded favors to get approval while in Watertown. It's shameful, and it's all a lie."

In the silence that stretched between them, Patrick scurried to find words that might help.

"I don't know if I can take it." Peyton spread her hands open. "The stares. The head shakes. The rumors and innuendos. This morning, women from our church shook their heads at me and made rude comments. And Mr. Turley called me a name I cannot repeat. Papa had heard even more but wouldn't say. The social backlash cuts deep, Patrick. Especially from my own hometown folk."

He stiffened, fisting and unfisting his hands. But then he took her hand and stroked the top of it lovingly. "You're in good company. Remember how the Scriptures tell us that folks in Nazareth were offended by Jesus too? Prophets and people who try to bring change aren't often honored by their own. Hopefully, a day will come when we'll laugh about this. Today is not that day." He bent and kissed her hand. Then he let go of it, picked up a stone, and tossed it in the still water. "Watch."

A tiny ripple where the stone entered the river expanded in circles. Wider and wider until it finally dissipated into a flat calm. "That's what a rumor is like. Give it time, dear one."

CHAPTER 16

PEYTON RUBBED THE BACK of her hand, warmed by the tenderness and encouragement Patrick had poured out on her like honey on toast. That's how she felt—like crumbly, burnt toast. And to think, she'd nearly said no to his request to join him on a walk.

She climbed the stairs to her room. Perhaps Rachel would be up and interested in talking. As much as Patrick had soothed her, she craved a female perspective just now.

She couldn't forget that Patrick had also given her verbal slaps in the face when she needed them. Was he right in warning her about society's current confines and measuring her words more carefully? Papa would agree wholeheartedly. He'd as much as said so. The two people who loved her most...

Maybe they were right.

She opened the door to her room to find Rachel writing a letter. "Good evening. Don't let me disturb you."

Rachel acknowledged her with a nod but turned back to pen a few more words. "All done. How are you, Peyton? Did you enjoy your trip to Clayton?"

She shook her head as she pulled off her bonnet and let down her hair. "That's a long and sordid story, I'm afraid."

Rachel grinned mischievously. "I love sordid stories. Do tell. And remember my promise to keep our words in this room."

Peyton gave her a weak smile. As she started to get ready for bed, she related her papa's declining health and her troubles with the local rumormongers. "Patrick was so kind as we spoke about it just now. I don't know what I'd do without him."

Rachel laughed, her eyes dancing. "I thought you and he had something special going on. You really do care for him, don't you? You light up like a firefly when you talk about him."

Peyton threw her hands up to her cheeks to cool them. "I do?"

"You do. I've observed it from the start. Even when you're vexed with him. Like my parents did when they argued. Though I was just twelve when Papa died, I still remember that they never failed to love one another even when they didn't agree."

Peyton plopped down on the bed. "My mother died just after I was born, so I don't know what couples do or don't do. I've only ever viewed marriage from afar. And much of what I have experienced has been none too pretty. Even the O'Clearys' marriage seemed on tenterhooks more than not, though they put on a good front with the public. So I don't know if I could ever marry. What I do know is that I couldn't be ruled and controlled by a man. I just couldn't."

Rachel climbed into bed, pushing back her coverlet to use just the sheet. "It's so hot and humid tonight." She wiped her brow before addressing Peyton's angst. "Not every husband is that way. My father wasn't, and I dare say the Emerys have a rather equal partnership. At least, that's what I've observed."

"If I were to marry, I'd make sure my husband understood my positions on the vote and the struggle for women's equality. Papa even told me that Mama participated in moving suffrage forward, and he was proud of her."

Rachel's eyes grew wide. "Was she ostracized badly? I've heard such women are beaten and worse. We're even labeled as radicals, so Edna taunts me every time we pass in the hall or happen to be in the same room. If my family didn't depend on my meager salary, I'd be tempted to leave this place just to be rid of her ridicule."

"I didn't know she was persecuting you like that." Peyton reached over and patted her hand. "I'll have her neck in a noose if she doesn't leave you be. I'll talk to her tomorrow and tell her—"

"Oh, Peyton, please don't. She's a vindictive bully. The more you push a bully, the more trouble comes your way. I don't want trouble. Please."

Peyton huffed her exasperation. "Oh, all right. But that girl needs to be put in her place."

"She does, but I'm not sure we're the ones to do it. Let's put that topic to bed and return to the one you seem to want to avoid. Patrick."

Peyton shrugged. "I don't avoid it. I just don't know what to do with it."

"You two make the perfect couple. You've known each other forever. And I can see in his eyes that he moons over you something fierce." Rachel giggled behind her hand. "I suspect you love him too."

Peyton shook her head. "We're childhood friends—that's all. He can be so exasperating—and opinionated. He told me I should be more careful about my unorthodox ideas."

"He's right, I'm sorry to say." Rachel bit her lip and paused. "This isn't the big city, Peyton. Folks 'round here don't fancy modern ways like they do in other places. Papa always told me that to bring lasting change, I was to be prudent in speech and action. I think that's wise advice."

"Prudence?" She sighed loudly. "Yes. I'm beginning to think that might be the right way to go."

Rachel smirked. "Back to Patrick. Just because he warns you about things and has opinions different from yours doesn't mean you're not a match. Proverbs tells us that iron sharpens iron. That's what friends—and good marriages—are all about."

Peyton tossed her a kind smile. "You appear to be too wise for your age, my friend."

Rachel shrugged, and a comfortable silence filled the room.

Might she broach another topic? Why not? "Are you a person of faith, Rachel?"

Rachel beamed. "I am. It's what carries me through even the darkest days and toughest times."

Peyton's heart raced, and tiny beads of perspiration formed on her brow. She swept them away with her sleeve. "My faith has faltered of late. I still believe, and I love God. But He seems so distant and silent."

"But He's always here, as close as your very breath—if you love Him and have given your heart and life to Him. The question is, have you stepped away from Him?"

Yes, she'd distanced herself from the Almighty, but how far? Too far? "When I was in Watertown, I was so busy, and all my friends and acquaintances there were not people of faith, so it just ... slipped away. I stopped reading my Bible and only went to church on Christmas and Easter. But now, I'm wondering if that wasn't folly."

Rachel slipped out of bed and sat next to her. "We all have our seasons. When Papa died, I was so mad at God that I refused to touch the Bible and pasted my lips shut during church. I wouldn't talk to Him for over a year. Even when Mother made us go to church, I recited poems in my head rather than hear about the God who took Papa from me. But then, I realized that was also folly. I told Him I was sorry, and He filled me with so much love and peace that I haven't been the same since. He can do that for you too. You just have to ask."

Peyton's throat constricted. Her eyes pooled with sorrowful tears. Could Rachel be right? Could it be that simple? She gave Rachel a hug so the girl couldn't see her tears. "Thank you, Rachel. You've given me much to think about. Now, I think it's high time we hit the hay and get our rest."

Rachel hugged her back. "I'll be praying for you, my friend. Thank you for sharing your troubles. It means a lot."

Peyton smiled as she pulled back the quilt, and Rachel slipped under her own covers. Peyton turned off the lamp and rolled toward the wall.

Could returning to faith really be as simple as saying "I'm sorry" to the Lord and starting over again?

Hours later, Peyton awoke with a start and yanked herself up on an elbow to look around. The early-morning light filtered through the open window, and a cool breeze wafting in brought the scent of rain. Thankfully, Rachel still lay sleeping.

Another night terror. Another drowning dream. But this time, a hand pulled her out of the abyss, and she was safe. Was that hand God's or Patrick's?

She lay back down and ventured to pray silently. *Lord, I've been amiss. Please forgive me for my waywardness. I'm so sorry. Turn my heart and mind back to You, forever. Help me to know what to do with everything— my faith, my words and work, my papa, and Patrick. I can't do this alone.*

As rain fell in heavy drops, Patrick stared out his bedroom window, recalling the times he'd ran away in the rain or hidden from his father in a snowstorm. Foul weather hadn't bothered him near as badly as his father's anger and strap.

Why couldn't he forget the pain of those moments? At the strangest times, the memories would rear their ugly heads and taunt him. Like now.

How could he be a good husband and father when all he'd ever known was abuse? Was the vice deep in his genes? Would he become just like the man whom he hated?

Dear God, no.

He loved Peyton. Dreamed of being her husband and the father of her children. But what if ...? Maybe he should stay a bachelor and save her and her children the same fate he and his mother and sister had endured.

He sighed, a hollow emptiness taking residence in his heavy heart. The thought of life without Peyton made his melancholy deepen, a patchwork puzzle of frenzied emotions filling his mind.

A cool breeze swept in from the river, and the rain mocked the tears forming in his eyes. He snuck a gander at Mitch, who snored softly in his bed.

Patrick shook himself, trying to dispel the gloom. But it didn't help, so he quietly dressed and headed for the ballroom. What would it matter if he started work before breakfast or after? Maybe he could work off some angst before seeing Peyton at breakfast.

Entering the ballroom, Patrick blinked in the gray morning light. He wiped the raindrops from his clothes and removed his jacket and hat.

First, he assessed his work. The walls and fireplace—perfection. The baseboard he'd worked on thus far—well done. Then his sharp gaze followed the path of his finished work to the part he'd been sanding yesterday.

Wait. What had happened here?

As he moved closer, hackles rose on the back of his neck. A near growl slipped out of his lips.

Stain splattered the wall and floor as if the can had somehow exploded. Brushes had dried hard as if he'd left everything to the elements the night before. Positive he'd sealed the stain can and cleaned his brushes well before leaving, Patrick fisted his hand over his racing heart. Anger boiled in his veins, and he fought back a sour taste in his throat.

The saboteur's evil hand. Again.

His hands trembled with fury as he touched the wall. Dry. The floor? Dry too. The brushes—ruined. Someone had done this hours ago, and it would set his work back days.

Why would anyone do this?

Patrick squinted toward Peyton's workstation. With the light so dim, he wasn't sure what he saw, so he hurried to the alcove.

The mayhem he beheld tumbled his stomach, and for a moment, he thought he might vomit the emptiness of it.

Peyton's station had been decimated as if a tornado touched down upon it. Fabric bolts tossed like toothpicks. Her tools scattered about. The stuffing she'd so carefully applied to the chair back flung in wads around the area. And worst of all, a huge slit in the upholstery she'd completed so nicely on the chair bottom destroyed her work.

He picked up a rubber mallet and heaved it across the ballroom floor, fuming at the wickedness of the person who did this.

But who? His mind whirled with questions. Henry wasn't on the island last night. And Edna? She had no quarrel with him as far as he knew. Though he didn't know everyone who worked on the island, he knew of no one he'd offended or had made an enemy.

Once his ire dissipated a little, Patrick cleaned up Peyton's area first. He carefully rerolled the fabric, tidied up the batting, and returned her tools to the table in the order he hoped was correct—including the mallet he'd tossed in anger. But the slit in the seat? There was nothing he could do about that.

As the dawn grew brighter and the sound of rain stopped, birds chirped in the new day, grating on Patrick's sour mood. Then his head snapped toward the door, where Mitch shouted at him. "What in tarnation are you doing in here? Been looking all over for you. We'll be late for breakfast if we don't hightail it over there."

Patrick sprinted to Mitch, and they dashed to the dining hall. The only explanation he offered his roommate for his absence was that he couldn't sleep. Thankfully, Mitch didn't press him for further details.

Breakfast didn't sweeten his mood one bit. All the seats near Peyton were filled, so he sat at the far end of the table. For the entire meal, he ruminated over the cruel, unjust wrong done to both Peyton and himself. When he returned to his post, Peyton was already at hers, in a dither.

Her voice sounded like a squeaky little girl's. "Patrick, someone tore the chair seat. Please come and see."

He joined her, a corner of his mouth drawing back. "I'm so sorry, Peyton. Looks as though the vandal has hit again."

She ran her hand over the damaged material. "Who would do such a thing? To me? To the Emerys?"

Patrick willed his voice to steady. "I don't know. We'll speak with Duvall and see what can be done to find the perpetrator. I did the best I could to put everything back as you had it."

Peyton blinked, her face tense. "He did more than this?"

She turned to her table and ran her hand along the spines of the fabric bolts. Then she examined and fingered her tools, adjusting a few of them to a different order. "You ... you fixed all this? For me? When?"

"I couldn't sleep, so I came early and found the mess. I did the best I could." Patrick took her hand and pulled her to him.

She slipped her arm around him and gave him a hug, then promptly retreated, her cheeks turning a pretty pink. "You did wonderfully. Thank you. If I'd come and seen more than this tear, I might have fainted dead away."

Patrick chuckled and took her hand again. Both felt good. "We couldn't have that, now could we?"

At that moment, Duvall entered the ballroom, and they dropped their hands to their sides like little soldiers and took a step away from each other. Patrick glanced at her, and she followed him to meet the butler.

Patrick raised his chin. "Sir. We've had an ... incident you need to be aware of."

Duvall's brows furrowed into one. "An incident?"

Peyton bobbed her head but stayed silent.

Patrick stepped toward Peyton's alcove. "Sometime between when Miss Quinn left for dinner and this morning, someone disrupted her workstation. I came here early and found it vandalized and the seat ripped."

When they got to the area, Duvall groaned. "That's not a rip. Someone slashed it with a knife or some other sharp instrument. What else did you find? Tell all."

Patrick described the mess, and when he showed the butler the stain, Peyton's face went white, her eyes brimmed with fear, and her hands knotted against her middle.

Duvall shot Peyton a reassuring look and placed his hand tenderly on her shoulder. "Don't worry. We'll find the culprit—just you mind that. I have ways of snuffing out rats and other such varmints."

The fear melted from Peyton's face, though worry still flickered in her eyes. "I hope you can. Mrs. Emery is counting on me finishing my work before the ball. It'd be a shame if I couldn't fulfill my duties."

Patrick picked up a handful of batting and squeezed it. "We'll pray you can. Won't we, Miss Quinn?"

When Peyton squared her shoulders and planted a confident smile on her face, Patrick tilted his head and smiled. "Yes, indeed. We will both pray."

CHAPTER 17

PEYTON BIT HER BOTTOM lip, trembling at the reality that no innocent prank produced such vandalism. Someone sought to ruin not just her but Patrick as well. But why? Perhaps Duvall could solve that mystery before any more destruction happened.

Patrick touched her shoulder. "I'm happy you said you'd join me in prayer. God can take this burden from us and expose the miscreant."

She ran her hand along the slit on the seat. "But in the meantime, the culprit has caused me a lot more work. You too. How will you remove the stain from the wall?"

Shrugging, Patrick appraised the defaced wall. "I have no idea. Perhaps I can find a solvent in the toolshed or powerhouse."

With that, her heart raced. Apparently, her fear showed on her face, for Patrick's eyes grew wide, and he sucked in a breath.

He squeezed her forearm gently. "I have a confession. I am aware it was Henry Applebee who accosted you at the powerhouse. Fear not, my sweet. He'll not harm you again—at least, not as long as I have breath in my body."

With the back of her hand, Peyton swiped at her lips, trying to remove the loathsome memory of the scoundrel's kiss. "I can't forget being forced into my first kiss from one such as he. It haunts me."

Patrick slipped his hand from her forearm down to her hand, then kissed it. "That wasn't your first kiss, my dear." His words hung in the air. "Remember?"

She blinked, searching for a memory, but drew a blank. "What?"

Patrick squirmed under her gaze, looking every bit the ten-year-old who hid a mouse in the schoolteacher's desk and got caught. "I have another confession." He paused as if trying to read her face, then continued. "I gave you your first kiss a decade ago."

Her mind whirled with the thought, trying harder to recall the moment. Yes, in her silly teener years, she'd wanted to kiss him more than once but quickly thought the better of it each time. A good little girl wouldn't be so bold. "I don't remember you ever kissing me."

Patrick shrugged again, shifting his weight from one hip to the other. "I stole a kiss."

Bewilderment rattled her already shaken body, and she stepped back as if slapped. She opened her mouth to object, but nothing came out.

He broke the silence with the tale of a childish kiss on that summer's day while she slept in the grass. His tone was tender and innocent, not bold and brash as a rogue would sound. Obviously, he cherished the memory. "Peyton Pie, that moment gave me courage to face each awful day at home." He shook his head. "I'm sorry, but—I'll have you know—I've never kissed anyone before or since."

For several long moments, Peyton didn't know how to respond. She should be mad—livid, even. But he'd been but a child, as was she. Besides, somehow that connection had helped him. Why should she scold him for that? "Well, better that be my first kiss than the other. But in the future, please inform me of your intentions ahead of time." She gifted him with a warm smile, which, in turn, brought a huge grin to his face. "Promise?"

He saluted her. "Certainly, miss." The twinkle in his eyes meant mischief was on its way. "But I have a question, Miss Quinn."

She acknowledged his statement with a raised brow. A dense tangle of intertwining thoughts crossed her mind. After this stunning revelation, she couldn't imagine what he'd ask her.

Patrick quirked a brow, a tiny muscle in his jaw twitching. "Shall there be a future for us? I pray it is true."

Her face warmed at the implication. Would there? A sudden, wonderful, blinding knowledge enfolded. "I think providence may have its way. But first, we must focus on the work at hand."

"How right you are, Peyton Pie. Back to work." He grabbed her hand and planted a long kiss on it. "And now, I'm off to find a solution to the damaged wall."

With that, he was gone, leaving her alone with too much to ponder—the vandal, the kiss, their future. Dizzy with an awakening, swimming sensation of hope for a future with Patrick mixed with a gnawing foreboding of more trouble, Peyton didn't know what to do with the simmering stew of emotions inside her.

Work. That always helped.

She turned to her station and picked up a tool to remove the damaged fabric and recover the seat—again.

Who would've done this? Edna? Henry? Another malefactor whom she didn't even know? Could Duvall really sniff out the skunk?

At the approaching footsteps, Peyton cringed inwardly but quickly relaxed when the missus entered the ballroom. Smoothing her skirts and swiping a stray hair away from her face, she hurried to meet the queen of the castle. She curtsied. "Mrs. Emery. How may I be of assistance?"

Mrs. Emery scowled. "It appears we have a rapscallion in our midst. Duvall informed us this very morning. The butler will find him out, but until he does, I do not want you alone, at any time. Is that understood?"

Peyton bobbed her head. "Yes, ma'am."

The missus assessed the room, her eyes taking on a measure of alarm. "Where is the carpenter?"

"Searching for solvent to clean the varnish from the wall, missus."

Mrs. Emery sighed. "Very well. But next time, stay with him. I'd rather have one less chair recovered than a staff member hurt. I don't know what this vandal has in mind next, and I don't want scandal on my island."

She could be in danger. Her voice quivered as she spoke. "Yes, missus."

"I'll have a maid come and stay with you until he returns."

"No need, missus. He should return presently."

Mrs. Emery gave her a sharp gaze. "There is need. She shall be here presently."

As the mistress turned and left the room, Peyton considered her situation. Was she truly in danger? Did the missus know more than she revealed?

Fear planted its cold fingers on her shoulders, weighing her down. Her scalp crawled as her eyes scanned the doors to the ballroom. She studied the circular stairway. Might the perpetrator hide on the upper floor undetected before striking again?

She willed her racing heart to calm as she clenched and unclenched her hands. No. She would not be consumed by fear. Slowly, she talked herself down from the cliff of terror and returned to the chair.

Before long, a maid entered the ballroom. Backlit by the morning sun, Peyton couldn't detect who it was. But as she drew closer, Peyton tensed.

Edna.

Of all the maids, the missus called *her* to come to her aid. She turned her back on the girl and pulled off the last of the damaged fabric. Inwardly, she fumed, her cheeks fiery. She pressed her palms to them. She would not let Edna perceive her angst.

Finally, Peyton turned and pasted on an insincere smile. "Why, Edna. Come to clean the ballroom?"

Edna rolled her eyes. "Just the windows. And babysit you."

Peyton shot her a glare, her hands trembling. Edna would not get the best of her. "No need. Do your windows, maid."

Her tone was a little too mocking, but she couldn't take it back. No doubt, she'd pay for that.

Enda stood her ground. "I see you have some repairs to do. Pity. At least, it'll keep you out of trouble for a while."

Peyton stifled words she shouldn't speak, pasting her lips together. She turned her back, waiting for Edna to leave, but she heard no footsteps.

"I'm sure you heard that Henry Applebee has joined us on the island today." Edna feigned friendliness, sidling back into view. "Such a nice man, and funny too. Seems muskrats chewed through the wiring and caused a short, so the keeper's house has no power to it. Do you know Mr. Applebee?"

Fearing she might explode in her growing anger, Peyton willed herself to not turn and look at Edna. But her voice held ire nonetheless. "I've met him but don't know him."

Edna giggled. "Oh, we've had several outings together. My cousin is his best friend, and though Henry is a bit of a rascal, he's very entertaining. If I could sneak out of here for a few moments and say hello, you wouldn't be so juvenile as to tattle on me, would you?"

Disgusted to the point of irritation, Peyton sounded more like a feral cat than herself. "I care not. Do what you want and leave me be."

No retort came, but neither did footsteps. After what seemed an eternity, Edna groaned and went back to cleaning the windows.

Patrick searched the tool shed but found nothing that might help him clean off the wayward varnish. He headed for the powerhouse to look for turpentine, but as he drew near, a group of several men lounged nearby, laughing and smoking as if they hadn't a care in the world. The man with his back to him seemed oddly familiar. Perhaps one of the boatmen who'd taken refuge from the storm?

When Patrick joined them, a yard hand named Tim addressed him. "Henry here is telling us all the news of the North Country. Wanna join us?"

Henry? Before Patrick could distinguish his face, he knew it had to be Henry Applebee. The cad.

"No, thank you. I have work to attend to." He clipped a look at Tim, then at Henry before scanning the other four men. "As do you all, I'm sure."

Henry blew a puff of smoke, his eyes narrowing like a snake after its prey. "Well, well. If it isn't the town drunk's little boy trying to bootlick the Emerys. You'll not make a very good carpenter by leaving your work undone and your things scattered around."

Implications of the treachery left Patrick in a tither and shaking. It had to be Henry's hand that vandalized the ballroom. "How did you know about the damage? Were you the culprit?"

Henry cackled—a mocking, gloating sound. "Me? I don't live here on the island. The boys here just informed me of your mishap. Right, boys?"

As if entranced by a hypnotist, one by one, the men complied, one murmuring, "That's right, Henry."

"Well, lad. Falsely accusing an innocent man is the kind of stuff the son of a drunk might do, but it's not at all becoming for a professional. Have a drink. You'll become just like your father. Sooner or later."

Patrick fought the desire to jam Henry's insults back down his ignorant throat. Before something terrible and irrevocable happened, Patrick skirted the circle and hurried away, fleeing the chortles and snickers of the men. The solvent could wait. He pounded his thighs with his fists as he climbed the steps to the castle. How he wanted to strike some fear into that scoundrel, but punches and words wouldn't work with the likes of him.

Before going back to his post, Patrick needed to calm down. If not, Peyton would sense his anger in a second.

Peyton. Just the thought of their conversation eased his angst and warmed his heart. She'd all but acknowledged a future with him. Could it be? After several deep breaths, his heart settled to its normal rhythm.

Like that of a three-year-old waiting for Christmas, Patrick's chest swelled at the mere prospect of seeing Peyton again. He hurried to the ballroom, but Edna stopped him on the terrace, batting her eyelashes and stepping in his path. "Why, Patrick. How nice to see you again, my handsome man."

"I'm not your man. Excuse me." He sidestepped her and returned to his station without addressing Peyton. He took several deep breaths and wiped his brow with a handkerchief. But before he even had a chance to pocket it, he sniffed the air, alarm ringing in his head. "Do you smell smoke?"

Peyton lifted her head from what she was doing and took a whiff. "I do, but it doesn't smell like leaves or wood. It smells like … oil. Do you suppose there's a boat on fire nearby?"

He sprinted to the terrace with Peyton close behind. He scanned the grounds, then pointed toward the lagoon. "There. The powerhouse. There's a fire in the powerhouse." Peyton's gaze followed his finger, her face turning ashen. He tossed her a warning glance and took off running toward the danger. "Not to worry. I'll be back soon."

On arriving at the building, he joined a bucket brigade that had already formed, Henry conspicuously absent. Thankfully, the fire was already almost extinguished.

Tim smirked at Patrick. "Missed all the excitement, chap. That one got the heart pumping."

Patrick closed the gap between them. "What happened? Is it badly damaged?"

Tim flicked his fingers to mimic someone tossing out a cigarette. "Someone left a smoke near some oily rags, and they caught fire. Lucky we were nearby."

The question soured on his tongue, but he asked, anyway. "Wasn't Henry working in there?"

Tim shrugged. "Appears he's missing at the moment. Haven't seen him since we were jawing there a while ago."

Patrick had started walking back to the castle when a titter of voices drew his notice to the old oak tree near him. Edna giggled and talked with someone hidden behind the girth of the trunk. Patrick stepped a few paces closer and to the right. Lo and behold, Henry leaned against the trunk, running his hand disgracefully along Edna's midsection.

She laughed again. "You handsome rascal. Shall we meet on my next day off? I'd love to see you again."

Patrick cleared his throat loudly. "Aren't you supposed to be in the ballroom washing windows, Edna?" He scolded her with a fiery glare. Then he turned to Henry. "And you. The powerhouse caught on fire under your watch. What will Mr. Emery say to that?"

After Edna blew Henry a kiss and scurried in the direction of the castle, Henry folded his arms across his chest, eyes blazing with a menacing taunt. "Say a word, fool, and you're a dead man. Her too."

The threat rattled Patrick, but more on Peyton's account than his own. Before he could reply, the caretaker, Mr. Fitzsimmons, strode up to the group near the powerhouse, his voice loud and angry. "What happened here?" Patrick strained to hear what one of the men said to him, but most of it floated away on the breeze.

It was Henry the caretaker should be talking to.

Patrick cleared his throat and spoke loud enough to draw the caretaker's attention. "Well, Henry, shouldn't you be in the powerhouse?"

Mr. Fitzsimmon's head snapped toward them, his eyes narrowing. He waved their way, his tone angry. "Henry? What in tarnation are you doing up there, man?"

Like an eel in murky water, Henry slipped onto the path. "Just attending to the call of nature, sir." He moseyed up to Fitzsimmons and patted him on the shoulder. "Good thing I was here, or this entire building might have gone up in smoke."

The nerve of that man. Patrick's temples pounded, and his throat tightened. Nothing made him more furious than a lying scoundrel taking credit for curtailing what he'd likely caused.

Over Patrick's dead body.

When he returned to the ballroom, Edna was absent.

Peyton, however, pulled the tacks from the damaged seat with a vengeance. She wiped her brow. "Is everything all right? From here, it looked like a pretty big fire."

He shook his head. "Some fool left a cigarette too near a pile of oily rags. There was damage, but the fire was contained quickly. But now I've lost half a day's work. It's almost lunchtime."

"I know." She stopped working and stared at her workstation, looking as forlorn as a street urchin. "With all these setbacks, how will I ever accomplish all the missus is expecting? It feels insurmountable, as though I shall fail at my first real position."

Patrick patted her shoulder gently. "You'll do it, Peyton. I believe in you. But when this summer is over, you don't have to keep working if you don't want to. You can always let someone else slap a piece of material on a chair and tack it down."

Peyton's green eyes narrowed. She shoved her hands on her hips and glared at him until he felt like a lizard atop an exploding volcano. "There's much more to my work than simply slapping and tacking. The material and pattern have to be just right, and … gracious! I don't need to justify my profession to you."

Blathers! He'd done it again. "I misspoke. I know you're good at your job, but you don't have to deal with the stress and hard work it brings. You know I love you, Peyton. Maybe it's time you give this up and let me take care of you. You can stay home and care for the house and the garden and, one day, our children."

"You, sir, misunderstand *me*! I *want* to work, whether part-time or full-time. I cannot sit around dusting and primping all day. I need purpose. And last, but certainly not least, I don't need taken care of."

"Oh, Peyton Pie, you already have purpose—serving God and your family. A job is just a job. I think that the grandest purpose of any woman is to be a strong, committed Christian who will teach her children the ways of the Word."

"Then I obviously fall short of your lofty expectations." Peyton's eyes brimmed with tears as she fled his presence.

Now what had he said?

CHAPTER 18

THE FOURTH OF JULY dawned sunny and hot. Peyton crawled out of bed and dressed, groaning at the prospect of working in the stuffy ballroom on such a day.

Rachel twisted her hair and pinned it. "Something wrong?"

Peyton shrugged. "Wishing I could do the fireworks with Papa, 'tis all."

Rachel rolled her eyes. "Can't imagine it. They scare me." She paused. "I miss my hometown folk today. They're like family. We'd have a community picnic with games and lots of fun. Are the Clayton folk that way?"

Peyton closed the door behind Rachel as they headed to breakfast. "They are good folk, 'cept for the gossipmongers."

"Yes. There are always tattling toadies."

Peyton put her finger to her cheek. "I remember a time in our village history when we came together in a special way. Five years ago, around Christmas. This island's caretaker attempted to take one of their hired help, Miss Minerva Robbins, back to her home on Grindstone Island, just a mile across the river. They were in his punt built for use on ice and in water. His little boy came with them while the boy's two sisters stayed home."

Rachel's brow furrowed. "I fear I'm about to hear a sad story."

Peyton sighed. "Unfortunately. About halfway there, a snow squall arose, and the punt broke through the ice and sank, never to be seen again. The worst of it, though, was that Mrs. Rogers witnessed the incident from her kitchen window. Can you imagine what it was like to watch your husband and your eight-year-old son die and not be able to do anything to save them?"

Rachel's face whitened as she sucked on her bottom lip. She shook her head slowly. "Weren't others on the island to help?"

Peyton waved an arm toward the caretaker's house on the far side of the island. "No one. Since they wintered alone on this very island, Mrs. Rogers tried to get help by sending night signals to the villagers. But no one came, and it must have been agonizing."

"The villagers couldn't see the signals?"

"Apparently, no one noticed. In the morning, she raised an inverted flag to draw attention. That worked, and when the folk of Clayton heard of the tragedy, skiffs of every size took to the frozen river in search of the bodies. They discovered the damaged punt, and Miss Robbins' body was found in seventy feet of water by my neighbor, Mr. Murdock. Several days later, they recovered Mr. Rogers' body. But they never located the little boy."

Rachel shook her head. "How tragic."

Peyton stepped aside and opened the staff dining room door, letting Rachel enter first. "The villagers stepped up like a community should, and Mrs. Rogers wrote to the town paper thanking all who helped and prayed for her. Papa was one of those people."

Rachel slipped into an empty seat. "That is quite a story, and to think, it happened right here on this island."

Peyton concurred as she sat next to her. When she looked up, Patrick stared at her from his seat across from them. "Good morning, Patrick."

He acknowledged Rachel, then Peyton. "Happy Fourth, ladies."

Duvall cleared his throat. "Your attention, please. We have a special guest this morning."

Mr. Emery stepped into the room, and the staff grew silent. He'd never before come down to their servant hall. Chairs clattered back as they stood before the master of the castle.

With the dignity of his status, Mr. Emery addressed the lot of them. "Happy Independence Day. My wife and I will be celebrating at the Frontenac Hotel, so I'm pleased to announce that you may have the day off unless your superior needs you here. I hope you enjoy this holiday gift from the missus and me. Duvall will give you further instructions."

After Mr. Emery departed, the staff resumed their seats and murmured their appreciation and excitement.

Peyton thrilled at the generosity of the Emerys. The entire day off? She couldn't believe their luck. She turned to Rachel. "I know what I'm going to do. I'm going to help Papa with the fireworks display."

Rachel's eyes grew wide. "I'll watch from the shore, thank you very much. I can't imagine being near such danger."

Peyton shrugged before sipping her tea. "Oh, I've been on the fireworks barge or around fireworks my entire life. It's thrilling."

Her friend shook her head. "It's scary. Why do you like it?"

Peyton took a bite of her flapjacks before answering. She peered at Patrick, who was obviously listening to the conversation. "My great-grandfather started the business. It was small back then. But when new-money industrialists like the Pullmans, the Bournes, and others who came to summer here wanted fireworks displays during their summers on their islands, Gramps grew the business. Then Papa took it over, but Quinn Fireworks already had a splendid reputation. Summers are the busy time, but, as I mentioned, Papa is sick and must retire."

Rachel touched Peyton's forearm. "Sorry, friend. I'd like to help, but I'm afraid of something as small as a match. I fear I'd be more trouble than worth."

Patrick piped up. "I'll go with you, Peyton. I can help."

Peyton sucked in a breath and assessed him with narrowed eyes.

Perhaps she could smooth things over. Perhaps he was trying to as well. "Really?"

"Of course. That is … if Duvall gives us the time off."

At that moment, Duvall addressed the staff. "As to the Emerys' wishes, you may all have the day off, but you must be back on the island by ten p.m. sharp. I will provide a shuttle boat this morning at ten and noon, and again at six and nine tonight."

The table erupted with whoops and hurrahs until Mrs. Milton hushed them all. "Enough, or I'll overrule this frivolous holiday and put you all to work."

Peyton held back a giggle, her tummy tumbling with joy. Patrick mirrored her delight with a hand-muffled chuckle.

Rachel patted her lips with her napkin and set it by her plate. "I'm going to write a letter to Mother, take a long nap, and read *Little Women*." She gathered her dishes but stopped. "And watch the fireworks tonight, of course."

Peyton picked up her plate, cup, and utensils, as did Patrick. The three stood side by side and washed their dishes before heading outside.

Rachel waved a hand before heading to her room. "Enjoy the holiday."

Peyton fell in behind her roommate but paused when Patrick followed her. He should've been going in the opposite direction toward the men's dormitory. "Can I help you?"

He wiped his brow with his shirtsleeve and looked to the sky. "Sure is hot today." He stole a sideways glance at her as if gathering courage. "Peyton Pie, I'm sorry for the wayward words of yesterday. I never meant to disparage your work. You're very talented. I only meant to encourage you. Please forgive me?"

"Forgiven. And forgive my hot temper. I get defensive when it comes to my profession. It was uncalled for."

Patrick grinned broadly. "Forgiven and forgotten." He took a step closer. "Now, to helping your papa. May I? I've always wanted to observe how he does such an amazing job."

She giggled at his boyish excitement. "I'm sure Papa would be pleased to have both our help. Meet you at the shuttle at nine-thirty? I want to be sure to get a seat."

"See you soon."

Peyton waved as the skiff pulled up to the Quinn Fireworks barge anchored about a half mile from the Clayton shore. "Hello, Papa. Patrick and I are here to help."

Papa squinted, shielding his eyes from the sun. "Merciful heaven! It is you." He put out his hand to help her aboard the barge while Patrick paid the boatman and then hopped on. The two young men who worked on the far end of the barge gave a wave and returned to setting up the fireworks. She waved back but focused on her grinning father.

Patrick told Papa how they got the day off, and after finding his house empty, they inquired at the dock, procured a boatman, and found him here.

"This is just grand." Papa hugged them both. "I admit, I was feeling a bit down in the mouth, but you coming has made the day one for celebration. And I'll have extra help, to boot. The Lord is smiling on me today."

Patrick rubbed his hands together. "I've always wondered how you make all this happen, Mr. Quinn."

"You should've told me, lad. I'd have hired you in a moment."

"Seems I might've missed my calling. What would you like us to do, Mr. Quinn?" Patrick grinned from ear to ear.

He chuckled. "Well, lad, the first thing you should know is that putting on fireworks displays is an art form. We're wonder-workers. We're visual symphony conductors. Fireworks is the art of extravagance."

Peyton giggled and feigned scolding. "Okay, Papa. Let's not go overboard."

"Oh, but it's a marvelous festival of fire and light." He waved his arms wildly in the air. "The skybursts. The rockets. The shells. They're chemical masterpieces."

"Papa. Enough. What should we do?"

Patrick shushed her with a gesture. "Hold on. I'm enjoying this unfettered enthusiasm, Peyton. So tell us about today's show, Mr. Quinn."

Papa laughed with abandon. "We usually shoot the fireworks from the barge, and every show is different." He waved toward the workers. "Each show gives me a new thrill, and my emotions vary according to the display. This year, though we won't have kamuros or horsetails, we will have five new-fangled willows. They're like a chrysanthemum but have long-burning silver or gold stars that produce a soft dome shape like a weeping willow."

Peyton slipped her arm into the crook of her papa's elbow. "I love your excitement, Papa. But show us how to help. Please?"

Clusters of tubes lay scattered around the deck—some large, some small. Some stood tilted at varying degrees, with others set like a fan.

Papa patted her hand atop his forearm. "Now, now. Stop being so bossy. We'll get to that in due time. As you can see, we've been setting up the display and are almost finished." He waved toward his assistants. "I'll send the boys home once the preparation is done, and we can have a jolly good time catching up until sunset."

"You don't have anything for us to do?" Peyton's shoulders sagged. "But we came to work. I wanted to work on the display, Papa."

"You will. We'll do the final security check and make sure all is well. Then the three of us will do the lighting and firing. How's that sound?"

"Splendid." Peyton rested her head on her father's shoulder. "But it's sad to think that Quinn Fireworks will end with you. If only I were a boy."

"I wouldn't trade you for a hundred boys. I can hire boys. I can't hire a daughter like you."

Patrick surveyed the massive barge. "I need a little instruction here, please. What are these?" He pointed to large tubes.

Peyton stepped up next to him. "They're called shells. They contain gunpowder and dozens of small pods. Each pod is called a star and makes one dot in the fireworks explosion. The firework's fuse ignites the gunpowder to send it aloft."

"Interesting," he murmured. "But how do they get their colors and shapes?"

Peyton slipped her hand into his, and he nearly exploded with joy. It was the first time she'd touched him that way. Sweat moistened the back of his shirt as his heart raced and his breath came out in little puffs. He gulped, trying to slow his breathing and pay attention to her.

Her eyes sparkled as she spoke. "Fireworks are designed to burn with colored flames and sparks, including red, orange, yellow, green, blue, purple, and silver. When the chemical colorants are heated, their atoms absorb energy, and then they produce light as they lose energy. Different chemicals produce different amounts of energy, creating different colors." Peyton bit her bottom lip as she often did when she was thinking. "Would you like to know more?"

His eyes widened. "You sound like a scientist. Maybe I should absorb that information for a moment."

Peyton *liggled*, and Patrick's stomach did a pleasant flip-flop. He basked in the moment, in the warmth of the summer sun, in her. The feeling of her small hand in his. Her sweet face looking up at him. Oh, how he wanted to bend down and kiss her right there. Indeed, her father was busy giving the two young men instructions. Patrick returned his gaze to Peyton, who offered a peaceful smile.

"During our long winter nights together, Papa used to read me the science of fireworks and explain it all patiently. I never grew tired of learning about what he loved, and I suppose I took in more than I realized. It's quite a fascinating science, don't you think?"

He nodded. "I think this whole day may prove interesting. Tell me, how do they launch into the air at different angles and heights?"

She pulled him over to the tilting tubes. "These aerial shells are angled to set the shells in various positions, and long fuses are lit to send them aloft. Different heights are achieved with various amounts of gunpowder. It takes about a minute from being lit until it blows up into the sky."

He touched one of the tubes. "It's made of paper? Doesn't it burn?"

Mr. Quinn joined them. "Yes, but by the time it's airborne, it doesn't matter. The shell is free to create its masterpiece in the nighttime sky." He patted Patrick on the back. "Did you know the Chinese invented fireworks using bamboo shells to drive out evil spirits? Some think Marco Polo brought fireworks to Europe in the 1200s, and after that, the Italians figured out the chemistry of colors. Many moons ago, I saw an ancient book on fireworks dating back to the 1600s that gave a fairly accurate recipe for making fireworks. Can you imagine?"

Patrick scanned the barge. "I guess I never really thought about it. I've just always enjoyed the beauty—and the sounds."

Mr. Quinn nodded. "Fireworks have specific sounds. The bang sounds like a gunshot, thanks to extra gunpowder. The crackle is made when I fill the fireworks with lead oxide, which vaporizes in the heat and makes the cracking sound when it expands. The humming sound is made from a tiny tube I tuck inside the firework. When the shell is shot into the air, it spins so fast it hums and whizzes. The screeching whistle is created by vibrating bursts of gas. It's pretty interesting, really."

Patrick chuckled. "That's an understatement. You sound like your daughter, full of scientific information that boggles my mind."

Mr. Quinn glanced at Peyton, then at their intertwined hands, and finally up to his face. Patrick let go of Peyton's hand and swept his through his hair. Would Peyton's father object?

Instead, Mr. Quinn laughed loud and free. "Well, Peyton, let's not boggle the lad. I dismissed the boys early, and they were thrilled.

Seems their cousins are having a party they would've missed."

"Good." Peyton clapped her hands. "Then we can work on this all afternoon, just the three of us."

For a long while, Patrick followed Mr. Quinn and Peyton around, feeling more like a puppy than a man. The two were in their element, chatting about mines and shells and all kinds of flower-named fireworks. For several minutes, they seemed to forget he was with them.

Then Peyton spun around and apologized, slipping her arm into the crook of his. "I'm sorry, Patrick. Papa and I can get so focused on fireworks. Forgive us?"

He smiled, giving her arm a tender squeeze and holding it tight in his. "Nothing to forgive. I take great delight in seeing you so happy. When I watch you upholster, you seem content. But here, with the fireworks, you glow."

Peyton's eyes grew wide, and she blanched. Did he say something wrong? That was the last thing he wanted to do on such a fine day.

Peyton glanced at her father, and her eyes held sadness. "I suppose you're right. If I were a boy, I'd be following in your footsteps, Papa, with joy and honor. As it is, upholstering is as radical as this community can handle. Can you imagine the gossiping geese if I were to take over your business?"

Mr. Quinn chuckled, took off his cap, and wiped his brow with his shirtsleeve. "That they would. It's our times, I'm afraid. A hundred years from now, they probably wouldn't bat an eyelash at a woman doing such work. But enough regret. Let's continue."

For the next few hours, they finished loading the shells the boys hadn't completed and added long fuses to each. They bundled the fuses of each group of shells—called zones—and marked them in the order Mr. Quinn planned for the fireworks display.

Suddenly, Mr. Quinn straightened and eyed him. "I'm putting you in charge of zone one, Patrick."

Patrick sucked in a breath. "Me, sir? But I know so little."

"I'll guide you. The boys already loaded these with comets and mines. And here are the Roman candles." Mr. Quinn pointed to a fan-shaped group of tubes. "A Roman candle consists of a long tube containing several large stars which fire at regular intervals. They're commonly arranged like this and set to explode closer to the audience." He waved a hand at the largest tubes. "These five Roman candles contain small shells, called bombettes, rather than stars."

Mr. Quinn clapped him on the back. "Don't worry—we'll be here to help. Before you know it, you'll be a professional. Say, maybe you could take over the company one day, son."

Son? Take over Peyton's father's business?

Patrick's mind exploded into fireworks of possibilities. He grinned wide as every one of them included Peyton.

CHAPTER 19

PEYTON WORKED ON THE foyer settee while daydreaming about last week's Fourth of July fireworks. Just seven days since that magical event with her papa and Patrick. But the joy she'd experienced in working with her father lingered like the sweet smell of honeysuckle.

Her cheeks heated as she recalled the closeness she'd felt with Patrick and witnessing his excitement as he learned all about Papa's business. The laughs they'd shared in the warm summer sun, out on the sparkling water, echoed in her memory. The camaraderie between Patrick and Papa had proved to be the icing on her Independence Day cake. And the cherry? A flawless fireworks display. Indeed, her best day in several years.

As usual, the local paper lauded Papa's work and raved about the new fireworks launched into the Thousand Islands sky. They called his business "the famously successful Quinn Fireworks" and said the community should expect "decades more wonderment to come."

They didn't know that soon, Quinn Fireworks would be no more.

She grimaced at Sam, who was busy shining the ballroom floor. Babysitting her, more like it. She didn't need watching over. Nothing more of concern had happened. Before long, Sam excused himself and left the room.

She pulled a row of tacks from the settee and sighed. Since sharing the fireworks accomplishment with the two most important people in her life, upholstering had lost its luster. Now the task left her exhausted and empty.

If only…

She scanned the ballroom, missing Patrick's presence. He'd been called to fix something in the caretaker's cottage, but what if Mrs. Emery came and saw he wasn't there? Though there'd been no vandalism in a few weeks, the missus made her promise not to be alone. Perhaps she should seek Duvall's counsel on the matter.

Peyton left her work to locate the butler. When she entered the foyer, Edna's voice interrupted her mission. Peyton tucked herself behind the heavy drapes to listen, peering at the horrible woman and another maid.

"It's disgraceful, I tell you. That floozy fawning all over Patrick and then having the audacity to spend the day—and the night—alone with him on a barge. Out in the middle of the river."

The other maid gasped. "Scandalous."

Edna cackled. "That's not the half of it. It's not bad enough that she's taken a man's upholstering job from some poor soul who needs it. On the Fourth, she worked on the fireworks display. Now everyone in Clayton is denouncing her actions as radical feminist hoopla that has no place in their civilized society. The women are up in arms over it, and the men mock her from the barbershop to the docks. I wouldn't be surprised if they don't write her up in the newspaper and forbid her to enter their lovely little village."

The maid put her hand to her neck, a shocked expression paling her face. "And the Emerys still employ one such as she? Will they not be implicated in her folly?"

Edna clucked her tongue. "We all will. How she can get away with such mischief is beyond comprehension."

Peyton held her breath until she could hold it no more, then slowly let it out. Surely, she was lying about the village naysaying. Should she confront Edna or let it be? The woman was an ignorant troublemaker, but would opposing her unleash a hornet's nest?

Instead of tiptoeing into the foyer, she retraced her steps to the ballroom. She'd talk with Duvall at dinner and deal with Edna later.

After lunch, Peyton and Rachel stepped out onto the servants' terrace. Low clouds and dark haze threatened a stormy day. A whoosh of wind moved through the trees, creating an eerie sound. Peyton couldn't help but be dismayed by the developing storm. Patrick had planned to go to Clayton to fetch her supplies.

Charlie, the young man who'd helped her move furniture a few times, clicked his tongue. "Looks to be a Greenie."

Peyton peered at the river. "A what?"

He chuckled. "The storms that come off Lake Ontario tend to be doozies. They turn the sky and the river a frightening green and bring a storm surge that often raises the river high over docks—high enough to flood the shoreline. They can sometimes be so fierce that they take out boats and ramps along their path. That's why Calumet harbor is so important to those seeking shelter."

Rachel scowled. "It's the ferocious thunder that gets me. Sounds like it's right on top of the island and echoes over and over until I can't stand it. But the lightning is even worse. Sometimes it hits the island and crackles like the dickens."

Charlie huffed. "We're on solid ground, miss, and this castle is built of stone. Besides, that's why there's a lightning rod on top of the tower."

Peyton shook her head. "I've observed such storms from Clayton but didn't know they were called 'Greenies.' Haven't seen one yet this year, though." She paused, recalling the summer storms that fascinated her so. "What I remember most is that spectacular rainbows and double rainbows often appear once the storm's fury abates."

"That's true, and here, when the sun comes out, I love how the pink granite sparkles and tints everything a pretty rose color." Rachel released a blissful sigh. "Then peace comes again to the river, and the birds break out in song."

Peyton slipped her arm into the crook of Rachel's arm as they walked back to their room. "That's something to look forward to. What assignments do you have today?"

Rachel smiled. "A thorough cleaning of the drawing rooms. They're such pretty rooms that I enjoy it as I daydream."

"I'm running out of supplies again, so Patrick is going to Clayton. But with this storm coming ..."

Rachel waved off her concern. "He's a smart man. He'll know whether it's wise or not."

Storm or no storm, Peyton was depending on him. Patrick shoved off and paddled the skiff, shivering not so much at the rising wind as at the possibility of chancing upon his father in town. With each stroke of the oars, he recalled the beatings, the berating, the barbaric way Father had treated him. He wanted to forgive the man, knew he should, but how? He'd prayed and pleaded with God to no avail.

The wind picked up, rocking the small skiff. He continued to fight the current, which was growing stronger by the minute. Ominous gray thunderclouds rose like huge towers in the sky and blew into the area with a vengeance.

Patrick picked up his pace. He must get to the mainland before the heavens opened. The wind groaned louder, and the first patters of rain mottled the green skiff cushions as he pulled up to the dock. Despite the wretched weather, he would gather Peyton's supplies and hurry back before the storm unleashed its fury. He observed the sky, and hope dwindled.

Patrick patted his pocket to ensure that the list remained safely tucked there. He sprinted to Burlingame's General Store just as the sky opened and buckets of rain flooded the street.

Mr. Burlingame leaned on the glass counter. "Afternoon, Patrick. Made it just in time. You might be here awhile. What can I help you with?"

"Hello, sir. I have a list. Mostly sewing supplies and the like. But a few incidentals for Mrs. Milton."

The man's belly shook with his chuckle. "How's that ornery woman these days? Glad you came instead of her. She sets my teeth on edge."

Refraining from agreement, Patrick handed him the list before browsing the store. Only one other customer shopped. With nothing new to peruse, he stood at the large picture window and watched the rain pour down.

He hadn't time to visit his mother today, so he tossed up a quick prayer for her, asking for protection from his father and for peace and rest for his poor, sweet mama.

Wait! Who was that? Across the street along the boardwalk, heading toward this very shop? Was he seeing things? He'd know that slicker, that shuffle, those bent shoulders anywhere.

Father.

Patrick's heart raced wildly, and he breathed with short, staggered puffs—but not in concern for himself. As a wagon came speeding down the street, splashing mud along the sidewalk, he pounded on the window. His head down, Father stepped off the boardwalk and into the path of the oncoming wagon. A strangled cry ripped from Patrick as a horse trampled his father like a ragdoll, and the wagon wheels crushed his body.

The driver leaned back, yanking the reins and commanding the horses to stop. Several people ran into the street. His father lay unmoving in the mud. Patrick's feet froze to the store floor, and he simply stood there like a shackled prisoner.

"What's the commotion out there, Patrick?" Hurrying over, Mr. Burlingame jerked him from his trance. "An accident?"

"It's Father!"

Like jumping into a nightmare, Patrick ran outside, parting the crowd gathered around the still form. "Father! Wake up. Wake up." He knelt, patting his father's cheek. No response. No movement. Blood oozed from his right ear and the right side of his head. His right leg lay bent at an awkward angle.

A lady's voice quivered in the rain. "Someone, get the doctor!"

A nearby man mumbled and removed his hat. "It's too late."

Patrick bent down to listen for a heartbeat. There was none. He pushed his ear tighter to his father's chest, but there was nothing but silence.

"No. Oh God. No."

Patrick rolled back on his heels and turned his face to the heavens. Thunder rumbled through the sky as a bolt of lightning struck somewhere nearby. The light of judgment. Two men lifted his father's body while another man tugged Patrick to his feet.

"Come, lad. There's nothing to be done, and this storm is raging. Your mother can't lose you too."

Patrick blinked back the rain as he allowed the man to lead him into the nearby barbershop. "Mama! I've got to be there for her."

Patrick barely acknowledged the man who'd rescued him or the men bringing his father's body into the shop. He gawked at the lifeless form one last time, emotions swirling like a hurricane. "I never ..." He wiped the rain from his face and stepped into the storm as thunder seemed to rock the boardwalk beneath his feet. "Oh, Mama!"

Another thunderclap pealed as rain engulfed him. He ran toward home, but a hitch in his side stopped him, and he fell to his knees.

"Dear God! Forgive me. I should've forgiven him long ago. Should have made peace with him. But no. My stubbornness kept me at bay. Oh God, forgive me."

Within minutes, the rain dissipated and the clouds thinned. Patrick rose and hurried to his mother's home—his childhood home— mere blocks away.

By the time he reached the house, blue speckled the sky, and humidity hung thick in the air. He opened the door and stopped. Mother stood washing dishes at the sink, her back to him.

She wiped her hands on her apron as she turned around and blinked. "Son? What in heaven's name are you doing here on a day like this? You're positively drenched to the gills."

His mama's face showed no sign of worry. No troubled heart. In fact, she seemed quite placid. Peaceful. Happy, even.

"Mama." He ran to her and wrapped his arms around her thin frame. Wisps of her graying hair brushed his cheek as a breeze blew through the window above the sink. "Mama."

She patted him on the back. "Son. What is it? Did something happen on the island? Do you still have your position there?"

Slowly, Patrick stepped back from her comforting arms so he could look her in the face. He took her tiny hands in his. "It's Father. An accident in town."

Mama's face grew ashen, her brows furrowed in confusion. "I sent him for eggs. Did he drop them?"

Patrick squeezed her hands. "Come and sit with me."

He led her to the rickety kitchen table, the chair creaking as she plunked down, a confused expression paling her face. He pulled out a mismatched chair, joined her, and took her hands. "Father isn't with us anymore. He stepped into the path of an oncoming wagon in front of the barbershop. I saw it all." Patrick's voice quivered and snagged, the lump in his throat almost cutting off his breath.

Mama sat still, as if she hadn't heard him, couldn't comprehend his words. A frenzied rap on the front door pulled her from her stupor. "Jenny? Are you there?"

Mrs. Skold, their neighbor and his mother's closest friend, stepped into the house and rushed to the kitchen. She stopped short when she saw him there. "Patrick? How did you hear about it so fast? Weren't you on Calumet?"

"Heard what?" Mother's voice sounded normal. Too normal. "What is it?"

Patrick held her hands tighter. "Mama, I told you. There's been an accident. Father has died."

Mother looked askance at him and then at her friend. "He's fetching me eggs. He'll return soon."

Mrs. Skold joined them at the table. "Jenny. Patrick is right. He's … gone."

Mama pulled her hands from his and stood. "Enough joking. And it's not a funny joke, either, Patrick! Haven't you learned by now what's funny and what's not?" She huffed, shaking her head as she turned back to the sink. "I must get these dishes done before he comes home."

Patrick frowned, his chest tightening.

Mrs. Skold shrugged her shoulders. "She's in shock." Then she addressed his mama. "Jenny, tell Patrick how Peter has changed of late."

"I have. Several times." She whipped around, dirty dishwater dripping from her hands. Anger flashed in her eyes. "Patrick, your father is a new man. He may be dead to you, but he's very much alive in body and spirit. He stopped drinking while you were gone and has turned his heart back to the Lord. He's become a kind, fine man. So stop dismissing him." Her face was scarlet, taut with anger.

"Mama, I …" Her sharp scolding added boulders of shame. The weight of his failing crushed him.

He couldn't breathe. He had to get some air. He pecked her on the cheek and fled to the small backyard. For years, ever since Father took to drinking when Patrick was a boy, the yard had been strewn with dilapidated equipment, broken furnishings, and trash. Patrick had always been the one to clean it up, to burn the refuse or haul trash to the dump. Now it was cleaner than ever.

Had Father really changed? Had Patrick missed knowing him again? His heart sank. He'd been so foolish, so stubborn, so unforgiving. He hadn't listened to Mr. Quinn or his mother when she tried to tell him.

A high-pitched wail came from the kitchen. Mama.

Patrick ran back inside and found his mother crumpled on the kitchen floor, rolled up in a ball, wailing unearthly sounds. Mrs. Skold rubbed her back. "There, there. God will take care of you."

Her wails turned into shivering sobs, so Patrick wrapped her in a blanket, stroking her hair. "I love you, Mama. I'm here. I'm here."

The rest of the day and the following days moseyed on in a hushed blur. Patrick sent word to Calumet of the crisis, and he never left his mother's side. His father was laid out on a table in the living room for those who wanted to say goodbye.

To Patrick's great surprise, the mourners who came to their humble home included dozens of neighbors, church members, and even prominent villagers—as well as Peyton and her father. All who came shared stories of how his father had truly become a new creation, a redeemed man. Even Peyton's father talked about how his father apologized to him for being such an angry man and rejecting his help in times past.

Patrick sat in the corner of his living room, and Peyton joined him, scooting close and keeping her voice low. "Oh, Patrick. I'm so very sorry for your loss. I wish I'd have known the new man he became. Isn't it wonderful to know he'll be in heaven when your mama goes there and when, one day a long time from now, you go there?"

Patrick conceded, heaving a great sigh. "It is, but I've lost so much through my foolish unforgiveness. I could have known that man."

Peyton slipped her arm in the crook of his and gave it a tender squeeze. "You will. For eternity."

CHAPTER 20

EVEN A WEEK LATER, Peyton ached for her best friend's loss. Judging by the dark circles under his eyes, Patrick hadn't slept in days. But that wasn't the worst of it. A dark cloud loomed over him. Was it grief? Regret? Or both?

She lifted a silent prayer for him as she worked on an oversized chair from the Emerys' master bedroom. She missed Patrick. He'd finished all his work in the ballroom, so when he'd returned from the funeral, Duvall had assigned him various repair jobs around the island.

Peyton shook her head. He was a finish carpenter, for heaven's sake, not a fix-it man. Though he could do almost anything, his downcast face confirmed that he didn't enjoy the work.

Indeed, Patrick's shoulders slumped, and he rarely spoke. He shuffled like an old man and barely talked to her. Even his once-hearty appetite seemed to have perished with his father. His cheeks bore a sallow hue, and his eyes lost their sparkle. Was he unwell?

No. Merely broken, and that could be just as bad—or worse—as being physically ill.

The setting sun drifted in through the windows, casting strange shadows and an eerie feel over the ballroom. She'd just work a few more minutes and call it a day.

Stomping steps drew her attention to the doorway. Mrs. Milton's militant gait betrayed her presence wherever she went. Indeed, the staff often mocked her. The woman puffed up like a frog. "Miss Quinn, come here at once."

What now?

Peyton rushed to her side and curtsied. "Ma'am?"

The housekeeper folded her arms over her ample chest and scowled as she stared at Peyton for a long time. What bee had landed in her bonnet?

"I had a long discussion with Mrs. Emery, and since there's been no mischief—that you call vandalism—in the past three weeks, the time has come to stop misusing staff to babysit you. You, miss, are on your own from now on."

Peyton ducked her chin. "I've thought it excessive as well, ma'am, but the missus insisted."

"I'll have none of your cheek. Get back to work." Mrs. Milton huffed, pointing to Peyton's workstation. "And no dawdling."

Peyton curtsied and sped to the alcove, picked up her hammer, and furiously set tacks as the woman glared at her from afar. Pretending not to notice that the woman didn't leave, Peyton worked as if being judged for a contest.

And judged she was. But why?

After several minutes, Mrs. Milton left the room. Peyton blew out a breath, wiped her brow, and huffed her own frustration. Indeed, what did the housekeeper have against her? A sense of control? Power?

"Peyton? Can you come?" Patrick stood in the terrace doorway silhouetted by the setting sun. She'd know that handsome frame anywhere, but his tone signaled anguish.

She joined him on the terrace, grateful he hadn't come moments earlier and given Mrs. Milton more fodder for her sharp tongue. She touched his forearm gently. "What is it, Patrick? Are you unwell?"

Patrick shook his head. "Only in heart." He appraised her workstation, his brow furrowing. Creases ringed his eyes. He pulled his lips into a tentative smile. "Why are you working at this hour? It's almost dark."

She shrugged, glancing at the long shadows of the trees. "I don't really know. Rachel had things to do, and you are ..."

He took her hand. "Distant. I know." He paused, motioning toward the shoreline. "Can we talk? I've been thinking about things and would like to speak with you."

She consented. "Of course. Let me tidy up my station, and I'll be right back."

His unfocused gaze alarmed her. "I'll wait here."

When he let out a deep groan, a chill ran down her back.

What was vexing him?

Peyton hurriedly cleaned up the alcove and returned to him within minutes. She slipped her hand around his elbow and leaned her head on his bicep. His muscle tensed and then relaxed as he glanced down at her, patting her hand.

Instead of heading toward the harbor as they usually did, Patrick turned toward the front of the castle. "The Emerys are at the Frontenac tonight. Let's explore this area."

His sharp tone allowed no room for discussion. But she didn't mind, so long as she spent time with him.

They walked toward the star-shaped garden below the front veranda and main stairs and stopped. The fragrance of hundreds of blossoms danced on the breeze and settled her heart. She breathed its bouquet of scents, closing her eyes to capture hints of rose, honeysuckle, and more. When she opened her eyes, she recognized black-eyed Susans, bee balm, butterfly bush, and purple coneflowers, even in the fading light. "Why haven't we come here before? This is a bounty of beauty."

Patrick nodded. "We're only allowed here when the Emerys are off-island."

She smiled, hugging his arm. "You're right, of course."

Anxious to hear his thoughts, Peyton rejected the temptation to force a conversation before he was ready. Instead, she prayed for him to be able to share his heart when the time was right. She exhaled. "It's beautiful, Patrick. Thank you for bringing me here."

Trees bordered a mowed, fan-shaped lawn down to the river. What must it be like to enjoy afternoon tea on the veranda, gazing across the shipping channel from Picton Island to the entrance of the narrows to Round Island, Clayton, and all the way to Lake Ontario?

He responded only with a nod, gently pulling them toward a clump of blackberry bushes heavy with fruit. He picked a few and held them out for her.

"Thank you." She popped them into her mouth, savoring the tartness. "Yum."

He picked a handful and ate them. So did she. They feasted on the berries for several silent moments until Peyton pricked her finger on the thorns. "Ouch."

When her finger bled, she sucked on it, wishing for a handkerchief. Patrick pulled one from his pocket and tenderly doctored her finger. He held her hand and gazed into her eyes as the sunset framed and glowed around them.

Then he pulled her to him, hugging her tight to his chest and rubbing her hair. "Oh, Peyton. I've been such a fool. The folly of unforgiveness will haunt me all my days, and the necessity of leaving you breaks my heart."

"*Leaving* me?" Peyton touched his cheek and caressed the shadow of stubble with her fingertips. "Whatever do you mean? You made a mistake and didn't reconcile with your father in time. That can never overshadow the wonderful man you are. Forgive yourself and move on, Patrick."

He shook his head. "I cannot. I am plagued by it, and I fear I'd do you more harm than good if I stay in your life."

Peyton forced a response past the tightness of her throat. "You don't mean that. This is only shock and grief talking. It will pass."

Patrick's eyes brimmed with tears—tears she hadn't seen since he fell out of a tree and broke his arm when he was twelve. "I must leave the island and care for my mother. She needs me and has to be my priority. My responsibility. I'm sorry. Let's always remain friends."

Peyton's heart thumped like a train coming to a sudden stop. Her eyes burned. "Friends?"

Patrick disengaged her arm from his and took a step back. Just then, a large black rat snake slithered out from under the bushes, a field mouse with its white chin visible in its mouth. It looked at them and wriggled in the opposite direction, still holding its prey.

She shuddered, shivering as if a winter wind blew in. "Eww ... I hate snakes."

He took another step toward the castle. "Coming?"

Peyton stood her ground. "We're not through with this discussion, sir."

He raised an eyebrow. "Yes, we are. Come. It's getting dark, and there may be more snakes where that one came from."

She hadn't thought of that. She scurried to his side, and they plodded up the hill to the castle in silence. What could she say to dissuade him from turning his heart away from her, just when they were drawing close?

When they arrived at the castle, Patrick turned and gave her a slight bow. "Good night, Peyton."

No. He couldn't leave it there. Her mind scrambled for something to say, a way to stop him. But her tongue froze, her mind went blank, and her confidence faltered. "Good night."

Without another word, Patrick shuffled in the direction of the men's dormitory, and Peyton fled to her room. Grateful Rachel wasn't there, she flung herself on her bed and sobbed. Great, heaving sobs that hurt in her chest. She groaned and wept and grieved, her shirtsleeve wet with tears, her heart breaking.

Why, God? Why did You dangle before me a future with Patrick and then yank it back?

Rachel opened the door and gasped. "What's the matter, Peyton? Can I help?"

Peyton wiped her face, gathering her composure with several deep breaths and a moan. "No one can."

Rachel's brows furrowed almost into a line. "Were you dismissed? Did someone die?"

Tears slid down Peyton's cheeks, and she wiped them away. "Love died. I cannot speak of it now. Good night, Rachel."

She turned her back to her roommate and readied for bed. Forcing herself to not catch Rachel's eye, she climbed under the covers and rolled onto her side facing the wall. Peyton lay there for a long while, willing herself to not whimper, whine, or cry. Her lungs heaved with hurt—not from exertion but from disappointment.

No matter how sweet Rachel was, Peyton simply could not abide pity just then.

Before long, a mighty storm arose. Horizontal rain blew into the window, sweeping her up and pulling her out the window and into a skiff on the raging river. Lightning so intense it appeared more like noonday than midnight lit up the St. Lawrence, the crack of thunder coinciding with the flash.

The skiff rocked on the waves, tossing her back and forth as it moved toward a waterspout that towered a hundred feet in the air with a girth wider than the island. She screamed for Patrick to save her, but no sound came out of her mouth. She was alone in the torrent, waiting to die.

"Peyton. Wake up. It's okay. You're safe in your bed."

Peyton opened her eyes to find Rachel hovering over her like a mother hen. She blinked and rose on one elbow. A dream. She wiped the perspiration from her brow and looked around the dark room.

She was safe.

Rachel still stood over her, waiting.

"Thank you for waking me. I had a bad dream."

Rachel chuckled. "I can see that. And no wonder, thanks to the state you were in when you went to bed. I've been praying for you. Whatever it is, Peyton, God will work things out. Trust Him."

Peyton groaned and flopped back down on her bed. "Good night, Rachel. And thank you."

Could He work things out?

Can a broken heart be sewn back together as neatly as she could sew fabric?

Patrick stared up at the Calumet Island Tower rising over a hundred feet in the air. It was the centerpiece of Clayton's river views, more of a lighthouse than a simple tower. He craned his neck to inspect the broken window he was tasked to repair. There it was, at the very top.

He sighed as he considered the pane of glass he'd have to haul up there. Working hard kept bad memories at bay. He hated when those thoughts reared their ugly heads. His father. Now Peyton.

The despair on Peyton's face when he'd left her last night had almost made him run into her arms and take back his difficult words. But he couldn't. She didn't deserve one such as he—one who denied his own flesh and blood and thought the worst of his father even when others told him different. He'd likely do the same thing to his precious Peyton one day, and he couldn't bear the thought of hurting her like that.

But hadn't he hurt her already? He saw it in her eyes—the way she looked at him and again today during lunch.

He swallowed a lump in his throat, entered the tower, and looked around. The first floor was big enough to house a small apartment. Thick, granite walls encircled him.

He climbed the stairs that followed the outside wall, round and round, hauling the heavy pane of glass and his tools to a many-sided room on the second floor. He paused there for a breather before taking another flight of stairs. He made two trips, one carefully carrying the pane of glass and the other to bring up his tools. The last three flights were steep, more like a ladder than steps.

Winded and too warm, he wiped the sweat from his brow and

gulped in several breaths of fresh river breezes. The air blew steady and strong, but it was refreshing and cool.

The Calumet Island light was famous to all who lived on or visited the river. People enjoyed its beacon at night, whether on the island, on the river, or in Clayton. Indeed, like a seaway lighthouse, it was visible for miles around from dusk to dawn. As instructed by the caretaker, Patrick checked the multi-faceted light firmly mounted on the floor to be sure none of the bulbs were blown.

One last ladder took him to the point of the cupola roofing on top of the tower. Unfortunately, a multitude of pigeons roosted on that level. How they got in was a mystery. The window had been broken for less than a week, but the stench, filth, and noise confirmed that they'd made this their home for a long while. Not welcome company. He chased most of them out before beginning his work. The task of extricating them actually eased a bit of his tension—tension that grew by the day.

As he turned to the window that needed replacing, he shuddered. So high up, the wind posed a formidable threat. He'd have to be extra careful.

This was his second-to-last task before leaving the island. He wanted to stay. Wanted to be near Peyton. But for what purpose? He refused to toy with her emotions. He'd done enough of that already. No. His mother needed him, and Peyton was better off without him.

The caretaker had also asked Patrick to climb onto the roof through a hatch and check for loose or missing shingles. The older man had sprained his ankle the week before and couldn't do it himself.

The wind tugged at his clothing, but Patrick's heart raced at the view from more than a hundred feet up. He could scan all the way to Lake Ontario and much of the main channel where boats went by. As one big-boy ship sounded its deep horn, Patrick waved, though he doubted anyone saw him.

He squatted on the roof and enjoyed a few moments of warm breezes, clear water, and the golden, shimmering summer sun. But it gave him little joy.

That had fled when he said goodbye to Peyton. With a heart heavier than the pane of glass, he descended the tower.

Peyton looked everywhere for Patrick, but no one seemed to know where he was. She had to tell him her news before others did.

Finally, from across the room at dinner, she caught a glimpse of the man she loved, the man who'd broken her heart. But he was also her friend and deserved to hear the truth from her.

Shaking off her sadness, she hurried to his side, pulling him far enough from the other servants that they could speak privately. "Patrick, I have news."

He stopped in his tracks, his brow furrowing. "Are you all right?"

She shook her head. "My workstation was vandalized again and the perpetrator apprehended."

Patrick's eyes grew wide. "Who was it? What did he do now?"

She groaned. "Not he. She."

He clucked his tongue. "A woman did such a thing? I thought surely it was Henry or one of his cronies."

"It was Edna." Peyton folded her arms and quirked her brow. She couldn't wait to see his surprise. He didn't disappoint her.

Patrick slapped his thigh and chuckled. "I'll be a monkey's uncle. I knew she didn't care for either of us, but I never thought she'd stoop to that."

"She did." Peyton paused. "What's more, Mrs. Emery was savvy enough to bait her by withdrawing my babysitters, as Mrs. Milton called them. But she made sure Duvall or one of his staff stayed on watch, and Duvall caught Edna in the act after I left for lunch. Can you believe it? She's been whisked away to the Clayton sheriff on charges of vandalism and more."

Patrick shook his head. "Goodness. And I thought island life would be peaceful and placid."

"It should be ... now." Peyton studied him, holding her breath.

Would this change his mind? Would he stay? Or would the fact that she no longer needed his protection convince him to follow through on his decision?

CHAPTER 21

THE NEXT DAY, PEYTON stepped into the lunchroom, hurrying to the seat next to Patrick. She acknowledged him as she set her napkin on her lap. "I haven't seen you all morning, and it's your last day with us. I wish it weren't true."

His eyes held a sadness that hurt her heart. "Mother needs me. It's my duty."

Duvall interrupted his words. "Attention, staff. It appears that we may have severe thunderstorms this afternoon. Mitch, Patrick, and Peyton, I'd like the three of you to oversee the comfort of our harboring guests."

Peyton and Patrick nodded, while Mitch voiced his agreement. "Glad to help, sir."

After additional announcements and a prayer, Duvall released them to talk while they ate. How she enjoyed Duvall's oversight during the meals rather than Mrs. Milton's.

Patrick leaned close to her. "The storm must be big for him to be forewarned. Usually, they spring up unawares."

"Papa's knee always informed us of snowstorms." She winked at him. "I wonder if Duvall has a bum knee too."

Patrick chuckled, his eyes releasing the gloom for a moment before it returned. "I'll miss you."

"I'm here. Just a boat ride away. And when the summer's done, who knows what I'll be doing?"

He didn't respond. He simply shrugged and took a bite of his fish.

Why had everything turned sour? Just because he needed to help his mother didn't mean they couldn't court, did it?

Peyton let out a sigh and sipped her tea.

Rachel studied Peyton from across the table. "Are you all right? You seem quite melancholy."

"I suppose it's the weather. Cloudy days do that."

Peyton glanced at Patrick, and Rachel nodded.

As Peyton finished her tea, Mitch sidled up to Patrick, slapping a hand on his shoulder. "We three musketeers had better gather blankets, towels, and such for our rescue plan."

Peyton shook her head as she stood. "I doubt we'll be rescuing anyone. Just giving them a cup of tea."

Mitch clicked his tongue, sidestepping Patrick as they left the dining hall and moved onto the terrace. "Don't underestimate Mother Nature. Look at that sky. A seasoned sailor like me knows such things."

Patrick rolled his eyes. "At ease, mate. Let's head to the harbor and evaluate what's there. Then we can decide what we need."

Peyton glanced at the sky and nodded. "Good idea. Looks like we have plenty of time."

As they surveyed the lagoon, Peyton stood between the men who bantered about their fishing failures the night before. She only half listened, though, her thoughts focused on Patrick leaving in mere hours.

When would she see him again?

As they took a few steps for a better view, Mitch walked backward in front of them, playing the wise tour guide. "Do you know this harbor was created by Mr. Emery? Calumet used to be two islands separated by a narrow causeway where the water flowed freely between. He formed this walkway to join the islands and had the harbor dug deeper for his yachts—with shovels, no less."

Patrick chuckled. "I didn't know that. You're just full of interesting trivia, my friend."

"I'm also an expert predictor of the weather." Mitch winked at Peyton, making her cheeks grow warm.

She raised her brows. "Oh? How so?"

"I can read it like tea leaves." He waved an arm skyward. "Just before a storm, the sky turns a bilious green, tinted with dark gray. The birds swoop around the tower in frantic circles. Then suddenly, the waves stop gently drumming on the stones of the west-facing beach and become an angry, growling beast. The temperature drops, and a peculiar smell scents the air around you. This is when you should find shelter and pray the island will protect you."

"Speaking of protection ..." Peyton pointed to the boats in the harbor. "They're so close. Where will the others dock?"

Mitch shrugged. "Some may need to anchor, and those at the docks must be tied down properly. Unfortunately, many casual river runners aren't too adept at the knots and ties needed to keep them safe. And many others think they can outrun these summer storms—much to their eventual misery. Some lose their boats. A few, their lives." He clicked his tongue. "There are but six boats here at the moment, but many more will undoubtedly come. Peyton, why don't you gather refreshments for twenty or more souls while I give Patrick a lesson on nautical knots?"

Patrick gave Mitch a shoulder bump. "I'm not an idiot. I grew up in Clayton, remember?"

"Yes, but did you live on a ship?"

Patrick shook his head.

Mitch snorted. "Well, a refresher course won't hurt you, lad."

Peyton rolled her eyes at the boy banter and headed to the castle kitchen. When she entered, Cook was railing at one of her charges. "Those suffragettes cause more harm than good. Don't let me catch you maids turning an ear to their propaganda. Why, it's only natural that men rule ... except in my kitchen."

Peyton covered a giggle with her hand. "Excuse me, but I've been tasked to serve the boaters finding shelter from the storm. What should I bring, please?"

Cook blinked as if trying to understand. "Yes. Duvall mentioned that. My staff are preparing traditional shore dinner appetizers and carafes of tea."

Peyton brightened, licking her lips at the memory of her papa's shore dinners he'd made when he filled in for his brother from time to time. "My papa makes fatback sandwiches. Do you use sliced red onions and a dollop of Thousand Island dressing?"

Cook nodded. "Yes, yes. And my thickly sliced fresh bread with plenty of fatback. Now go about your work, miss. I'll have everything delivered fresh and hot once the storm gets underway. You'll be in the boathouse, correct?"

Peyton curtsied. "I expect so. Thank you, ma'am."

Cook waved her off and turned to stirring something in a large pot. "Mildred, get out the fatback and start frying it up, girl."

Out of the kitchen, Peyton allowed herself to laugh with abandon while she returned to the harbor. Thank goodness she wasn't a kitchen maid. She'd been given wonderful opportunities many girls didn't get—schooling until she was sixteen, apprenticing as an upholsterer, and now this fine position. So why was she unsatisfied? She lifted a prayer to heaven, asking for peace and contentment. But would it come?

Patrick waved from halfway up the main dock. "Over here."

As she turned in his direction, something glistened at her feet in a ray of sunshine that had broken through the clouds. Bending down, she ran a finger along a seam between the cement squares of the grooved walk. The hard walkway forever entombed a beautiful purple stone. "Patrick. Mitch. Look at this."

She motioned for them to join her as she ran her hand along the flat, smooth gem.

Patrick arrived first. "What do you know about that? An amethyst set forever in concrete. I heard it was put there by the architect's daughter. I've walked this path a hundred times and never noticed it."

Mitch joined them. "Nor I. Takes a woman to find a fancy thing like that, but no matter. We have work to do."

Just then, a fat raindrop hit the top of her head. Then another. Before she could straighten, the birds flew frantically around the tower, a greenish-gray haze blew in with the wind, and the temperature dropped. She sniffed the air.

The tempest had begun.

As the storm kicked up in earnest, Patrick hurried Peyton to safety. "Better get into the boathouse."

Thunder clapped so loud it vibrated the dock. Lightning struck close—too close—with a flash of light and a crackle so loud his ears rang. Peyton squealed, covering her head. The lightning bolt had hit the far dock, burning a hole through it, but the heavy rain doused the sparks. The air sizzled and cracked as they grabbed the boathouse doorknob and scurried inside.

Peyton wiped the water from her face. "Did you see that lightning strike? Goodness. Duvall was right."

Patrick handed her a towel from the stack on the table. Next to them sat several blankets, extra ropes, lines, buckets, a life preserver, and a large first-aid kit.

Mitch punched a thumb to his puffed-out chest. "Duvall was right because I warned him. I've got a nose for these kinds of things."

Peyton feigned a deep curtsy. "I apologize, your high-nose. Thank you for saving our lives."

Mitch chuckled. "Say, where are the refreshments?"

Peyton waved a hand. "Cook said her staff would deliver them once the storm got going, so I guess that'd be any time now."

Patrick assessed his friend. He had to admit that Mitch was a boating expert. Minutes earlier, while they had tied down the anchored boats, several more slipped into the harbor. How many more were out there, and how many would find their way here?

Before long, strong winds howled through the harbor. Even inside the safety of the boathouse, the clang of sailboat riggings against masts and the debris flying from one end of the marina to the other painted a grim picture.

Peyton peered out the window next to him. When she shivered, he grabbed a blanket and wrapped it around her shoulders, then he turned to Mitch, who appeared unconcerned. "Where are the boaters? Shouldn't they be in here?"

Mitch shook his head. "Most huddle below decks on their boats. They want to be there in case they need to save their boats."

Suddenly, the boat nearest the icehouse broke loose and almost sailed through the air toward the river. In seconds, it disappeared into the storm's darkness.

Patrick touched Mitch's arm. "Should we beckon the boaters to take shelter here? It's dangerous out there."

"Good idea." Mitch grabbed a slicker and handed one to Patrick. "The Emerys would have our necks if anything happened to one of them."

As they left the shelter of the boathouse, chain lightning reflected off the water and zigzagged forked, angular weapons of destruction all around them. The rain came down sideways, assaulting them as they hurried from boat to boat, offering safety. Some people accepted and scurried to the boathouse. But many, especially the men, refused.

Another boat and then another entered the harbor. Where would they dock? Patrick had no idea, but he'd invited every soul already sheltering there to the safety of the boathouse.

The storm had strengthened even more, roaring downriver like a freight train, eerie and intimidating, raining almost at a forty-five-degree angle. Boats tugged on their lines, fighting the wind. Another lightning bolt hit the north side of the dock, and a puff of smoke rose as he got to the boathouse and closed the door, pushing it hard against the wind.

He strained to see out the window, praying for the boaters still in the harbor and out on the river.

Peyton grabbed his slicker. "You're soaked to the skin. Get out of this and dry off so you don't catch your death."

Mitch entered the boathouse with a family of five. Peyton helped Mitch out of his wet slicker, then handed the family towels and beckoned them to partake of the refreshments.

The refreshments had indeed been delivered. Patrick took a whiff of something wonderful. "Is that what I think it is?"

Peyton bobbed her head, her eyes dancing. "The kitchen staff delivered them just a few minutes ago, so they should still be warm. Come and enjoy with the others."

Near the rear of the boathouse, a dozen boaters sipped tea and munched on fatback sandwiches despite the hints of fear and anxiety in the air. Children, including two toddlers, hung close to their mothers, while several men chewed and conversed in the corner, still in their slickers. Patrick understood the need to distract themselves from the raging storm.

Peyton flitted about, like a bee to a flower bed, fetching whatever people needed, a sweet smile on her face. Patrick basked in the beauty before him. Her eyes shone with fear even as she graciously served the guests. What a lovely woman. If only he wasn't such a failure, such a buffoon, she could be his.

Mitch handed Patrick a cup of tea. "Drown your angst in this, old boy." Then he pulled a sandwich out from behind his back and gave it to him. "And this will soothe what ails you."

Patrick took them but shook his head. "'Fraid not, friend."

Thunder continued to boom and rumble, and suddenly, a blinding flash of eerie, bluish-white light came through the boathouse windows. The loudest crack Patrick had ever heard almost made him drop his teacup. A collective gasp followed.

Someone near the windows yelled, "Did ya see that?"

Patrick hurried to the windows. Lightning had struck the tower.

After a moment of silence, a man who'd recently docked began telling his story of peril, so Patrick joined the group. "I be anchored off Grindstone and had to get out of the boat to try and hold it off the rocks. We had five twenty-pound anchors out but had to leave them behind and head out into the river. It was raining so hard that raindrops ricocheted off the river and bounced up from all directions like bullets. As we made our way to this harbor, we passed all kinds of debris, including pieces of a dock."

An older man raised his glass. "I was making a run from Wolfe Island. Hit the storm right at the border. Saw it coming but thought I could outrun it. The sky went from sunny to almost night, almost in a blink of an eye, and then came hard rain. We bailed, but the water came in faster than it went out. Thank God we found this harbor."

A young man near Patrick's age motioned toward the river. "We got caught on the river coming out of Canada. The wind and waves were like an ocean storm. I'll always remember this being so exhilarating, so exciting."

Brows furrowed as the men shook their heads and stared at the foolish young sailor. Mitch joined them. "Phil? What in tarnation are you doing here?"

Phil slapped Mitch on the back. "My old shipmate. Good to see ya."

Sailors. Whether foolish or wise, they sure are brave.

Patrick left the group to join Peyton at the tea service. "Can I help?"

Peyton pointed toward the window. "It appears the storm is dissipating. I can see clear across the harbor, and it's only pitter-patting on the roof."

"Good thing. This storm has been one for the records, I reckon."

Mitch stepped next to him. "With this doozy, who knows what mess we'll encounter? But at least we didn't have hail ... or fog."

Once the storm abated, they bid their guests safe travels and ventured out to assess the damage. The tower appeared intact, but tree branches and debris littered the island. And congers writhed over the surface of the dock nearest the harbor's opening.

Mitch rubbed his chin. "Would you look at that? I've heard about eels being pushed in from Lake Ontario but never seen it."

Peyton scrunched up her face. "Eww ... hate those things. Always have. Always will."

The sun broke through the clouds, now low on the horizon. "It's getting late. I'd better go." He turned to Mitch, casting a sideways glance at Peyton. "Keep an eye on her for me, will you?"

Peyton slapped her hands on her hips, but her lips quivered. "I can fend for myself, thank you very much. Fetch your things, and I'll meet you on the dock."

Patrick bid Mitch farewell and gathered his packed bag from his room, swallowing his sadness. As promised, Peyton waited on the dock. The sunshine highlighted her blonde tresses, but her tear-streaked face betrayed her quivering smile. He steeled himself against her tears. He had to go—not only for his mother and himself but also for her.

She wiped her eyes with her shirtsleeve. "Please tell me we have a future."

He shook his head. "You don't need me. I'm not the same person I was. I'm unforgiving. Stubborn. Heartless. I'm broken, Peyton. You deserve better, and I don't want to hurt you."

As if he'd struck her in the face, her eyes grew wide and her face pale. She raised a palm in surrender to him as her glazed expression said it all.

"Perhaps so. Goodbye, Patrick." She tossed him one last glare and walked away.

CHAPTER 22

FOR THE LAST SIX days, Peyton had scolded herself for daring to open her heart to Patrick, to dream of him and hope for a future with him. She vacillated between anger and anguish. Anger that she'd allowed herself to care. Anguish because caring had crushed her.

She picked up her scissors, but her hand shook. How could she go on?

What was wrong with Patrick that he felt so broken and undeserving of her love? Surely, it was merely the grief of losing his father and would abate soon. Or would it?

She groaned her frustration as she cut the costly art nouveau fabric patterned with little green trees. It would soon cover the seat of an overstuffed ottoman that went with the chair she'd just finished.

Yes. She'd simply return to her former plan—to grow old, alone, as a successful businesswoman. She'd had nearly three years of enlightenment, learning to dispel the idea that a woman's place was only beside—and often behind—a man. She'd have to settle for being a career woman, despite the community gossip and opinions.

Yet, with each day that passed without Patrick's soothing presence, hope faltered, and by week's end, she'd retreated into a strange shroud of apathy. Her work didn't matter. The castle lost its shine. Indeed, there wasn't the faintest flicker of interest in her for anything, save

Patrick. What had happened to her? Where was her conviction to be her own woman, to enjoy her work and be free of society's encumbrances?

Patrick was the one who had pursued *her*, wooed her. She had withstood his advances at every turn. Then, when she gave in, he rejected her and fled.

Lost in an engulfing river of complacency, Peyton longed for home, for her papa's embrace. For a cup of tea and his deep, loving voice telling her everything would be okay. But it wouldn't. Not without Patrick.

Mrs. Milton clip-clopped into the ballroom, a duster in her hand. She waved it toward Peyton. "Come here, girl."

Peyton shook herself from her sullenness and approached the housekeeper. She curtsied. "Yes, ma'am?"

The woman's narrow-eyed glare accosted her. "I've had enough of your distracted, pathetic disinterest in your work. You've been down-in-the-mouth for a week now, and it's affecting your productivity." Her piercing gaze condemned her. "Indeed, the staff have even noticed how you barely talk or interact at meals."

Peyton's heart didn't even skip a beat. What did it matter, even if the missus dismissed her? Not a ripple of agitation touched her. "I'm sorry, ma'am."

Mrs. Milton quirked a brow. "What has you in such a state, child? Are you unwell?"

Peyton wanted to be honest, but she wouldn't reveal the whole truth. "No. I will try harder." Her dispassionate indifference surprised even herself. How could she pull herself from these doldrums? She hadn't a clue. "Thank you, ma'am."

The housekeeper touched her arm gently, her tone almost kind. "Please do." She ducked her double chin benevolently, but her dark eyes held an expressionless gaze. "And now, to the purpose of my visit …" She waddled to the center of the room.

Peyton returned to her place, puzzled by Mrs. Milton's kindness.

She peeked back at the woman. Had she misjudged her?

The housekeeper evaluated the ballroom, taking notes on a little pad she'd pulled from her pocket. She surveyed the walls, the windows, the furniture. She walked over to the fireplace and assessed it for several moments. Then she returned to the alcove where Peyton worked.

"It is but a week until the Grand Ball, and this room must be spit-spot for the event." She paused, inspecting Peyton and her workstation. "You have one more chair to finish. When you're done, move your workstation to your bedroom so the staff can properly prepare the ballroom. You'll need to finish by Saturday."

Two days? So soon? Had she lost track of time? She'd have to work steady and hard. "I'll do my best, ma'am."

Mrs. Milton pursed her lips. "Good. You'll be working on napkins for the ball once you're done with this. We need at least two hundred." She patted the brown-striped wingback chair. "Carry on, then."

Napkins? She hadn't signed up to be a seamstress. What else might she be asked to do?

Peyton blew out a breath and continued working. By mid-afternoon, she'd completed the ottoman. Next, to tear apart the wingback. She might be able to finish the chair by tomorrow if nothing went wrong.

She worked with her back to the doorway, but when she heard not one but two pairs of footsteps, she turned to observe Mr. and Mrs. Emery step into the ballroom. Behind them, Charlie carried a Gramophone. Sam followed with a small table. The two set up the table and music player and left.

Apparently, the couple had come to practice their dancing for the ball. Should she leave and afford them privacy? She took a few steps toward the door to the terrace.

Mrs. Emery stopped her. "Miss Quinn. A word." Her tone was flat.

Oh no! Had the missus noticed her slacking too?

Then she smiled, and Peyton's heart started to beat again. "Mr.

Emery and I wanted to thank you for your fine work. You have transformed the furnishings of this fine castle into a twentieth-century wonder."

Mr. Emery raised a brow. "I thought it an unnecessary folly when the wife informed me of her plans. But she was right. Your work has made a difference in the atmosphere of our home."

"Thank you both." Peyton curtsied low, warmed to her toes. "It has been a pleasure."

Mrs. Emery gazed at her husband but addressed Peyton. "You needn't leave. Continue your work. My husband and I are simply brushing up on our dancing."

"Thank you, missus." As they headed to the center of the ballroom, Peyton returned to her workstation but placed herself facing the couple. She worked as she watched, slowing her progress.

The elegance of the Viennese waltz had always intrigued her, and the Emerys made it look effortless. Mr. Emery gracefully held his wife's hand by his side as they glided around and around the room. They danced the one-step and then the two-step.

When the music stopped, Mrs. Emery held her husband at arm's length. "Darling, why don't we make this a more traditional ball? Let's open with the Grand March and lead couples around the room. Then we can dance the March in File and the Star. I just love those, even if they are fading in fashion. Throughout the evening, we'll alternate the group dances and couple's dances, just like old times. What do you say?"

Mr. Emery pulled her close, but Peyton could still hear his deep voice. "Yes, let's. I can show off my new bride, and it should be delightful. I dare say the Thousand Islands has yet to enjoy such a private ball, though the Frontenac regularly hosts open galas."

Mrs. Emery giggled as she moved toward the Gramophone. Peyton couldn't be caught eavesdropping on the Emerys, so she snapped her head down and returned to her work. When the music began again, so did their dancing. So elegant and romantic.

Growing up, Peyton had enjoyed dancing Irish jigs and reels with abandon. When she lived in Watertown, she'd been invited to a square dance now and then. She'd also learned the one-step, mastering its moves with ease, though she'd never participated in an actual dance. What would it be like to attend a ball like the Emery's Grand Ball?

That was far above her social standing.

She continued working on the chair until the music stopped and the Emerys left the room. But the music lingered in her mind, so she tentatively went to the center of the ballroom, curtsied, and pretended to accept the offer of a dance. From Patrick. How regal he'd look in a black tailcoat and bow tie, his shirt pure white and well-starched vest crisp.

And she? She'd choose a pale pink gown, bell-shaped with a gored skirt that fit closely at the waist and gradually widened to the hem. The bodice—close-fitting with a low-cut neckline and soft, feminine, puffed sleeves—would make Patrick fairly swoon.

She touched her hair. It would be drawn up in a knot on the top of her head and dressed with delicate ribbons and fragrant, petite flowers.

Breathless at the very idea, she danced. 'Round and 'round, she circled to the music in her mind, whirling and twirling with abandon, allowing her feet to remember the steps—dreaming that, one day, she could be in the arms of Patrick, perhaps dancing at their wedding.

Then—her high-button shoes caught the hem of her long skirt and sent her tumbling in a heap to the floor. "Goodness!" She giggled at her own folly. "I'm an idiot."

Mitch appeared as if out of nowhere. "May I help, miss?" He extended his hand and helped her out of the heap while her face burned. The back of her neck tickled with perspiration.

Peyton wiped her hands on her apron and pasted on a smile. "Thank you, kind sir." She checked the room to make sure no one else had seen her tumble. "What are you doing here?"

Mitch chuckled, putting out his hand again. "Shall we?"

She took it, and he led her in a music-less but perfectly executed waltz. The man had many talents, to be sure.

As they danced, Mitch answered her question. "Fulfilling Patrick's instructions to watch out for you. He loves you, you know."

Peyton stopped, causing Mitch to bump into her and almost trip them both up. "Sorry. What did you say?"

He took a step away, plunging his hands deep into his pockets. "He loves you. Never seen a man so over the moon. But he's hurting, Peyton. Blames himself for his father's accident. Blames himself for not forgiving the man."

Peyton frowned. "But it's not true."

"True or not, he feels himself unworthy of your love. It's not you. It's him. Give the lad time to come to his senses."

Peyton took a deep breath and let it out slowly. "Thank you. I'll try."

Mitch pulled his hands out of his pockets. "I came to take you to supper, and I'm starving." He swept a hand toward the terrace door. "Shall we?"

The moon's reflection on the rippling water became a backdrop for an ache so deep, Patrick could barely breathe. Nothing seemed the same without Peyton, without hope for life with her. In the past week, he'd brought his mother a measure of comfort. But she'd been so independent and responsible for everything during his father's wayward years, as she called it, that Patrick felt rather useless being there. Odd jobs around town filled his time, and evenings spent with a silent, grieving woman brought him no joy.

Standing on the Clayton shore facing the castle, Patrick followed the beam of the Calumet Tower across the river as a large freighter came into view and passed back into the darkness.

From light to darkness. Yes, he could relate.

The fireflies that danced all around reminded him of Peyton. Everything reminded him of her, whether he liked it or not. She loved the tiny creatures. Could she be outside now, enjoying their blinking lights, the warm evening, and the moonbeams on the river? If only he could be there with her. If only he was worthy of being there.

But no. He'd smashed to pieces a dream of life with her, and now it was beyond repair. He'd watched her expression change from sadness to anger to resignation. Felt the tingling shiver of finality run down his back. He'd severed their relationship, and it would never be the same. The reality of it grew so strong he choked on the unnerving thought.

Gooseflesh bristled on his forearms, and he rubbed it away. Why did his stubborn bravado hurt the most important people in his life?

"Why, God?"

He jerked at hearing his own bitterness seep out.

"Good evening, Patrick." Pastor Moreno joined him from the shadows, standing silently beside him for several moments surveying the heavens. "Have you ever wondered at all the eyes that have beheld the moon's reflection on these mighty waters? How many souls have turned to their creator as they gazed upon its beauty? The St. Lawrence continually beckons me to consider God's handiwork, His power, His healing. That's why I love living here. He created this river to bring life to so many of us."

Patrick continued staring at the river but cast a sideways glimpse his pastor's way. "What are you getting at, sir?"

"Our Lord spoke often of water. He was baptized in it, washed with it, drank it. But He also turned it into wine, walked on it, and promised us living water. And He said we can be cleansed by the water of His word. Do you need that, my friend?"

Did he?

Pastor Moreno placed a hand on Patrick's shoulder. "You've been through a lot, and I'm sorry for your father's passing. But accidents happen, and you aren't responsible for his demise."

Patrick glowered at him. "It's more than that."

"Then what?"

"I didn't forgive him." Patrick's eyes moistened, but he willed back the tears. "I treated him like a stranger. Avoided him. Hated him."

His pastor nodded. He knew what Patrick's father was like. "You and your mother have had some tough times in the past. But take comfort that your father is in heaven."

Patrick shook his head. "I don't think I understand my earthly father or my heavenly Father."

Pastor Moreno pressed. "I can help with that. Your earthly father was a changed man, and your heavenly Father is more than you can imagine. The Psalms say He's a father to the fatherless, and that's you. It also says He never changes. He's compassionate, merciful, and comforts us in times of trouble. Can you imagine? If you'll but reach out to Him, He's there."

Could this be true? Patrick understood Jesus the Savior, but the Father God was a mystery to him.

Pastor Moreno interrupted his ponderings. "My favorite passage is John 3:16-17, which you memorized as a child, Patrick. God loves you so much that He gave you His Son—and not to condemn you for your mistakes. Not to beat you up for being angry at your earthly father or punish you for your bitterness or even your hatred. He wants to save you from those feelings. Free you from their power."

Patrick had to admit that the more he dwelled on his hatred, anger, and unforgiveness, the more powerless he felt—as if those things were taking over his life. He'd pushed Peyton away based on those feelings. He was despondent and hopeless in the wake of them.

"How, then, can I know my heavenly Father, Pastor?"

Peyton strolled the island aimlessly, pondering Mitch's words. If Patrick truly loved her, why had he pushed her away? She couldn't reconcile the two.

Fireflies flitted around her, and tufts of dandelion seed drifted on the breeze like fairies dancing free. Oh, to be free of the confusion that befuddled her.

The starry August sky reminded her of the ballroom where she'd spent so much time working—women dancing on the dark floor, wonderfully ornamented and sparkling in their glittery gowns. Would she be able to catch a glimpse or two of the illustrious affair? She hadn't heard if her job would end before then or if she'd be asked to play a part in the Grand Ball. She hoped the latter.

As Peyton rounded the corner of the castle, moonlight reflected on the sandstone exactly right. Something appeared stamped on some of the bricks. Upon closer inspection, she discovered stars imprinted on them. How had she not noticed them before, and why were they there? What a curious embellishment. Now on a scavenger hunt of sorts, she found several more. Several bricks had two stars, and others had just one. She'd heard they were there but never happened upon them. An inconsequential distraction, to be sure. But an interesting one, nonetheless.

Pulling herself from her find, Peyton prayed for Patrick, for herself, for them. Perhaps, God willing, the stars would align for her and Patrick, after all.

CHAPTER 23

PEYTON TUGGED THE MATERIAL into place, tucking the edge under the chair's seat just so. She'd become an expert at creating the right tension the fabric needed to look perfect while also allowing enough give for even the heaviest sitter to leave it unaffected.

Though she no longer found joy in her work, still, she was good at it. Perhaps she might find satisfaction in having her own shop one day? Perhaps she could find success in a city? She might, but the idea made her nauseous.

No. She'd dreamed the dream of a life with Patrick. Now nothing could compare.

As she hammered one of the final tacks into place, Duvall stepped into the alcove. "A missive, miss." He held out a silver plate upon which sat an envelope.

She stood, took the correspondence, and curtsied. "Thank you, sir. I feel like a princess with you delivering my letter on a silver tray."

Duvall smiled. "You are, miss. In God's eyes." Without giving her a chance to respond, he left the room.

She giggled. A princess? What a kind man! She slipped her finger under the envelope flap, withdrew the letter, and unfolded it.

Miss Peyton,

Your father has been hurt. He is under my care and will recover in time.

But his eyes have been affected and his hands burned. He discouraged me from informing you since he didn't want to take you away from your duties on Calumet, but I convinced him that you have a right to know and to come to his side if you so desire. Please consider visiting him soon.

Sincerely,

Dr. Whitmarsh

Peyton gasped, her heart speeding to a dither. "No. Dear God, no!" Peyton cried out, covering her mouth at the sound of her voice, tears welling up, a giant lump filling her throat. She surveyed her work, not knowing what to do.

Suddenly, Patrick appeared in the doorway, and she gasped as he hurried to her side. "Peyton, your papa's been hurt. He will heal, but I think you should visit him."

She blinked and thrust the letter at him, whimpering like a lost child, feeling like one. "I just found out. You're right. I must go to him."

Patrick viewed the letter and nodded. "I'll take you immediately." He evaluated the work she was doing. "Perhaps you should add that one final tack, so the chair is finished?"

Peyton wiped her eyes. "You're right. It shouldn't take but a moment."

Patrick gave her a reassuring hug, which she gladly received. It soothed her soul a little, and at the moment, she didn't even care if Mrs. Milton—or anyone—saw them embrace.

Peyton banged in the tack and mumbled, more to herself than to Patrick. "I should straighten my workstation, then I'll talk to Duvall and gather my things from my room."

He bent down and kissed her forehead. "So professional and accomplished. I'm proud of you, Peyton. I'll tidy up here while you do that."

She agreed and rushed off. After she showed Duvall the letter, he released her from her duties.

As she hastened to collect her things, concern for her papa grew by the moment. *What if he's blind? Is he in great pain? What if infection sets in?* Questions pounded in her head with each step she took up to her room.

Peyton opened her door and frantically stuffed her things into her suitcase. She wanted to let Rachel know, but she didn't have paper and pencil handy. With a sigh, she grabbed her bag and left. Halfway down the stairs, she met her roommate. Peyton dropped her bag on the second-floor landing, and Rachel gave her a tender hug.

"Oh, Peyton. I just heard and came to see if I can help. I will miss you. I hope you come back soon."

"Thank you, friend. I don't know what the future holds, but I'm glad to have known you." Peyton gave her a squeeze before releasing her. "I must hurry."

"I'll walk down with you." Rachel took her bag.

"Thank you."

At the bottom of the stairs, with another quick hug, Rachel handed her the bag, and they parted ways.

Where should Peyton meet Patrick? She returned to the ballroom but found Mrs. Emery standing there instead. Peyton curtsied.

The missus opened her hands. "I've heard of your trials. Godspeed to you, and don't fret about the rest of the work. You've accomplished all I had planned ... and more. And whether you return or not, you will receive the highest recommendations—no matter what Mrs. Milton thinks." She wrinkled her nose, smiled kindly, and slipped Peyton a thick envelope. "And I will pray for your father and you."

Dipping her head, Peyton pressed the envelope into her pocket. "Thank you, missus. I hope to be back soon, but if not, thank you for this opportunity and all your encouragement. It has been such a blessing to be here."

"And you, in turn, have blessed us." Mrs. Emery waved a hand. "Now go." She motioned toward the terrace door where Patrick stood waiting.

Before long, they were in a skiff and on their way to Clayton. Peyton held back tears by biting her bottom lip. She grasped her seat until her knuckles turned white. When she noticed them, she relaxed her hands and rubbed them. Patrick stared at her as he rowed, bringing sudden heat to her cheeks.

Patrick blinked, his face serious. "You know you must oversee the Grand Ball fireworks next week. Your papa will be in no condition to do it."

Peyton's heart sped faster than the soaring gull overhead. "Are you mad? Help him, yes. Command the entire thing? Absurd."

Patrick pressed. "Think about it. I've observed your skills and listened to the knowledge you hold inside that beautiful head of yours. You can do this, Peyton, and if you'd like, I will be by your side to assist you in any way I can."

Peyton felt as though a fuse that had been lit, then extinguished. She looked to the heavens for a clear, simple answer. How could she say yes to a thing that ought not to be done? At least not by her, a mere girl, as society would say.

She'd gone against social norms and stepped into the unknown when she apprenticed for the O'Clearys, learned the upholstery trade, and embraced the ideas of suffrage. But taking on her father's very male job?

What would people say to such an audacious thing? What would they do? Surely, she'd be laughed out of town.

Yet how could she say no when her papa needed her? Her kind, faithful papa. First the palsy and now injured, never to do the job he loved again. She had to honor his final commitment.

Peyton made the decision without flinching. She relit the fuse. "I'll do it, and I appreciate your willingness to help. If Papa wants me to, that is."

Patrick dipped his chin as he pulled up to the dock, tethered the boat, and hurried with her to see her father. When they reached the porch, he kissed her cheek—igniting a flare of hope—and took a step back. "I'll leave you to it. May I visit this evening, please? I have some things to say."

What things? Peyton would have to ponder that later. "Certainly. Thank you for coming so swiftly."

"Of course." Patrick handed her the suitcase and smiled tenderly. "Until this evening, my Peyton Pie."

After waving him off, Peyton called out as she opened the screen door. "Papa? Are you here?"

"Up here, darlin'. In my room." Her father sounded weak, sad.

She climbed the stairs to her papa's room and found him lying on top of his covers, both of his eyes and his hands bandaged. "What are you doing here alone? Is there no one taking care of you?"

"Mrs. Nelson just left to feed her son. She'll return soon. I'm fine, especially now that you're here."

Peyton planted a gentle kiss on her father's weather-worn cheek. A slight smile crossed his lips. Thick gauze covered both eyes, and a thin strip of gauze held the patches in place. Both of his hands were also wrapped, although the left hand only had a small strip around the palm. "What happened, Papa?"

He groaned. "Foolishness, really. I was packing a Roman candle for the Emery's Grand Ball, but my hand shook a lot. I'm still not sure what happened—probably, friction set it off—but it exploded." He lifted his bandaged right hand. "Should've stopped when I saw I was having a bad day. No excuses."

Peyton patted his shoulder. "Don't beat yourself up. Accidents happen. The doctor says you'll be all right with time."

Papa shook his head, his angst palpable. "I don't have time. The Grand Ball is next week."

Peyton rubbed his head soothingly. "I'll do it, Papa. Patrick and I can do it. You can talk us through each step. You can lead us, and we'll be your hands and eyes."

Papa began weeping as his breath convulsed and caught in his throat. She had never heard him sob before. Her heart ached for this stalwart, steadfast man who'd been brought low.

Witnessing him so helpless and hurting, tears ran down her

cheeks. But she wouldn't let him hear her cry. She wiped her tears, squared her shoulders, and rallied her strength.

"Even if the old hens gossip or the town fathers run me out of the village, I'll finish this job for you, Papa. Together we'll put on the most successful fireworks display ever. You can count on it."

Patrick knocked on the frame of the Quinns' front door, his nerves prickling. He'd been pondering what he'd say to Peyton all day. He rubbed the back of his neck.

When he raised his hand to knock again, Peyton scurried down the stairs quickly but quietly. She whispered as she opened the screen door, "Papa just fell asleep. Let me get some lemonade, and I'll meet you in a moment."

He kept his voice low. "Sounds delightful."

The Quinn's' covered porch overlooked the neighborhood, a large oak tree shading both it and much of the front lawn. If he craned his neck, his childhood home was visible from where he stood. A rag rug, two Adirondack chairs, and a small table made a comfortable sitting area. He took a seat in the far chair, wiggled the table to center it between the chairs, and waited.

Peyton opened the door holding two tall glasses of lemonade and a plate of cookies, which teetered precariously on top of one of the glasses. Her smile wobbled a little, then she groaned.

Patrick jumped up and hurried to take the plate and a glass. "Don't want to lose these oatmeal cookies. With raisins? My favorite."

Peyton *liggled*. Oh, how he'd missed that sound. She batted her long lashes. "I know."

They sat and sipped their drinks for a moment, and Patrick munched on a cookie. "Freshly made? How did you have time for that?"

Peyton shrugged. "Papa's sleeping a lot. Probably for the best. He's in a lot of pain, and there's not much I can do for him. Our next-door neighbor, Mrs. Nelson, is helping. She used to be a nurse, you know.

She changed his bandages while I watched."

"How bad is it?"

Peyton brushed a flyaway strand of hair back into place. "His eyes have minor burns, so they'll heal in a week or two. His left hand has a few blisters. But his right hand took the brunt of it. A Roman candle exploded while he was working on it."

"Blathers." Patrick raked his hand through his hair. "He still has his fingers, yes?"

Peyton nodded, her face scrunched up as it always did when she was worried. "Yes, but they may be pretty scarred."

He placed a hand on hers and patted it. "Poor man." He took her hand and pulled it over to kiss it. "Did you mention our willingness to help with the Grand Ball?"

Peyton's face relaxed. "Yes, but I'm worried about the community's attitude toward a woman taking on such a dangerous job."

He waved his free hand in the air, still holding half a cookie. "The tattling toads will have hysterics, I'm sure, but I'll protect you from their retribution. You can count on that."

Peyton's brows furrowed, her eyes questioning. "I ... I thought we had no future together. I thought ..."

He blew out a deep sigh. "I'm a fool, Peyton Pie. My father's death hit me pretty hard, you know."

She dipped her chin, gently squeezing his hand. Her tender green eyes implored him to continue.

"I was so confused. And mad. At my father. At myself. At God. I couldn't understand how a loving God would let that happen—would let me fail to make amends before Father died."

Peyton pulled his hand to her lips and kissed it as he had hers, sending a wave of warm bliss through his veins. "He is a loving Father, Patrick, even though yours was not."

Patrick gave her a reassuring smile, then stared at the darkening sky for a long while, gathering his thoughts. "God has begun to heal my heartache over my father, and I'm learning to truly forgive the man. And also to give myself a little grace."

Peyton rubbed Patrick's hand, her fingers delicate and soothing. "I'm so glad to hear that."

"I had a long talk with Pastor Moreno, and I think I've had a revelation, of sorts. God loves me so much more than any earthly father can. He wants me—all of us—to be free of our earthly heartaches so we can become the unique people He's meant for us to be—in our careers and life choices, but also in our relationships. And yes, He might allow us to go through some things to grow us. But it's not to be mean or because He's ashamed or mad at us. It's to help us become who He's intended us to be."

Peyton's twinkle lit up the evening like a full moon. She beamed, bidding him continue.

Patrick chuckled. "I think I understand now that God isn't like my father or even like yours, Peyton. He's so much more than that. If we can imagine a father who only wants the best for us and then we magnify that a million times, we might get a glimpse of the depth of the Father's heart for us."

Peyton nodded, then furrowed her brow. "That's true, Patrick. But where does that leave us?"

He reached over and took both of her hands in his. "In God's hands."

Peyton lay on her bed, muddling over the words Patrick had spoken. *In God's hands? What does that mean? Why couldn't he just be clearer?*

She punched her pillow, trying to find a comfortable position in the middle of her uncomfortable thoughts. By the end of the evening, the two of them had renewed their friendship. But would there be more? Could there be more?

Patrick had been right that her spiritual moorings needed repair. Her years in Watertown and the world of modern enlightenment had battered her faith more than she'd realized. Now, based on circumstances, it ebbed and flowed like the St. Lawrence.

She got out of bed and went to her window, where an almost full moon shone on her face. How had she strayed so far? Did she know the Father God of whom Patrick spoke? And how did her convictions on suffrage square with faith?

She'd become like a ship battered and beaten by the storms of life. From people's opinions of her. From being ostracized, belittled, mocked. From being judged. Even, if she were honest, from the teasing she took as a child.

Where was God in all of that? She wasn't trying to rebel against Him. She was merely trying to find the right route for her life. Yet in the process, had she drifted far from the way?

As awareness dawned, tears welled. She'd read of her Southern sisters who saw suffrage as God's divine calling to bring equality to women. Their faith motivated them, and they took it on as a righteous cause. They even viewed Eve as the first suffragist and saw Jesus as the emancipator of women.

But she had been influenced by those who largely kept faith out of the discussion, even censoring those who tried to connect it or add their personal faith to the movement. The O'Clearys certainly disparaged faith. Indeed, they had disengaged from the church altogether, spewing bitterness from the persecution they'd endured from elders and churchgoers alike.

On the other hand, the anti-suffragists she had met called suffragists disobedient—even un-Christian—and declared that women's suffrage violated the rules of creation. They said that giving women the vote would bring social disintegration.

Why couldn't faith and freedom go hand in hand? Yes, God wanted women to be treated better. Men and women were equal before God, both bearing His image. She'd plead that cause until her dying day. But would Patrick approve? Did his reluctance about her views bring about his reluctance to commit? Or was it something deeper?

Chapter 24

A FEW DAYS LATER, PEYTON headed to the store, a list tucked in her pocket. As she passed Mrs. Fillmore's house, the woman hollered from her porch in a rather unladylike way. "Peyton Quinn. May I have a word with you?"

That woman will present me with an earful, to be sure. I haven't time for this. Maybe Peyton could pretend she hadn't heard. But no.

Do unto others ...

With a sigh of concession, Peyton opened the picket-fence gate and slammed it closed. She pasted on a smile and climbed the four porch steps. The decades-long choir member in their church stood with her arms crossed over her ample chest, her pug nose high in the air.

The woman huffed. "I know you want to help your father with the fireworks, Peyton. But it isn't proper. You may have been without a nurturing mother all your life, but I should think a girl of your life experiences would know what an embarrassment you would be to this community. To our church. Moreover, you are going against God's laws."

Peyton swallowed her anger, measuring her words—and her tone—carefully. "What laws, ma'am?"

The gray-haired, gray-eyed woman tapped her foot. "Men hold positions such as your father's, and, I might add, the positions of upholsterers and many other jobs not fit for females. A proper woman should be under her husband's rule, caring for the home, not shooting off fireworks and recovering furniture. 'Tis a sin, I tell you."

Her face stinging as if from a slap, Peyton took a step back, almost off the porch. She teetered on the edge and stepped down. "Thank you for your concern, madam. I must be on my way. Good day to you." She hurried off the property, fairly running down the street to avoid the woman's retort. She ignored the words Mrs. Fillmore continued to toss her way.

The nerve of opinionated old biddies. This was the twentieth century, not the Dark Ages.

Some women had nothing better to do than tear people down and gossip. How Christian was that?

Peyton entered Joseph Brabant's Drug Store with her heart still in a tight ball. She'd quickly gather the paper and glue she needed to finish the last few shells for the Grand Ball fireworks before anyone— Oh no.

Two of Mrs. Fillmore's cronies, Mrs. Price and Mrs. Gordon, stopped chatting and glared at her. Mrs. Price shook her head, her eyes narrowed. She turned to Mrs. Gordon. "Why, there's our town Jezebel now."

A Jezebel? Jezebel was a wanton, promiscuous, shameless woman. Peyton most certainly was not.

Mrs. Gordon clucked her tongue. "We must remember, she's but a poor, motherless child."

Mr. Brabant examined Peyton and then shot the women a scowl that silenced them.

Could Peyton be silent in the midst of such persecution? For now, she'd ignore the women. "Good day, sir. I need some paper and glue, please."

The shopkeeper reached over the counter and patted her hand. Then he whispered, "Take no mind of them, miss."

At his kindness, Peyton's eyes burned, but she blinked back the tears threatening to spill over. She'd not let those women see her cry. She cleared her throat. "Thank you, sir."

Before long, Mr. Brabant bagged her purchases and bid her good day. She'd take an alternate route home, circumventing Mrs. Fillmore's home. She'd had enough ill-treatment for one day.

As she entered her front door, a woman's voice drifted from the kitchen. "But Mr. Quinn, don't you understand what a mark this puts on your daughter? She'll forever be branded a malcontent, a radical."

Not again. In her own home? To her papa? She stood at the doorway and listened, gathering what little emotional strength she had left after her jaunt to the store.

Papa's voice quivered with anger. "Mrs. Sanford, you may be the president of the Ladies' Temperance League, but you have no jurisdiction over my daughter. As you can see, I am in no condition to fulfill my obligation to the Emerys in just two days. Peyton is merely acting as my eyes and hands, and Patrick Taylor will also be helping. There is nothing improper about a daughter helping her ailing father, is there?"

Mrs. Sanford let out a loud huff. "Very well. If it's just this once. Perhaps we can overlook such unconventional actions under the circumstances. But you'd best get control of her, sir."

Had the cronies coordinated this web of oppression, or had they ganged up on her the same day by coincidence? She'd guess the former. Peyton slammed the screen door to alert them. "I'm home, Papa."

Papa's tone was flat. "In the kitchen."

Mrs. Sanford stepped into the front room and smirked, looking down her nose at her. "Peyton." The woman addressed her father as she walked to the door. "Best be on my way. I hope you'll heed my counsel, sir."

Peyton silently acknowledged the woman. She wasn't about to get involved in a conversation with her. Instead, she opened the door for her to exit. After Mrs. Sanford descended the porch steps, she let the door slam behind her and mumbled, "Good riddance," before hurrying to her papa.

She kissed her father's forehead and brushed back a rogue curl. "What are you doing out of bed, Papa? You need to heal."

Papa shook his head. "Stuff and nonsense. I'm not an invalid. We have work to do. There are still a dozen shells unfinished, and the Grand Ball is in two days." He stood, but Peyton urged him to sit.

"I know, Papa. Patrick will be here within the hour, and we'll finish them in no time. You've taught me well, and I remember every detail of assembling the shells. But I'm sorry. Things would be so much easier for you if only I were a boy."

Papa reached for her hand that still laid on his shoulder. He pulled it around and kissed it. "My girl. Don't ever regret being who God made you to be. You're a wise, beautiful, talented woman, and just because others voice opinions against you, you must give them no heed."

Peyton plopped down on a chair. "I heard what old Bertha-the-biddy said just now. She had no right to come here and lecture you. And I've already had two earfuls from Mrs. Fillmore and Mrs. Price during my trip to the store."

Papa groaned. "They're all of the same camp, Peyton. Old cronies who complain about anything that runs counter to their self-centered, self-appointed proprieties. But remember, they are only a small handful in this community. I daresay most in Clayton would either applaud you or think nothing of your unconventional ways. I, for one, adore you for them."

"Thank you, but their words hurt, and those women are powerful people in the community, Papa. I try to ignore them, but ..." Tears slipped down her cheeks. She was tired of ignoring, fighting, and hoping others would accept her for who she was.

Papa reached for her and pulled her into an embrace. With a bandaged hand, he patted her back. "I know, daughter. It's not right, but we live in a fallen world where so much is wrong. People can be mean, and anything—or anyone—different threatens them. And I'm sorry to say that, in a small town like this, change in action or thought comes slowly. We just have to move forward and find peace to overcome the injustices we may face. In time, things will change."

"I don't have time. It's happening here. Now."

Patrick marveled at the skill it took to make firework shells. They had set up two worktables in the far corner of the backyard under the shade of a large oak tree. He sat at the table that held the supplies. Peyton sat at another table, rolling, gluing, and pleating down the ends of the shell casings, with Papa by her side, encouraging and reminding.

What would it be like to have such a dangerous but exciting job? A job that entertained, brought joy, celebrated beauty, and caused people to wonder at the mystery and magic of something exploding in the sky.

Peyton bit the tip of her tongue as she worked, concentrating on each detail, smiling when she accomplished a step. Patrick warmed at the memories of her quirky little traits. Traits he adored.

She worked on each casing methodically, inspecting it multiple times, so intensely that she probably didn't realize he was watching her. That was all right with him. He'd be happy to observe her anytime.

At first, Patrick had hesitated to even touch the explosive materials. Carpentry work was safe, secure, and somewhat rewarding. Besides, he was good at it. For the past hour, he'd quietly helped the Quinns any way he could. He'd lined up the paper, glue, fuses, and the boxes of gunpowder and what was labeled 'stars' and handed Peyton whatever she needed.

But after watching Peyton deftly create such intricate combustible devices, he was ready to try. "May I make one?"

Peyton stopped working and snapped her head toward him, surprise brightening her face. Did she think that he was incapable of creating one?

Mr. Quinn chuckled. "I wondered when you'd be ready to give it a try. Come here, son, and we'll lead you through it."

Patrick left the supply table and joined Peyton and her papa at the worktable.

Mr. Quinn eased back in his seat. "Ready, Patrick? I'll talk you through it. You and Peyton can make shells together. She'll show you, and you can follow her lead."

Peyton mouthed the words *you can do it* and tossed him a wink. His heart danced in double time. Yes, with that affirmation, he could do just about anything.

As Peyton demonstrated how to make a simple fuse called a *spolette,* Mr. Quinn narrated the steps. She handed Patrick a tube, showing him how to fill it with a tiny scooper, ramming fine black meal powder down and stuffing it solid. After completing several more steps, it looked like a little candle.

Peyton assessed his work and nodded her approval. "Excellent job, Patrick. Truly. Next?"

Papa cleared his throat. "The shell casings."

Peyton handed Patrick a tool called a case former, some paper, and a knife. They rolled the paper around the case several times, cut it, and glued the paper onto the case. After several more rather intricate steps, Patrick wiped his brow.

Peyton winked her encouragement. "Now let's add the stars." She motioned for the box of black chunks of material resembling coal.

"Stars?"

Peyton *liggled.* "Yes. They're made of different chemicals that create the different colors and shapes of the fireworks."

Patrick whistled. "I had no idea this process would be so intricate, interesting, and fun."

Mr. Quinn waved a bandaged hand. "Whoa on the fun. This is serious—and sometimes dangerous—work, as you can see."

Patrick's face warmed. "Sorry, sir. I only meant that ..."

Peyton's papa laughed. "I know what you meant. Just teasing. Doing things with the one you love is always fun."

Peyton sucked in a breath, her face turning crimson, her eyes like saucers. "Papa!"

Patrick raised an eyebrow and shrugged. "He's right, you know."

Peyton scolded him with a whisper. "Patrick ..."

Papa interrupted them. "Let's finish these shells, shall we?"

They did, adding a layer of coarse black powder, carefully tamping it level, and pleating it shut.

Peyton inspected Patrick's shell, rolling it on the table. "Very good work, Patrick. Tight and solid. Now it's time to spike it."

Befuddled, Patrick laughed. "Like a football?"

Mr. Quinn shook his head. "We want to make sure the shell is spiked—tightly wound with flax string so that it explodes up, not out."

Peyton demonstrated. She handed him a roll of flax string and showed him how to wind the string tightly onto the shell until it was securely covered. Then she passed him a roll of brown paper. "Now we paste the shell."

Again, he followed her lead, thoroughly pasting a strip of paper, rubbing it firmly onto the shell, and enclosing it in the paper. Peyton's instructions and precise production were as professional as her upholstery work.

She was an amazing woman, to be sure. So talented. So beautiful. So—

Her papa interrupted his thoughts. "Once the glue is dry, we need to weigh each shell to determine the lift charge."

Peyton weighed each of the shells on a small scale and scribbled down the number. "We'll now make piped matches that are a part of the fuse we attach to the shells. And then we'll add the lift charge."

Patrick ran a hand through his hair and blew out a breath. So many steps. So many dangerous, important steps.

And Mr. Quinn wasn't yet done explaining. "The lift-charge rule is one ounce of powder for every pound of shell weight." He talked them through a few more steps before they were done.

Peyton assessed Patrick's shell. "You've made your first firework shell, Patrick. Bravo. Now, all we need to do is carefully put the shells into the tubes when we set up the show tomorrow."

Patrick held the shell in his hand, admiring the finished product. "Amazing. And how long have you been doing this, sir?"

Mr. Quinn clicked his tongue. "I was probably nine or ten when my father first taught me, and his father taught him. It's been three generations of Quinn Fireworks." He sighed, a frown forming on his bandaged face.

Peyton went to him and hugged him. "I'm so sorry, Papa. If I were a boy, we could carry on the company. But I doubt people would allow me to."

He stood. "The Lord knows, child. Now, I need to rest. I assume you two can safely make the rest of the shells while I nap?"

"Of course, sir." Patrick rose, brushing off his slacks. "May I walk you back to your room and get you settled?"

Mr. Quinn grinned. "Of course, son. I'd be much obliged."

Before long, Patrick settled Mr. Quinn in his bed, but he lingered by the door, his heart in his throat. "May I ask you something, sir?"

CHAPTER 25

PEYTON POURED A CUP of coffee, setting it in front of her father and guiding his hand to it. Poor man, still bandaged and unable to see. Her heart ached seeing him like that.

She touched his cheek, several days' stubble scratchy against her fingers. "This may prove a long day for you. Are you up for it, Papa? Patrick and I aren't professionals in setting up fireworks displays, but we could try it on our own."

Papa sniffed and slurped his coffee, then chuckled. "You're not professionals *yet*. But you've assisted me enough to know how it's done. I'll be there to answer any questions."

She took a seat next to him and sipped her tea for a moment. "Truth is, we couldn't do it without you."

Papa shook his head. "Someday you may, my girl. Someday."

Patrick's voice interrupted them. "Hello. Anybody home?"

Peyton hurried to the front door and greeted him with a hug. "I'm so glad you're helping us with this. I'm so nervous, my hands are shaking like Papa's. You'd think I was planning a stagecoach robbery. After all the criticism and village gossip, I can't bungle this."

Patrick smiled, took her hands in his, and kissed them. "Settle down, Peyton Pie, and don't worry about the prattle. We'll do a fine job of this. I'm certain."

If only she shared Patrick's confidence. When he put his mind to something, he exuded courage. Why had that same gallantry faltered with their relationship?

When they entered the kitchen, Papa greeted Patrick. "Well, son, are you ready to learn the nuts and bolts of fireworks displays?"

"Hardly slept a wink, sir." Patrick grinned. "After making the shells, I'm eager to learning the tricks of the trade."

Peyton slipped her hand into the crook of his arm, leading him to the back porch cleared of everything save a long table and stacks of crates. "You've been busy, my girl. Why didn't you have me help?"

"I couldn't sleep either." Peyton shrugged. "First, we need to sort and count the shells so we know what we're working with. After lunch, we'll go to the island and set up the display."

Papa laughed through the screen door she'd propped open so he could be part of the conversation. "You young people worry too much. I slept like a baby."

"But this profession is much more complicated than carpentry, sir." Patrick took off his cap and scratched his head.

Peyton raised her pointer like a teacher would. "And far more dangerous."

"But also much more fun." Patrick tossed her a wink.

Papa called out from the kitchen, "Enough, you two. We have work to do."

For the next few hours, Peyton and Patrick counted and double-checked each shell Papa had meticulously created before his accident. He spoke through the screen door again. "When those are lit, they can shake like the dickens, so they all need to be tight and secure. We never want an errant one to take off in another direction, especially toward us or other fireworks. That can be disastrous."

Patrick gingerly touched each tube to make sure they were sound. "Only one questionable shell out of hundreds? Mr. Quinn, you're amazing."

"Ah, thank you, son." Papa tilted his head upward. "Just doing what I love. Fireworks make me well up inside with patriotism and pride. Each show is a one-of-a-kind piece of art."

Peyton stepped into the kitchen and hugged her father, but she gazed at Patrick. "Isn't he wonderful? Such an amazing man and businessman but still with the wonder of a child." She planted a kiss on the top of his head.

"He is." Patrick joined them and placed a hand on Papa's shoulder. "I think the world would be a better place if we all kept more of our childlike wonder."

Papa patted Patrick's hand. "Enough prattle. Let's count the big guns."

She and Patrick returned to the porch and assessed the large shells. Some were only four inches in diameter and looked like they'd be rather harmless. But other shells were bigger than Patrick's arm, a few even longer and broader. Peyton shivered at the power they'd have and handled them with great care.

Papa cleared his throat. "This afternoon, you will load the shells into large tubes with a stick attached that anchors and positions them to shoot in the right direction. Notice how each shell already has a fuse and a charge, just like the ones you created yesterday. Only, these are much larger and more complex."

"And more dangerous." Despite her dire proclamation, Peyton spoke with confidence. "What kind are these, Papa? They're tagged with yellow ribbons." She handed him a large shell.

Papa fingered it gently. "I think they're the chrysanthemums I imported from Japan." He turned his head toward Patrick. "They explode into a sphere of colored stars that leave a visible trail of sparks. The pink tags are the dahlia. They have larger stars that travel farther before breaking out of the shell. They're stunning."

Patrick's eyes grew wide as perspiration formed on his brow. "And the blue tags? What are they?"

"I know what they are." Peyton raised her hand like a schoolgirl, then plunked down in a chair. "They're my favorite, right, Papa?"

Papa nodded, a huge grin lighting his face.

She pretended to place an invisible crown on her head. "They're diadems, a type of chrysanthemum with a center cluster of non-moving stars of a contrasting color." Peyton's heart raced with memories of seeing them. "They burn without any tails and explode into a sphere of colored stars that resemble a crown. They're the best, in my book."

"My girl." Papa feigned scolding her. "You'd use nothing but diadems if you had your way. As a little girl, you clapped your hands and giggled whenever they exploded in the sky. Then, for the next week or more, you'd draw crowns and play princess incessantly."

Clicking his tongue, Patrick shook his head and joined them at the table. "So that's why you so often wanted to play prince and princess in the summertime. I never knew."

Peyton blinked as she recalled those times. "I never realized that, either. But yes, Patrick, I made more than one crown for you and had you wear a towel cape. Sorry." She reached over and touched his hand. "You were always a good sport about my silly games. And a good friend."

Papa grew somber. "Your mother was my best friend, Peyton. I think friendship makes the best marriage. That and shared faith."

Peyton sat up straighter. "You were best friends? You so rarely spoke of her, I didn't know. But you always told me that shared faith is like the roof of a house—it keeps you warm and safe from the dangers beyond."

"I like that." Patrick scooted his chair closer. "What was your wife like, Mr. Quinn? Was she as beautiful and clever as your daughter?" He snapped a grin at her.

Papa sat back in his chair and tried to fold his arms over his chest, but the bandages got in the way. He sighed. "She was a beauty and brilliant. And so kind. Peyton reminds me more of her every day."

Peyton patted his forearm. "Thank you, Papa. I'd like to hear more about Mama sometime."

Papa hung his head. "Your aunt never liked her and resented it when I spoke of her. So I guess I just never bothered creating a fuss. And after Auntie was gone, I never found the right time or the words. Forgive me? In the days to come, we will speak of her more." He waited until Peyton nodded in agreement. "And now ... back to work."

Aunt Bess. Such a persnickety woman and so opinionated. With a huff, Peyton returned to the porch, where she handed Patrick one of five large shells. "These have green tags, but I've never seen them before."

Papa raised his voice to answer. "They're the new ones I mentioned. They're palm shells that feature a thick tail that looks like a tree trunk as the shell ascends. Then the stars fan out like palm tree branches. I saw these last year at a show in Montreal and just had to have them."

Peyton studied them. "They sound lovely. But only five?"

Papa nodded. "They're quite expensive, child. So are the crossettes and the bouquets. But the Emerys were more than generous with their fireworks budget. Do you know that there will be over two hundred prominent people descending upon our little community?"

Patrick whistled, shaking his head. "They've been coming for days, sir, from New York City, Syracuse, Albany, Philadelphia, and even Chicago. Can you imagine? The hotels are full to the brim—at least, that's what Mr. Braxton, the station master, told me this morning."

Peyton wrung her hands. "Goodness. Now I'm more nervous than ever."

Patrick moored the barge on the southeast side of Little Flower Garden Island so the wakes of the passing ships along the northwest shipping channel wouldn't batter it. Since this tiny island lay in front of Calumet Island, the Emery's Grand Ball guests would have a perfect view of the fireworks show—and so would the people of Clayton. Unlike the Fourth of July fireworks, Mr. Quinn had chosen to use the tiny island to launch the spectacle instead of his barge. "Closer to the spectators and more room to perform," he'd said.

Once Patrick finished unloading the fireworks from the barge onto the shore, he stood back and assessed everything needed for the show. No wonder Mr. Quinn was ready to retire. The work that went into just this one show was more than Patrick ever imagined. Peyton's father had been successfully accomplishing several shows every summer for decades with little more than a few unskilled lads to help. Good thing he didn't have to do New Year's or other snowy North Country events like the big cities.

His own father had hopped from job to job, never keeping a steady position or providing a regular income for the family. Peyton had a good, faithful father who had done both all his life. A wave of jealousy washed over him, but he pushed it away.

I forgive.

Patrick picked up his toolbox and carried it to the small hut he and Peyton had set up on the far edge of the island. It wasn't much more than a wobbly four-foot by four-foot barricade that the three of them would hide behind when they lit the fireworks. Mr. Quinn had used it for years, and its age showed.

Today he'd use his carpentry skills for staging the fireworks display. He took out his hammer and waved it in the air, calling out to Peyton's father, who sat on a crate under a shady tree. "Ready to help."

Just then, someone slapped a hand on his shoulder. "Need a hand?"

Patrick jumped. "You scared me half to death, Mitch." He heaved a few breaths before smiling at his friend. "But welcome. How did you come to be here, anyway?"

"Duvall sent me to see if you needed a hand." Mitch pointed to a small skiff and saluted. "At your service."

"That was nice of him." Patrick grinned. "May I introduce you to Peyton's father, Mr. Quinn?"

"Pleased to meet you, sir." Mitch put out his hand.

Mr. Quinn stood and shook it. "Thanks for coming, young man. Patrick, if you and your friend would be so kind as to add a few nails to secure the hut, I'd be much obliged. And the racks have a few loose boards. The shells need to be tight in the rack so they don't shimmy out and explode in the wrong direction."

Patrick saluted him. "Aye, Captain."

Mr. Quinn chuckled. "This ain't no ship, son. At ease."

They all laughed. It felt good to expel the strain that crept into working with such dangerous material.

After he and Mitch sturdied the hut and racks, Mr. Quinn handed them the diagram for the display. Thank goodness, he'd created it before his accident. "There are three display zones. Zone one is loaded with the vertical shell racks holding Roman candles and a fan."

Peyton pointed while her father explained, then tapped the diagram. "Zone one starts the show with ground fireworks that expel hundreds of stars into the sky. The Roman candles have several large stars that fire at regular intervals. It's a great way to get everyone's attention, right, Papa?"

Mr. Quinn grinned. "You're right, and I've made these shells so that they shoot in crisscrossing shapes closer to the audience on Calumet. That should get hearts pumping and eyes searching the sky."

Peyton slid her finger along two lines to the left and right of the paper. "This is zone two. Here's where we'll shoot off the chrysanthemums, dahlias, and diadems."

Her father patted his notes. "Zone three is the battery for the racks of crossettes and bouquets." He paused as if picturing it in his head. "The crossettes will split into four pieces which fly off symmetrically, making a cross. After that, the bouquets burst and scatter shells across the sky before they explode."

Patrick rubbed his chin. "I can see it now. What a spectacle. The guests will *ooh* and *ahh* so loud, we'll hear them from here."

Peyton pointed to two areas drawn on the plans. "We'll use one long fuse for each group so they light at the same time. It's rather dramatic."

Mitch's eyes were big as saucers. "And dangerous."

Patrick acknowledged his friend's reticence with a gentle smile.

"That too." He'd felt that same way just hours ago. How had be become comfortable with this so quickly? Was that a good sign—or a bad one?

Mitch gave him a raised eyebrow and turned to Peyton's father. "Mr. Quinn, may I ask a question?"

"Of course."

"I've always wondered about the colors of fireworks. How do you achieve those?"

Peyton's father fiddled with the bandage on his hand. "Different chemicals create different colors. Compounds of sodium burn yellow and orange. Copper yields blue, and barium blazes green. Strontium turns red. The blues and golds are largely thanks to the Italians. It's simple, really."

Mitch slapped his thigh. "Well, what do you know? Thanks, sir."

Peyton turned to her father, getting them back on track. "And what about the finale, Papa?"

Mr. Quinn sniggered. "The finale for the Emery's Grand Ball will be a large battery of the two- and three-inch shells I made and the ones you and Patrick made yesterday, plus the large palm shells. Should be magnificent."

"That it should." Patrick turned to Mitch. "Thanks for coming. As you can see, the fireworks are in quite the disarray. Peyton, how about if you supervise us while we set it up according to your father's plans?"

"Thank you, gentlemen. That'd be helpful." Peyton rubbed her hands together. "Then I'll teach you how to match the zones."

Mitch elbowed Patrick in the ribs before winking at Peyton. "You've got yourself quite a special lady."

Patrick nodded, winked, and elbowed him back. "What about Rachel? Any new developments?"

Peyton's gaze jerked up from the plans she'd been studying. "What about Rachel?"

Patrick chuckled. "Mitch is sweet on her."

Peyton feigned offense. "How'd I not know this? I was her roommate."

Mitch shrugged. "It's rather new in the past week. We've taken two strolls already. She's a charming young lady."

Peyton *liggled*. "She is, and you'd be lucky to have her, Mitch. Truly. But now, let's set this up."

For the next few hours, they worked on creating the fireworks display with intermittent comments and suggestions from Mr. Quinn. They arranged the zones as Peyton's father planned, then took a short break before matching everything.

Mitch guzzled his lemonade. "Did you know that one of Queen Victoria's former ladies in waiting is here?" He pointed to the castle. "Seems she sailed up the St. Lawrence and is staying in Kingston. When the Emerys heard she was so close, they invited her to be their guest for the Grand Ball. The maids say she's been regaling the Emerys with stories of Queen Victoria and her son Edward's coronation. She even talked about how wonderful the coronation fireworks were over the Thames."

"Goodness." Peyton put her hand to her mouth and bit her index finger. "Our humble affair may seem provincial to her."

Papa sat up straight, his brow furrowing. "Now listen here, missy. Don't be comparing the two. I can only guess the Brits' fireworks didn't have palm shells."

Mitch laughed. "Oh, and Rachel heard the woman talk about a newfangled machine that the royals' maids use to clean the floors and rugs. They call it a vacuum cleaner."

Peyton's eyes grew wide. "We live in an age of wonder. What a marvelous time to be alive."

Mr. Quinn cleared his throat. "I agree, but I sense it's getting late. Let's get this finale chained and ready, shall we?"

CHAPTER 26

THE EMERYS' GRAND BALL was finally here. For months, Peyton and the staff had prepared for this night. But she wasn't there. She was on Little Flower Garden Island, just a few hundred yards from the party.

Calumet Castle twinkled with electric lights, candles, and glittery gowns. The streetlamps along the concrete walkways revealed elegant couples exploring the island. But she saw them only from a distance.

She sighed, closed her eyes, and imagined what it must be like.

Just before dusk, two hundred guests arrived at the main dock and ascended the long walkway through the woods rising gently to the castle. In their fanciest finery, couples would catch their first glimpses of the castle from the massive, paved terrace below. The pink sandstone towers and orange terra-cotta roof would gleam in the moonlight. After climbing the steep stone steps to the expansive verandas which were enclosed by stone balustrades leading to the main entrance, the guests would likely pause in awe.

One by one, the partygoers undoubtedly would turn to view the majestic river, the elaborate gardens, and the manicured lawns below. They'd behold Clayton lit in the early evening, and if they looked downriver, they might glimpse the massive, white Frontenac Hotel. They might even be tempted to linger on the wicker veranda furniture to enjoy the view.

But no! The open door to the great hall of Calumet Castle awaited them. Ceremoniously, they would step in line, waiting to be announced as the honored guests to the Emery Grand Ball. Cut flowers would decorate every nook and cranny, and the wait staff would stand at attention, ready to attend to the guests' every need.

Patrick interrupted her musings. "Isn't it beautiful, Peyton Pie?"

Peyton strained to view those milling about on the veranda and meandering around the lawns. "I wish I could peek in the ballroom. I can only imagine what it might be like."

Papa chuckled. "Why don't you and Patrick sneak over there for a quick peek? It'll be at least an hour before it's time for the show. We're ready. You've filled the shells properly and completed two safety checks. Besides, I need a catnap."

"Shall we?" Patrick stood and reached for her hand.

Peyton giggled. "That'd be wonderful. But do you think the Emerys would object? What if Mrs. Milton catches us?"

Patrick waved a hand, scrunching up his face and rolling his eyes. "What'll she do? Fire us? We already have great recommendations. Besides, you have a way with both Mrs. Emery and Duvall. I doubt either would think a thing of it. We'll keep a low profile and blend in."

Peyton inspected her dark blue skirt and white shirtwaist. "I'm not so sure about that." She removed her apron and sleeve protectors and smoothed her skirt.

Papa cleared his throat. "I don't have my sight back just yet, but I'm sure you'd be the belle of the ball in whatever you're wearing, my darling daughter. Now go—before you waste any more time."

Patrick took her hand and pulled her toward the skiff. "Your father's right. On both accounts."

Peyton's cheeks burned with the compliments of both men she loved. Itching to see the ballroom and guests, she hurried ahead of Patrick and climbed into the skiff without waiting for his help.

"And do you want to row too?" Patrick folded his arms over his chest in mock offense.

Peyton shook her head. "I'm just excited. Listen. The music and laughter bounce along the water as if the river were a megaphone. Do you think we can watch the dancing?"

Patrick shrugged. "If I have to carry you in and announce you as the queen's niece, I shall take you to the ball, my princess."

Within minutes, they were on the Calumet Island shore. Patrick moored the skiff and helped Peyton out of the boat. He took her hand and spoke softly. "Let's skirt the castle and stay in the trees so the guests won't notice us."

When they got to the ballroom terrace, they hid behind the wide-open doors. The violin, piano, violoncello, and cornet blended in perfect harmony as the orchestra played a Viennese waltz from the inner balcony.

With no one nearby, Peyton peeked around the corner. The waltzing couples skirted each other as they glided gracefully around the room. She whispered near Patrick's ear. "Observe how the gentlemen don't hold a lady's hand behind them or high in the air—or move her arm as though it were a pump handle like the Clayton boys do? A gentleman holds the lady's hand gracefully by his side. See?"

Patrick chuckled. "I'll have to remember that the next time we dance."

His whisper tickled her face, making her shiver. She loved being so near to him. "The ball is as I imagined. So elegant and magical. The men in their black tailcoats and polished shoes. And the ladies? They look like a flower garden all in bloom, with their exquisite, light-colored gowns with décolleté revealing their shoulders and arms." Had she said that aloud? She put her hand to her mouth, her cheeks warming. But the beautiful vision carried away her senses. "So elegant with hands in long gloves holding a fancy fan and dance card. Just like the old days."

What would it be like to wear such a gown?

Patrick blinked, tapped her on the shoulder, and pointed to Mitch as he approached them, a wide grin lighting up his face. What was he doing here? She sighed, reluctantly following Patrick away from the beautiful sight and into the shadows where Mitch stood.

"Why are you here?" Mitch scratched his head. "Aren't you doing the fireworks?"

Peyton nodded. "In an hour or so. I wanted to see the dancing."

Patrick slapped Mitch on the shoulder. "Why are *you* here?"

"Just caught a glimpse of you and wondered if something was wrong with the fireworks show."

Patrick shook his head. "No, everything is ready to go."

"Good. Before you leave, let me show you something." Mitch led them to where four crates of lotus-flower-shaped candleholders sat at the water's edge. "These are Japanese lanterns. Ten thousand arrived yesterday. After I got back from helping you, Duvall put Sam, Charlie, and me on the task of scattering them along the shore and lighting them when the fireworks start. Can you imagine?"

Peyton bent down and touched the delicate creations. "They're beautiful. And they float?"

"Sure do." Mitch grinned.

"Then I guess you'll be a part of the spectacle too." Patrick rubbed his chin.

Peyton scanned the darkening sky. "Heavens. We should be getting back. Our most important job of the year is about to commence."

Upon returning to Little Flower Garden Island, Patrick moored the boat and gazed heavenward. One by one, stars popped out on the black velvet canvas above him. Fireflies awakened, twinkling their tiny lights, and the dazzling night sky danced with beaming stars as if all creation cheered them on. Peyton joined her father near the barricade, but Patrick needed a moment to gather his wits. Could he do this job without injuring someone or bumbling something?

Hands shaking and breath coming quickly, he paced the tiny island, waiting for it to be dark enough to start the fireworks. He was merely an assistant to Mr. Quinn, but what if something went wrong? What if Peyton were hurt? He took several deep breaths to calm his racing heart and worried mind.

Where was his faith? He stopped, then prayed for peace, protection, and success.

Before long, a city of boats joined them to enjoy the spectacle. They floated all around the island—hundreds of vessels, tiny lights quivering onboard each one. A huge ship steamed along the main channel, creating a dark hole, dividing the boat lights as it passed.

Patrick joined Mr. Quinn and Peyton. "Look at that. It's like the ship is parting the waters of the Red Sea."

Peyton slipped her hand into his, sending waves of pleasure up his arm. "And now that it's passed, the boat lights wobble like ducklings learning to swim." She *liggled.*

Mr. Quinn stretched. He'd been snoozing. "'Tis a pretty sight, to be sure. How was the ball?"

Peyton told him all about it, her excitement bubbling up like a beautiful brook. Even in the twilight, her eyes danced with joy.

Once she finished her tale, her papa pulled her close and kissed her cheek. "I'm glad you had a pleasant outing, my dear." Mr. Quinn turned his head toward Patrick. "Are you ready for this, son? I love how fireworks over water amplify the beauty, the sound, and the spectacle. It's as if the display is being duplicated on the water. And the spectators, their faces … well … I sure wish I could see it all, but I'll have to settle for enjoying the sound."

Patrick touched his shoulder. "You do see it. You've just painted a picture few have witnessed."

Mr. Quinn shifted in his seat, rubbing his chin before grinning wide. "Thank you, Patrick. I wish I could take these bandages off right now."

Peyton rubbed her father's shoulders, letting out a slow sigh.

Mr. Quinn mumbled to himself before clapping his hands. "By gum, let's try. It's dark, so the sun won't bother my eyes. And if it's painful, we can rebandage them."

"If you're sure, Papa." Taking a shaky breath, Peyton gently unrolled and removed the bandages.

Mr. Quinn's eyes were red, and a few blisters remained, but the swelling was down. Slowly, he blinked, and two tears rolled down his cheeks. Several moments passed before he spoke, his expression unreadable. "They're tender, but I can see just fine." His face relaxed. "Let's leave the bandages off."

Peyton threw her arms around her father and hugged him tightly. "Oh, thank God. If they get tired or sore, I'll rebandage them, okay?"

He nodded. "Okay." Mr. Quinn took out his pocket watch and turned it toward the moonlight before snapping it shut. "Now, are we ready for the show to begin? We'll start in five minutes."

Patrick and Peyton said *ready* at the same time and laughed about it. It was as if Peyton was the other half of him, the part of him he needed to make him whole. Alive. Free.

Mr. Quinn kept his seat behind them, reminding them of cautions and conditions and reiterating that the two of them would execute the entire fireworks show without him. He'd stated over and over that he was just the supervisor.

Now Patrick's stomach churned. Could they do this?

Mr. Quinn cleared his throat. "One minute, folks."

Patrick took Peyton's hand and kissed it. "I'm ready if you are."

Peyton responded by kissing his before letting go. "Let the show begin."

Mr. Quinn counted down. "Ten. Nine. Eight. Seven. Six. Five. Four. Three. Two. One. Light zone one."

Patrick and Peyton lit the fuses to the first zone. The sound of gunfire echoed in the sky as explosions of light and color burst in the night. The Roman candles followed, popping and crackling in the air. Crisscrossing fireworks soared close to Calumet—but still at a safe distance.

Peyton turned to her father. "You didn't tell me you put bombettes in the candles. Nor did you mention the salute."

Mr. Quinn threw back his head and laughed. "You didn't ask."

Patrick quirked a brow.

Peyton explained. "A salute is made of flash powder that just made that very loud report—the bang."

"Ah." Patrick nodded.

Mr. Quinn clapped his hands. "Zone two. Go."

Patrick and Peyton lit the next set of fuses, setting off the chrysanthemums, dahlias, and diadems.

Peyton's professional demeanor amazed him. She patiently instructed him on which fuses to light and when, then she watched, brows furrowed, as the fuses scurried along the ground to meet their end.

But her proper manner altered as Peyton *liggled* with each explosion. "Look. A spider. And another."

Patrick laughed with her as the stars burst into a series of radial lines much like the legs of a spider, and its twin followed.

Nudging him to transfer his attention from the sky, Peyton pointed toward Calumet. "Look. The Japanese lanterns. The guests are setting them off. How fun."

After that, several crossettes and bouquets burst in the sky. Patrick leaned close to Peyton. "What makes that whizzing noise?"

"The tiny tube fireworks are ejected into the air, spinning with such force that they shed their outer coating, and that makes them whizz and hum."

The sulfur tickled Patrick's nose, and smoke burned his eyes, but he didn't care. He gazed at his Peyton Pie, alight with another burst of fireworks. He burned the beauty of the scene into his brain. This. This amazing moment.

He'd never forget it.

Peyton patted his hand. "Ready for zone three? Wait till you see this."

Patrick smacked his palms together. "Ready when you are."

On a count of three, Peyton lit one long fuse, and Patrick lit the other. The fat line sparkled and popped, then divided to the two separate batteries. Smaller fuse lines continued until—for a split second—nothing…

Had they failed? What would they do?

Bang. Pop. Bang. Simultaneously, the batteries exploded into a series of fireworks shooting all over the sky. Beautiful, magical chaos lit the night with colors and lights. Yellow. Orange. Green. Blue. Gold. Red. Hot chemicals. Excited electrons.

Patrick sucked in a breath. The scene echoed his feelings just then.

Mr. Quinn chortled. "Now for the grand finale of the Emery Grand Ball. Are you ready to light the shells you two made? And the palm shells? I can't wait for you to see the work of your hands."

Peyton and Patrick complied. They sizzled and popped, then exploded into dazzling gems in the heavens. Before the shells vanished, the palm shells soared high in the sky as if a giant finger drew five tall palm trees from the trunk up. Once they faded into history, silence hung in the air.

Patrick wiped his eyes—from tears of joy or the smoke, he wasn't sure. The Japanese lanterns encircled the island, the entire area now, and so did the hundreds of boats, but for that moment, time seemed to stand still.

Then, another explosion erupted. The guests on Calumet Island began cheering and clapping. Some whistled and hollered—likely, the staff—while others shouted, "Hurrah."

Peyton and Mr. Quinn glowed with pride and joy. Then Peyton noticed Patrick, and the intensity of her gaze made him shiver in a most pleasing way.

Mr. Quinn interrupted the perfect moment. "Well done, both of you. A flawless execution of a grand event. I must admit, I was rather apprehensive when I woke this morning, but that was for naught. I am duly impressed."

Peyton hugged her papa. "Thank you, Papa. I bet I was more worried than you."

Patrick guffawed. "And I was more terrified than the two of you put together."

They burst into laughter and stretched away the stress. They hugged. They laughed some more.

Mr. Quinn shook Patrick's hand. "What we talked about before? It's yours, should you want it."

Patrick's heart exploded like a diadem. "Thank you, sir. I will consider it deeply."

Mr. Quinn winked, then returned to business. "Let's check the island for sparks, douse anything questionable, pick up our things, and head home. Tomorrow, we'll clear the island of debris."

Patrick rubbed his chin. "Sounds good, sir. You rest. You, too, Peyton. I can do this."

Peyton shook her head, planting a hand on her hip. "I'm as able as you, my friend. Let's get this done. I'm hungry."

In short order, they did as Mr. Quinn bid them. Within the hour, they were docking in Clayton.

When they had disembarked, Patrick blinked. Was he seeing things? "Mother? What are you doing here?"

His mother wrapped her arms around him. "Those fireworks were spectacular. You did this?" She pulled back and raised her hand to cup his cheek, then patted it and turned to the Quinns. "Hello, Mr. Quinn. Peyton. The show was wonderful."

Patrick gave her an extra squeeze before letting go. "It was quite thrilling, I'll give you that. And I have a whole new respect for Mr. Quinn's profession."

Mother slipped her hand in the crook of Patrick's arm. "I thought you three might be hungry, so I made Irish stew and soda bread. And your favorite, Patrick, blueberry pie. How about it?"

Peyton licked her lips. "Oh, thank you, Mrs. Taylor. I'm starving."

Patrick playfully bumped Peyton's shoulder. "Well, we can't let this wee spit of a thing starve, now, can we?"

Mr. Quinn chuckled. "Thank you, ma'am. I'm much obliged. Lead the way."

Patrick's mother assessed Mr. Quinn. "I thought your eyes were bandaged."

"We took the bandages off just a few hours ago." Peyton clasped her hands against her chest. "He got to see the show. Isn't it wonderful?"

Patrick rubbed his chin. He prayed their future would be wonderful too.

Peyton kissed her father's cheek before he headed upstairs. "I'll be up in a few minutes. Just want to say good night to Patrick."

"That delicious meal sure made me sleepy." Papa rubbed his belly. "Take your time, my girl. Good night."

Peyton stepped out on the porch, joining Patrick where he leaned against the railing, staring up at the night sky. "What a day this has been. Did you enjoy it, Patrick?"

Patrick took her hand in his, his lopsided grin affirming her question. "Unforgettably. As you are. I'm so impressed by how professional and accomplished you were during this entire event. Thank you for allowing me to be a part of it."

Peyton shook her head. "It is I who should thank you. We couldn't have done it without you."

Patrick kissed her hand. "I think we make a pretty good team, don't you?"

Peyton bobbed her chin. What would it be like to work together all the time?

Magical.

"Oh." Patrick reached for a thick envelope on a nearby table and handed it to her. "I found this here. It's addressed to you. From the O'Clearys." A strangled laugh escaped his throat. "Hope it's not a job offer."

Peyton opened the package and scanned the contents. She blinked and then giggled. "It's … your letters." She read the attached note.

Peyton,

Please forgive Mr. O'Cleary's abhorrent error. He'd meant to give these to you upon your leaving but forgot. Said he kept them so they wouldn't distract from your work. You can bet he received a severe tongue-lashing from me. Forgive us, dear.

Sincerely,
Mr. and Mrs. O'Cleary

"Goodness! They were right under my nose all this time ..." She held them to her chest and scowled. "That man ... I can't wait to read them."

Patrick gently took the package from her and set it on the table before he slipped his arm around her and drew her close, pulling her a little off balance. She grabbed his strong upper arms as his muscles flexed. So did the muscles of his jaw.

She slipped into his embrace, and he hugged her tightly, but just for a moment. Then he drew back and gazed into her eyes.

Would he steal another kiss or wait for her? How could she tell him she wanted a kiss—yearned for it?

His eyes softened, and his breathing sped up. She put her hand on his chest, and his heart raced faster than the trains that brought the city folk to their village. He tilted his head down, and the slightest smile crossed his lips.

What would those lips feel like? Taste like?

As if he'd read her mind, he wet them with his tongue, and her craving soared higher than the rockets they'd sent into the sky.

A tiny moan escaped her lips, and fire lit her cheeks. She raised her face, inviting him, imploring him.

His hand rose from her arm to her face, and he cupped her jaw so gently it almost tickled. As he dipped his chin, his eyes never left hers, and her heart raced too. Probably outran his.

Time stopped.

A brush of lips, barely perceptible. Then he deepened his kiss. It wasn't grasping but giving. It was his gift—for her.

Her senses exploded in a shivering, quivering dance of joy, and she smiled, then giggled, unexpectedly breaking the kiss.

Patrick pulled back, his brow furrowed. "Is it so bad you *liggle?*"

Peyton shook her head. "No. Oh, not at all. The joy of such a wonderful, magical kiss just bubbled up inside me and overflowed. Forgive me?"

He nodded, almost imperceptibly.

This time, she kissed him. Passionately. Completely. Fully. When she was done, Patrick's bottom lip quivered. "My Peyton Pie, I love you."

Peyton swallowed, tears forming in her eyes. "And how I love you!"

CHAPTER 27

TWO DAYS LATER, PEYTON donned her best Sunday dress, a light blue damask she'd made herself, embellished with the lace she'd tatted during the long winters in Watertown. She tugged the blousy top into place to accentuate her slim figure and smoothed the front before adjusting the bell-shaped skirt. She looked in the beveled-glass mirror on her dresser—and approved. Pinching her cheeks, she donned a wide-brimmed, straw cartwheel hat and hurried to join her papa in the parlor.

As she descended the stairs, Papa closed his Bible and beckoned her near. "My lass, you haven't worn that in a while. It's my favorite. Makes your green eyes sparkle like emeralds in the sunshine."

She swatted at a rogue fly. "Thank you, Papa. And look at you. You're looking better every day. I love how God created us to heal like we do. I barely detect any burns on your face." She stepped closer to inspect his hand. "Or on your hand." Patting his still-wrapped right hand, she quirked a brow. "Did you change the bandage?"

"I did." Papa shrugged. "And it's healing, too, though I fear it'll never work the same. My fingers are severely stiff."

She helped her father out of the chair. "Perhaps they'll heal with time. I'll pray they will. Ready to go?"

Papa nodded, and they set out for church. Several neighbors walked ahead and behind. Perhaps Clayton was the place for her to be, rather than the city with so many strangers. Why, she could name every person in each house she passed. Save for a few busybodies, her hometown was a fine place to live. Perhaps she'd set up a tailor and upholstery stop or just work from her father's home until deciding what to do.

Peyton's heart raced as she neared Mrs. Fillmore's white picket fence. Hopefully, the woman was already on her way to church.

No such luck. Standing on her porch, Mrs. Price and Mrs. Gordon stepped aside as Mrs. Fillmore closed her door and joined them. Jezebel, indeed. Mrs. Gordon was terribly unkind to make such comments. So were the others, for that matter. Mrs. Black, the gossip from the shop, headed toward Mrs. Fillmore's from across the street. A fine gaggle of geese they'd make.

With a huff, Peyton slipped her hand into her father's arm and hurried him along. But Mrs. Black stepped out in front of Peyton and Papa. "Good morning, Mr. Quinn. Peyton." When the woman said *Peyton*, her tone said volumes. Condemnation. Judgment.

Papa patted Peyton's hand. "Pay them no mind. They are a bitter bunch of biddies."

She laughed. "Quite the alliteration, Papa. But a good name for them. Still, I must forgive and not pass judgment on them."

"Remember the Irish proverb, 'Everyone is wise—until he speaks.' God knows your heart, and most of the townsfolk do as well." Papa's voice cracked as he spoke. "You're a jewel in my crown, Peyton."

She hugged her father's arm as Patrick and his mother waved from the other side of the street. She and Papa crossed to join them, glad to at least have a road between them and the biddies.

Patrick shook Papa's hand. "Good morning, sir. You're looking well." He turned to Peyton. "And you're most exquisitely lovely, my lass." He bowed as if she were royalty.

A warm flush rose from her chest to her temples at his kind words. She giggled, then turned to Mrs. Taylor. "And good day to you. Isn't it a beautiful morning?"

Mrs. Taylor kissed Peyton on the cheek. "A perfect day, my dear."

They chatted until they reached the church, and Peyton bid them quickly take a seat to avoid any gossip that might spoil the day.

Patrick sat next to Peyton, leaning close to whisper to her. "May I take you on a picnic today, Peyton Pie?"

She sucked in a breath. The warmth of his breath, the invitation, the nearness of him nearly made her lightheaded. "I'd love that, thank you. But I must check with Papa first."

He rubbed his chin. "Of course, my dear."

Something about the way he spoke and acted on this fine summer's morning gave her butterflies—no, more like hummingbirds—in the pit of her stomach. She placed her hand on her middle as her breakfast of fruity oatmeal rumbled. Papa tossed her an amused grin. He'd heard it too.

Thankfully, the organ began the service, and everyone stood to sing, drowning out any further tummy noise. She blew out a relieved breath right before she felt someone staring at her. Mrs. Fillmore tossed her a narrow-eyed glare and then shook her head.

As if she'd heard Peyton's stomach. Good heavens.

Shaking off her frustration, she focused on the music and the company beside her. Treasured, all. She glanced at Patrick's mother, who glowed as she sang. *Thank you, God, for the change in her from anger and depression to a peace that passes understanding.* Next to her, Patrick had his eyes closed, singing the hymn with his deep, joy-filled baritone. He, too, had been transformed—once he had forgiven himself and his father.

A second hymn began with just the organ, so she stole a peek at her papa. He'd been through so much in his life but always kept a deep, abiding trust in the Almighty. Now, with the palsy and burns, he still showed no lack of faith. What about her?

Yes, she'd grown, but oh, how much further she had to go. Edna passed through her thoughts, so she whispered, "I forgive." She scanned the biddies, sighed, and joined the song. She'd forgive them too.

"Be still, my soul, the Lord is on your side. Bear patiently the cross of grief or pain; leave to your God to order and provide; in every change, God faithful will remain. Be still, my soul: your best, your heavenly friend through thorny ways leads to a joyful end. Be still, my soul: your God will undertake to guide the future, as in ages past."

Tears flowed, washing away so many harsh words, so many of her fears for the future. Patrick tenderly handed her his handkerchief, brushing his hand against hers, pausing until she looked up so he could give her a reassuring smile.

She'd been striving to prove herself to others her entire life, always trying to convince and demonstrate and justify her thoughts and actions to others. Others who chose to judge her and condemn her for being different. She wasn't rebellious. Didn't choose to be different. She just was.

Be still, my soul. Through thorny ways He will lead me to a joyful end.

At that moment, all the cares of the world slipped away, as if washed by a gentle rain. She lifted her head, amazed how a moment, a song, could change so much.

After prayers and Scripture readings, Pastor Moreno took his place at the lectern, greeting the congregation he had served since Peyton was a young girl. "Our passage this morning is from Romans eight, verse one. 'There is therefore now no condemnation to them which are in Christ Jesus, who walk not after the flesh, but after the Spirit.' What does it mean to walk in the Spirit, to live free of condemnation?"

He turned the page. "Remember the stormy weather a week ago? The low-hovering, dark clouds swept in, the wind howled, and the sky rumbled. Then came the lightning, flashing here and there at will. I'm sure you read in the paper that a nearby boathouse was burned to the ground by a rogue lightning bolt."

He waited until the murmurs and gasps from the congregation quieted. "My friends, our tongues, our thoughts and actions, our judgments can be like those lightning strikes. By them, we can bring much destruction and even destroy people's lives."

Peyton held her breath, then blew it out.

The pastor glanced at several of his parishioners. "We don't have to live under continuous, low-lying black clouds of condemnation and judgment. Life in Christ, like a strong wind, can clear the air and free you—and others—from the brutal tyranny of judging one another. We must learn to hold our tongues and rein in our thoughts and opinions of others. God is our judge. And we must never forget that."

He pointed an index finger to nobody in particular. "Is Mrs. Smith too worldly because she has extra doilies in her house and entertains more often than others?" Another jab in a different direction. "Is Mrs. Jones sinning because she strives for her sisters to live a better life?" And another. "Is Mr. Brown errant because he cooks and helps his wife with the children?"

Pastor Moreno shook his head. "We are a family in Christ and should live our lives free, with faith, hope, and love as our foundation. So today, I pose a question to you. Will we, as a community and as individuals, walk in our fleshly nature, enslaving ourselves and others by condemning and judging? Or … will we choose daily to walk and talk and live by the Spirit of God who has given us freedom?"

Silence thundered in the church until a baby cooed—the sweet, innocent sound of life.

As the midday sun drifted through the windows of his childhood home, Patrick paced the floor, wiping his brow. His clean, white shirt had too much starch, and his best pants were well worn. He'd have to buy new clothes soon. "Do I look all right, Mother?"

She adjusted his tie. "You're as handsome as ever. And don't worry. I've fixed a lovely picnic basket—fried chicken, potato salad, lemonade, and berry tarts. I'm sure she'll be pleased as a rabbit in a lettuce field. And there's one other surprise for her." She winked, her eyes twinkling.

"Thanks." He planted a quick kiss on her cheek. "Are you well? You seem ... at peace."

His mother beamed. "I realized that I have a choice—to make life bitter or better. I've chosen the latter. I've also chosen to trust God." She paused and scrutinized Patrick. "In the past few years, your father worked hard to make up for the past. Thankfully, he saved a tidy sum. 'For a rainy day,' he said. We had no idea that day would come so soon, but I'm taken care of, son. Just you mind that."

He grinned as he picked up the heavy basket. "I'm grateful to Father and happy for you. Enjoy your afternoon, and pray for me, please."

Mother put her hand to her heart, her eyes sparkling. "Oh, you can count on it, son."

Before long, Patrick had fetched Peyton, and they were on their way to the fishing hole in a little cattail-sheltered inlet of French Bay just blocks from their homes.

When she saw their destination ahead, she *liggled*. "I wondered if you'd take me here. I hoped so."

"Good." He chuckled, but it sounded jittery. He took a deep breath to calm himself. "We haven't been in years. I've been a few times without you, but it doesn't feel the same."

Peyton slipped her hand into the crook of his arm. "Are you unwell, Patrick? You don't seem yourself today. Even in church. We can postpone our picnic if you need to rest."

"No." The word came out so strained and loud that Peyton jumped, and he hurried to explain. "I mean, I'm fine. I've been looking forward to this for some time."

She squeezed his arm. "Good. So have I."

When they got to their special spot, Peyton's eyes gleamed at the surprise he'd prepared. Early that morning, he'd cut the wild grass and spread a quilt under a nearby willow tree. A bouquet of fresh-cut asters lay in the middle, tied with a white satin ribbon. He set the basket on the edge of the blanket and picked up the bouquet, handing it to her. "For you, my precious Peyton Pie."

She smiled and put her face almost in the middle of them. She sneezed several times, *liggling* like a child. "Excuse me. I always do that. You'd think I'd learn."

How he loved her laugh. "'Tis true, my dear. You've inflicted yourself with sneezing fits as long as I've known you." He waved for her to sit. "What did you think of the sermon?"

Peyton sucked in a breath as she settled, straightening her skirts about her. "Gracious. I know we should only think about our own part in whatever is being taught, but today I felt as if a dozen eyes were burning a hole through the back of my head. Have you ever felt that way?"

He nodded as he spread the feast before them. "I think that allowing God to guide us—walking by the Spirit, as Romans calls it—is the key to so much of life. Those who think they can do it all on their own become obsessed with comparing their own moral righteousness against that of others. They seem plagued by do's and don'ts and try to impose their standards on others, whether valid or not. If I ever do that, my love, please bop me over the head or shake me to my senses."

Peyton *liggled*, throwing her head back and closing her eyes. "I'll try to remember that." She paused, chewing her bottom lip. "Patrick, I … I need to confess that I only recently forgave you for the day you left to apprentice. I'm sorry I was so angry and unforgiving."

He grasped her hand. "It is I who need to apologize. I was such a dunderhead. So selfish and eager to start my career that I hardly considered your feelings or needs. Forgive me?"

She kissed his hands. "Forgiven and forgotten." She pushed her hat off her head until it hung by the ribbons around her neck. "The sun speckling through the willow tree feels so magical."

Forgotten, indeed.

Patrick touched her hair, silky and warm against his hand. He halted his fingers near her ear. "You're so beautiful. So precious."

Peyton leaned into his hand, just a bit. She bit her bottom lip, eyes brimming with tears. "Thank you, Patrick. I do love you so."

Patrick pulled his hand back and tossed her a not-yet grin. "And I love you. But let's eat this before the bugs realize we're here."

Peyton blinked. "Yes, let's." She sat upright and fiddled with her hair. "That chicken smells scrumptious."

He handed her a too-thick napkin—the surprise his mother had mentioned. Then he placed some of everything on both plates, pleased to serve her. Unknown to him, his mother had also provided them with pickles, carrot sticks, and slaw.

Peyton shook her head, putting out an open palm. "Go light on my plate, please. I eat about a third of what you do, remember? Though it all looks yummy." She opened her napkin and shrieked. "My letters? How in ..."

He guffawed. "Mother found them in Father's things. I've been itching to read them but thought you'd like to give them to me in person."

Peyton radiated joy as her eyes darted from him to the letters and back. She flipped through them as if to make sure they were really hers. Then she hugged them and ceremoniously handed the pile to him.

He held them to his chest. "I will treasure them forever, and tonight will be the best reading of my life, I'm sure."

Peyton's brows furrowed. "You ... you don't want to read them now?"

"Nae. I want to savor every word. I've waited this long. I can wait until tonight."

Peyton shrugged. "You've more patience than I. When you're done, I wouldn't mind reading them again. It's been so long." She took a sip of her lemonade before picking up her plate.

For a long while, they ate in comfortable silence save for the crackle of the crusty chicken and the crunch of crisp vegetables. He savored each bite, but not as much as he relished the closeness of Peyton.

Finally, she dabbed her lips with her napkin. "Isn't this day glorious?"

He agreed and took a sip of his lemonade. How could he start?

He'd rehearsed the speech over and over, but now he couldn't recall any of it. His heart thumped hard in his chest as drops of sweat tickled his temples. He wiped them away.

A gentle breeze cooled his nerves and kept the bugs at bay. He took a deep breath and munched on a carrot to give himself time to think. Peyton seemed content with the quiet—thank heaven.

When they finished their meal, Peyton picked up their plates, but he wouldn't have it. He waved a hand. "I'm serving you today, my lovely lass. Relax and enjoy. It likely isn't often you get to be served."

She smiled. "You're such a fine gentleman. Thank you. It's quite a treat—I'll give you that." She eyed him with a tilt of her head as if to ask him something. But she didn't. She made a sweeping gesture. "I love how the river sounds like soft music. I can listen to it for hours. Not even Handel could create such a beautiful melody."

He leaned back and closed his eyes. "I agree completely." After a few minutes, he sat up, then got to his feet, reaching a hand toward her. "Shall we stretch our legs?"

She stood, wobbling on the soft grass and almost bumping into him. The scent of lemon verbena tickled his nose. She shrugged. "Sorry."

Patrick offered his arm, and she took it, but they didn't walk. Instead, they stared at a pair of geese gliding over the water. "Do you know they mate for life?"

She smirked, her brows furrowed.

A team of ducks, followed by a dozen or more ducklings furiously trying to keep up, swam nearby. He pointed to them. "They don't."

She blinked, and her brows furrowed even deeper. She quirked her mouth to one side. "So?"

Patrick took both of her hands in his. It was now or never. Slowly, he got down on one knee. "I'd like us to be like those geese, gliding along through life together."

Peyton's eyes brimmed, one little tear sliding down her beautiful cheek.

"I love you, my Peyton Pie. Always have. Always will. But just being friends isn't enough." He swallowed, fumbling in his pocket for a tiny velvet bag. His fingers finally found it, and he pulled it out. The midnight-blue velvet shimmered in the sunshine.

Blasted thing. Why couldn't it be easier to handle?

His fingers quivered as Peyton patiently stood there, her green eyes outshining the sun, tears flowing freely, but with a smile so wide he knew he'd hit the mark. When he finally got the thin gold band out of the bag, he held it up to her. "Marry me, please, Peyton Quinn, and make me the happiest man on earth."

Peyton gawked at the ring and then focused on his face before bobbing her head intensely. "Yes. Oh, yes, a million times, my love."

Patrick stood and gently took her face in his hands. This angel, this woman, would be his wife. He bent down and kissed her forehead, brushing his lips against her right temple and down to her cheek. He had waited so long. Dreamed of this moment. Longed for it.

His blood surged through his veins, his heart pumping faster and faster. He leaned her into his arm and swept his lips across hers. Gently. Softly. As she deserved.

But then, she kissed him back. Passionately. Hard. Dizzyingly intense.

The Grand Ball fireworks paled in the light of that moment.

CHAPTER 28

PEYTON THOUGHT SHE'D SWOON as she melted in Patrick's arms, even as she shivered with the joy of it. She'd be his wife.

His kiss—glorious. She tried to speak but words failed. Instead, she responded with all her emotions, emotions that exploded within her with such intensity that Papa's biggest fireworks seemed inert in that moment.

She'd thought the porch kiss—the one she deemed her first—held the greatest emotion and latter ones wouldn't matter so much. But this ...

Her lips trembled as she pressed them against his. She'd had no idea she could feel such intensity about anything. The world faded, and only she and Patrick mattered.

He groaned softly and drew her closer. She, in turn, held tight to him. When he released his hold, she opened her eyes, the world spinning as if she'd run too fast around a Maypole. She blinked when a hummingbird hovered over Patrick's head. It made her laugh, and the magic of the moment faded.

At her giggle, Patrick opened his eyes and drew her toward him again. She wanted to return to that magical moment and kiss him again and again.

Instead, he winked and kissed the tip of her nose. "I love you, my soon-to-be wife."

She wrapped her arms around him and hugged him tightly. "I love you, too, my future husband."

They sat and laughed with abandon, needing to rest as if they'd played a game of tag for an entire afternoon. Then, when her grin made her face ache, she poured them each a glass and took a sip of lemonade. "That was ..."

Patrick clanged his glass on hers. "... heavenly. I can't wait to get married. When shall we do it?"

When? Peyton swallowed wrong, choking on her lemonade. Once she recovered, she shook her head. "Always in a hurry, you are. I need time to make my dress, and ... Did you talk to Papa?"

He smirked like a young lad. "Remember that night I helped your father to bed? I asked for your hand then."

She quirked a brow. "That's what took you so long."

He shook his head. "That took moments. Your father wholeheartedly consented. What took so long was talking about the business."

"The business? He's still retiring, right?"

Patrick nodded. "He wants us to carry it on, Peyton—the Quinn-Taylor Fireworks—and I tentatively agreed. During the off-season, I can still do my carpentry work, and if you'd like, you can still do upholstery, sewing, or whatever you desire. Even fight for the rights of women."

Could it be? How could a lifetime of dreams come true in one afternoon?

Two butterflies flitted around each other just feet from them. They seemed to be dancing. Could she and Patrick waltz around three businesses—and have a family?

Perspiration trickled down her back. So many decisions to make. "Where would we live?"

Patrick glowed. "Here's the thing. Mother has decided to move to Rochester and live with Aunt Kay. Surprisingly, my father paid off the house, and she's giving it to us for a wedding gift. It needs work, but I'm a carpenter, and you're an upholsterer, so we can make it our own in no time."

Peyton swallowed hard. Was she dreaming? "Your mother knew about today?"

He shrugged. "She's praying for us now, and so is your papa." He reached into the basket and pulled out a brown paper package wrapped with a blue ribbon. "Mother made this for you."

She unwrapped it to find a cross-stitched tea towel with the words, *May the strength of God pilot us. May the wisdom of God instruct us. May the hand of God protect us. May the word of God direct us. – an Irish Blessing.*

She held it to her chest. "Oh, Patrick. It's beautiful. Please thank your mother. I'll treasure it forever."

Could everything she'd ever hoped for, dreamed of, desired, be coming to pass?

He kissed her again as gently as before. Tingles tickled her spine until a dark cloud hovered over her thoughts. "But what would the biddies think of us doing fireworks?"

Patrick yanked his head back as if slapped. "Peyton. Do you seriously care?"

She absorbed the gentle rebuke and shook her head. "I just had to ask. There's so much to think about. So much to do. So many decisions."

Patrick kissed her cheek. "Still your soul, my love. We'll make each decision together, one by one." He stood and held out his hand. "Come. Let's go and share the good news."

A month later, Patrick ran his hand through his hair before closing his new suitcase. Trousseau planning was supposed to be for the bride, not the groom, but he was well overdue for new clothes, and his honeymoon was the perfect time to have them.

He assessed himself in the small mirror, rubbing a hand along his chin, checking in case an errant whisker was hiding in the cleft. He'd shaved twice, just to be sure. He adjusted the flip of his hair and snickered. Peyton now said it made him look rather roguish, but she liked it, anyway.

Peyton would be Mrs. Patrick Taylor in just hours—his dream come true.

Mother yelled up the stairs. "Patrick, you're going to be late for your wedding, son. Let's get going."

He buttoned his single-breasted frock coat over his double-breasted vest. "Coming, mother." After wiggling his wide tie in place, he grabbed his gloves and top hat. With a free hand, he carefully closed the door.

Taking the steps two at a time, he reached the bottom, where he almost bumped into his mother.

She laughed, her eyes twinkling. "Eager to start your new life?"

"Most definitely." He kissed her. "You look lovely. Thank you for everything. Let's not be late."

Mother adjusted his celluloid collar before stepping off the porch. "You're welcome. Such a handsome groom. You know what they say, 'Marry in May and rue the day, but marry in September's shine, your living will be rich and fine.' This is a perfect autumn morning for your wedding, son."

Patrick shook his head. "Any day would be a perfect day for marrying my Peyton."

Inside the pastor's office at church, Peyton smoothed her high-necked, frilly bodice and wide, puffy, gigot sleeves. Patrick loved blue and ruffles, so she'd handmade her wedding dress to please him. The soft, flowing Messaline silk had just a hint of blue—just the way she wanted it. She tugged at her long train before donning her hat, veiled the same length. She pinched her cheeks before slipping on her white kid gloves and tucking them under her sleeves. Joyful tears welled in her eyes, but she blinked them back.

Papa knocked and opened the door, his smile so wide she could barely see his eyes. "You are the most beautiful bride I've ever laid eyes on." He walked over, picked up her bouquet, and handed it to her but raised a palm and shook his head. "Don't smell them, or you'll sneeze."

"Aren't asters the happiest flower in all the world? Patrick gave me a bouquet just like this one when he proposed."

Papa thrust the crook of his arm toward her. "Let's get you hitched." He kissed her cheek as she took his arm, then laid his hand gently upon hers. "I love you, daughter."

She lifted up on her toes and kissed his cheek in return. "And I love you, Papa. Thank you for making this day magical."

He groaned. "I almost forgot." He reached into his pocket and retrieved an extravagant double strand of white pearls. "This was your mother's. I gave it to her on our wedding day." With some struggle, he unclasped it and put it around her neck, adjusting it among her lacy ruffles. "To remember her, my girl. She'd be so proud of you, so pleased you're marrying Patrick. She would have loved him, too, you know."

A tear escaped and slid down her cheek, so her papa brushed it away. "Don't cry yet. I have one more gift."

She shook her head. "You've done so much already, Papa. We need nothing more."

Papa shrugged. "You'll be spending your first night as husband and wife at the Frontenac Hotel."

She nodded. Patrick had already told her that.

A wide grin spread across his face. "But after that, I've arranged for you to take a steamer up the St. Lawrence for a week at the Windsor Hotel in Montreal. How does that sound?"

She blinked. "Really? You know how I've dreamed of visiting Montreal. Does Patrick know?"

He chuckled. "We've been scheming for weeks when you thought we were just fishing." He touched her cheek gently. "When you get back, you can settle into your life together with plenty of sweet memories."

She hugged her father. "Thank you, Papa. But we already have a lifetime of sweet memories from the time we were children. These memories will be extras."

Papa snapped his chin up. "But my girl deserves the best."

She sighed. "We've already received so many wedding gifts, Papa. I don't feel as though I deserve any of this. I even received apologies from every single one of those biddies acknowledging their transgressions and offering to help us in the future. Truly, an unexpected bouquet of blessings."

"Yes. Those *are* gifts. Starting your married life without that cloud of judgment is God's gift to you."

Just then, the organ began to play, and Pastor Moreno knocked on the door. "Ready?"

Peyton beamed. Ready.

Ready to marry her best friend.

Ready to become Mrs. Taylor.

And ready to see what else God would do.

The End

AUTHOR'S NOTE

IN THE 1980s, I had the privilege of staying on Calumet Island when it was a bed and breakfast. My time there was so inspiring that I knew I had to write a story about it one day. Then, last summer, the caretaker graciously brought me over to the island for an afternoon of touring it, hearing stories, and recapturing the essence of the island.

I'm also grateful for *Toujours Jeune: Always Young* by Rex Ennis, a fine piece of non-fiction about the Emerys, Calumet Island, and the castle. The many historical details helped make *Peyton's Promise* accurate and interesting.

Calumet Castle actually predated Singer Castle on Dark Island, the setting for my last novel, *Devyn's Dilemma*, and Boldt Castle on Heart Island, a popular tourist attraction today. Construction on Calumet Castle began in 1893 and finished a year later. Though not as elaborate as the other two, Calumet Castle had thirty rooms plus the ballroom, as well as the many outbuildings you read about.

The Emerys are real. Charles Goodwin Emery was a New York City resident, entrepreneur, and tobacco tycoon. He made The New Frontenac Hotel on Round Island near Calumet Island a world-class hotel that provided a wide variety of amenities and high standards of service. He also donated to many causes and was a prominent benefactor around the islands.

In 1907, five years after this story, Mrs. Emery died on her husband's birthday, July 20. She'd been ill, and it was her wish to spend her last days on the island. After that, Mr. Emery closed the castle.

Thanks to high taxes, the heirs abandoned the castle, and in 1956, the castle burned to the ground. Fortunately, the outbuildings, including the caretaker's house and the tower, remained unharmed. Since then, the island has been a marina, a bed and breakfast, and a restaurant. It is currently a privately owned summer retreat.

Patrick and Peyton and their parents, as well as the other servant characters, are fictional. I had lots of fun creating these people, many from bits and pieces of friends and family I love so dearly. (Watch out, friends—you may be in my next book.) I hope you enjoyed hearing their stories and learning about this Gilded Age family, castle, and island.

Please visit www.SusanGMathis.com/fiction for all of my Thousand Islands stories, including: *The Fabric of Hope, Christmas Charity, Katelyn's Choice, Sara's Surprise, Devyn's Dilemma, Reagan's Reward,* and more.